Sallust

The Catiline and Jugurtha of Sallust

Translated into English by Alfred W. Pollard

Sallust

The Catiline and Jugurtha of Sallust
Translated into English by Alfred W. Pollard

ISBN/EAN: 9783337189594

Printed in Europe, USA, Canada, Australia, Japan

Cover: Foto ©Andreas Hilbeck / pixelio.de

More available books at **www.hansebooks.com**

THE

CATILINE AND JUGURTHA

OF SALLUST

TRANSLATED INTO ENGLISH.

BY

ALFRED W. POLLARD, B.A.,

ST. JOHN'S COLLEGE, OXFORD.

London:

MACMILLAN AND CO.

1882.

PREFACE.

THE text used in this translation is that of Dietsch's last edition. The system of division into paragraphs is taken from the same source. Wherever possible, the square brackets which Dietsch uses for marking words which he suspects as interpolations, have been retained in the English version.

Besides my obligations to the usual works of reference, and to the suggestive essays of Professor Tyrrell in the introduction to his edition of Cicero's Letters, and of Professor Beesly on " Catiline as a Party Leader," there are two heavy debts which I wish specially to acknowledge. The first of these is to the edition of Cicero's Orations, and the Roman history of the late Mr. Long. To any one who desires to make a detailed study of any portion of the period on which Mr. Long has written, the latter work cannot be too strongly recommended. By its clear arrangement of the materials to be found in the various ancient authorities, and scholarly discussion of all the points they raise, it has considerably lightened my labour in writing the notes to this volume. My second debt of gratitude is due to my friend, Mr. Watson, of St. John's College, Oxford, for his kindness in revising the whole of the translation, a revision, I may say, by which hardly a page has been left unimproved.

A. W. P.

CONTENTS.

NOTE ON SALLUST.

THE facts which we know about our author's life are sufficient to prove that he was at no time an important man at Rome. A member of a plebeian family, Gaius Sallustius Crispus was born in the year B.C. 86 in the town of Amiternum.   Until B.C. 52, when he was one of the tribunes of the commons, we hear nothing of him, but he then took an active part against Cicero's client, T. Annius Milo. Two years later he was removed from the Senate by the censors, Appius Claudius, and Lucius Calpurnius Piso, but his expulsion was probably only a party measure, as other Caesarians were similarly treated, and even if the story about his intrigue with the wife of Milo is true, adultery was at this time too common at Rome to exclude the offender from the Senate. It is said, without much authority, that immediately after his expulsion Sallust joined the army of Caesar ; anyhow, in B.C. 48, we find him in command of a legion in Illyricum. The following year he was one of the praetors elect (when he had been quaestor we do not know), and thus regained his place in the Senate. In September he was employed by Caesar to check the mutiny in Campania, but his efforts to do this were unsuccessful. Sallust took part in the African war, and on its conclusion was appointed the first governor of the newly

formed province of Numidia. In B.C. 45 he returned
to Rome, so enormously enriched as to give colour to
the charges of extortion which were vaguely, though
probably never formally, brought against him. He
now laid out the Horti Sallustiani in the valley between the Quirinal and the Pincius, and lived here in
retirement until his death in B.C. 35. It is probable
that these ten or twelve years comprise the whole
period of his literary activity, and that during them he
wrote, not only the " Catiline" and "Jugurtha," but the
other essays which were joined together into a con-
tinuous account of about twenty years of Roman
history. On Sallust's death, his property all went to
his grand-nephew, who became a man of some note
under Augustus and Tiberius. The story that the
historian married Terentia, the wife whom Cicero
divorced in B.C. 46, is worth mentioning, though the
authority for it is not good, and it seems intrinsically
improbable.

The preceding brief sketch of Sallust's life enables
us to gather that throughout his career he was a
consistent democrat and supporter of Caesar. This
Caesarism is often alluded to as detracting from the
value of his work, but it would be much truer to say
that it constitutes his first qualification as a historian.
There is a wrong and a right side in politics as in
everything else, and in the struggle which brought the
Roman republic to an end the partisans of Caesar, as
we now see, were in the right. It need not greatly
alter our estimation of Cicero and Cato as men, or
even as statesmen, that in that struggle they did
battle for a constitution whose continuance would

have been Rome's ruin. Their position was intelligible, consistent, justifiable ; as it appeared in the heat of the contest, even noble, for they were fighting for an idea, and Caesar for his personal gain. But despite Cicero's literary power, and Cato's force of character, a history of Rome for the century which followed the fall of Carthage, if written by either the one or the other, would have been a very lamentable production. They would have misunderstood everything, and consequently misexplained everything. The way in which Cicero alludes to the men and events of the period of the Gracchi should be sufficient to convince us of this. Sallust, though vastly inferior as a man to either of the optimate leaders, was extraordinarily successful in seizing the thread of events. The chapters on politics in Rome in the year which succeeded the Gracchan revolution, and again after the consulship of Pompey and Crassus in B.C. 70, can hardly be too highly praised, especially when we consider how soon after the events narrated they were written. Sallust, indeed, except when speaking of the dictator himself, never allowed his Caesarian sympathies to carry him away, and it is difficult to understand how Professor Mommsen could permit himself to speak of the " Catiline " and "Jugurtha " as partisan pamphlets. If Sallust was a party writer, then Defoe himself must yield him the palm for cleverness in concealing his real object, and one could almost wish Mommsen's theory correct, for the ingenuity of the elaborate contrast which Sallust draws between Caesar and Marcus Cato, the one man for whom the dictator entertained an uneasy hate, would then be without a parallel. But the whole tone of Sallust's two essays forbids the idea that he was writing for any immediate purpose. The elaborate care bestowed on the style, the recurring pompousness, the affectation of an extraordinary virtue, all betray the vanity of a man who wrote with Thucydides' "to be an everlasting possession" ringing in his ears, and who probably esteemed his own work little less lightly than that of Caesar. Over passages in the latter's career which he might not care to have revived, Sallust was sufficiently prudent to draw a veil. The different manner in which he alludes to the rumours of the complicity of Caesar and of Crassus in Catiline's conspiracy is an instance of this ; and, certainly, we should never have learnt from our author how close was the political connection of Catiline and Caesar down to the end of 64. But, when not dealing with the dangerous subject of the dictator's conduct, it is difficult to find any trace of partiality in Sallust. Allusion has already been made to his character of Cato, a like impartiality marks his sketches of Metellus, of Marius, and of Sulla : and there is hardly a single passage in the two essays he has left us in which one political party is unjustly exalted at the expense of the other.

So far we have been dealing with Sallust as a political historian, and here there is little to do but praise ; there are, however, other aspects of his work in which it appears less satisfactory. Of his defects as a military historian, and of the excuses which may be alleged for such defects, something is said in the introduction to the "Jugurtha" ; his contempt for details of chronology and geography forms the subject of many of the notes; neither of these points therefore need be more than alluded to here. There is, however, another side of his writings on which a few remarks may, perhaps, be profitably made. If by the pains which he takes to link together events and their causes, and to find the key of each period of history in that which preceded it, our author has justly earned himself the title of a philosophic historian, it must unhappily be added that by the way in which he draws on his imagination, he exhibits himself as the earliest of historical novelists. It has been remarked that there are often two ways in which the same set of facts may be described : " we may say that we saw a man snatch up a stick and strike a dog ; or, that we knew the man was angry and resolved to punish the dog;" in very simple cases it does not much matter which form of expression we use. Sallust, however, has a perverse propensity for using the second form where it is entirely inapplicable. To speak pedantically, he interprets material in terms of mental phenomena in a most illegitimate manner, and often seems to do this merely to conceal his ignorance of some historical detail. He is constantly supplying motives and reasons, constantly telling us what his characters thought, and describing mental conditions of which he could by no possibility have known anything. In the history of the Jugurthine War the effect of this is chiefly ludicrous. The elaborate account of Micipsa's motives in sending Jugurtha to Numantia, the ascription of Hiempsal's murder to the terror he caused Jugurtha by his supposed remark, the mental pictures of the Numidian and his opponents presented to us on each change of tactics on either side—all these we may value as highly or as cheaply as we like.   However we rate them, they will not alter our views as to the nature of the war.   In the case of the "Catiline" it is different.   Here, much depends on the opinion we hold as to the personal character of the conspirator ; and Sallust, in his foolish straining after effect, has perhaps done more even than Cicero to elevate Catiline into the portentous stage villain with whom we are familiar.   To trace the conspiracy to the madness which resulted from a guilty conscience, to portray the man whom Caesar and Crassus supported for the consulship as a kind of dissolute maniac, to say that he made his followers commit aimless crimes in order to keep themselves in practice, to alter the date of a speech in order to give the conspirator an effective exit from the Senate-house, to introduce some foolish talk about the Roman women as an excuse for a dashing sketch of Sempronia—all this is characteristic of an historical novelist, not of a philosophic historian.   It detracts from the value of Sallust's work, it makes us receive his statements with suspicion, and treat his soberer judgments of men and things with less attention than they deserve.   Enough, however, has been said as to Sallust's defects, especially as in the notes, from the nature of the case, it is chiefly to his defects that attention is called.   He may not be the equal of Herodotus, Thucydides, and Tacitus, but by his combination of excellence of style and of matter, he is at least worthy to be ranked in the same class with them.

INTRODUCTION TO THE CONSPIRACY OF CATILINE.

THE history of the years B.C. 66 to B.C. 62, in which the activity of Lucius Sergius Catilina was chiefly manifested, like that of every other period in any nation's existence, can only properly be understood when viewed in connection with the history of the years which preceded and followed them. The century which elapsed between the final establishment of the provincial system and the battle of Actium was occupied at Rome with the struggles of a people, great in themselves, greater still in virtue of the dominion over which they ruled, to throw off a system of government which had become antiquated, and to find one which should be capable of satisfying the new wants that had arisen. But the change from the rule of the Senate to that of the Caesars was no easy one for such an unwieldy mass as the Roman empire to accomplish, and from the tribunate of Tiberius Gracchus to the assumption of the tribunician power by Augustus, we have to watch the miserable experience by which, blindly but surely, it was led to accept the government which alone could bring it peace. No mere fluctuations in Roman politics, persecution of the democrats by the Senate, or persecution of the Senate by the democrats, could bring this change about.   These had their place, their necessary place, in the chain of causes, but in themselves were only one element out of many which contributed to the result.   Rome was not like Athens, where the eloquence of a Pericles could gain its possessor a practical dictatorship for life ; the voice of an orator in the Forum was insufficient to change the destinies of an empire which stretched from the Straits of Gibraltar to the River Euphrates.   Such a change could not be effected without bloodshed, and that on a larger scale than the breaking of a few heads in street riots at Rome.   Sulla and Marius had first to battle for dominion in Italy ; Pharsalia, Thapsus, and Munda had first to be fought ; and even so the tale of horrors was not complete till Antony and Octavianus had finally wearied the world with war.   Then, at last, the empire was firmly established, and Rome had peace for a hundred years.

Let us look at some of the causes by which this momentous change was brought about.   Abroad, the rapid succession with which, in the middle of the second century B.C., nation after nation was reduced to the form of a Roman province, made their government by the two hundred thousand demoralised men who had the right of attending the comitia in the market place of a single city, an absurdity which could not long continue.   The extent of the Roman empire demanded a ruler, who would not only govern his subjects for their own good rather than for the wealth to be gained by their plunder, but who would, in some sense, represent them far more truly than could be done by any pseudo-representative assembly in which Greeks and Spaniards, Africans and Asiatics should come together in unsympathetic union. At home, on the other hand, there was needed a strong executive government to meet the existing distress with some measures of relief, to keep the disorderly rabble of the capital in check, and to render travelling in Italy and on the high seas at least a little more secure. The government actually in power at this time was composed of the grandsons of the men, who, in Rome's long struggle with Carthage, had been their country's bulwark. With the close of that struggle the Roman aristocracy had lost their excuse for existing, at any rate as a governing body ; and the inevitable conflict had already begun, the end of which was to see the Senate reduced to impotence. The nobility fought for their privileges with unex-ampled pertinacity, and had they only shown a little temperance in their exercise, might have postponed their extinction almost indefinitely. As Professor Gardiner[1] remarks of an epoch, not altogether unlike in our own history, " the overthrow of the predomin-ance of the aristocracy would not come from a mere jealousy of their supremacy. It is not in this way that great constitutional changes are effected. There must be some actual sin of omission or of commission on the part of the rulers to stir up the desire for change." It is only, indeed, because it supplies the record of such sins and of their effects that the history of Roman politics during this century of transition is really interesting.

[1] Introduction to the Study of English History, p. 176.

The objects for which the democrats strove against the Senate were sometimes good, sometimes bad, but always, in themselves, comparatively unimportant. To one of the two really great measures of Gaius Gracchus, the enfranchisement of Italy, both parties, alike, were opposed, and the Italians had eventually to win it by their swords ; to the other, the establishment, namely, of transmarine colonies, the Senate was opposed, while the people were only lukewarm and half-hearted in its favour. The allotment of land in Italy to the poorer citizens, which formed the great feature in the legislation of the elder Gracchus, was successful as a measure of temporary relief, as we see by the sudden addition of five-and-twenty per cent. to the diminishing muster-roll of Roman burgesses. The very frequency, however, with which such proposals were repeated, shows how little permanent good they effected, and how fruitless was the endeavour to maintain a system of peasant-proprietorship side by side with the huge farms of the capitalists. This, in fine, in common with every other measure of domestic reform, which formed the subject of contention between Senate and Plebs, was ultimately useful only in so far as the struggle it occasioned helped to diminish the power of the aristocracy, and paved the way for the abolition of its rule. Of the effeteness of this aristocracy the provinces, meanwhile, had their experience in the exactions practised upon them by each successive governor, and at home the people were learning to despise it by their success in bringing its members to trial after such disasters to the Roman arms as those which occurred in the Jugurthine, and the early part of the Cimbrian war. Sulla gave the aristocracy one last chance, but this also it threw away ; and its impotence in the face of Spartacus and his gladiators, and of the pirates of Cilicia and Crete, proved to Italy and the whole Roman world its unfitness to rule.

At the date when Sallust's narrative begins, the end of B.C. 66, this feeling on the part of the people of the utter incapacity of the aristocracy, had just taken decisive effect. The Gabinian and Manilian rogations had been passed ; the generals of the Senate had been superseded ; and the whole forces of Rome were placed at the disposal of Pompey. The object for which the democrats had unwillingly fought was practically attained, and the end was beginning slowly to come into sight. By the immense powers conferred upon him Pompey was placed in a position to enact on his return from Asia Minor the part which Caesar subsequently played on his return from Gaul, and nothing but his own sluggishness and timidity of disposition stood between him and the perpetual dictatorship of Rome. By these two laws a new power was created in the state, a power which, though in the hands of Caesar it became essentially democratic, in the hands of Pompey, as the popular leaders clearly saw, might become a fatal agent of reaction. With the rise of this force the power of the Senate was definitely crushed, and, as a consequence, the old democratic battle-cries lost all their meaning. The authority against which they had been useful as levers was overthrown, and to quote the evils against which the Gracchi had striven as the object at this period of the popular party's attack, is as idle as it would have been to support the Reform Bill of 1868 with the arguments used for that of 1832. In B.C. 67 the partisans of Pompey had forced the hand of the popular party, and compelled them to support the proposal of Gabinius. The proposal became law, and for the next five years it was not the Senate, but the suspected military dictator, that was the object of the democratic hatred and fear.

It is at this conjuncture that Catiline appears on the scene. To say, with Professor Beesly, that " he was the successor in direct order of the Gracchi, of Saturninus, of Sulpicius, and of Drusus, of Cinna," is in one sense true, for every great political movement has its temporary side, which ends in a caricature, as well as its lasting side, which does not end, but only merges itself in a higher order. The legitimate successor of Gaius Gracchus in his noble aspiration towards Italian unity, and in his clear perception of the necessity for Rome of an absolute ruler, is Caesar or Augustus ; his legitimate successor on his lower side, on which he pandered to the Roman mob, is Catiline. Nor was it only the leaders of the democratic party who found here their fitting and final caricature. Catiline was a Sergius, a member of one of the noblest families in Rome ; and in his selfishness, his incapacity, and his unclean life, he only exaggerated the vices which had been prevalent among the aristocracy for the preceding century. Alike in the character of its prime mover, in the blindness and feebleness of aim which it indicates in the democratic party, and in the impotence which the Senate displayed in their measures for its suppression, the conspiracy of B.C. 63 forms a fitting prelude to the new epoch, which dates from Caesar's departure to gain himself an army in Gaul.

On his return in B.C. 66 from the government of Africa, Catiline, according to Professor Beeşly, assumed the leadership of the democratic party at Rome. Mr. Beesly is undoubtedly right in pointing out that at this time the leadership was not possessed by Caesar; but we are not for this reason bound to conclude that it lay with Catiline. If Caesar is mentioned in no oration or letter of Cicero's before B.C. 63, on the other hand, until the delivery of the election speech before the Senate about June, 64, Catiline's name only occurs in connection with his trial for extortion. If we may argue back from the latter's being engaged in a democratic plot to the likelihood of his being the democratic leader, the same argument would apply equally well to Caesar, and several other members of the party; in fact, either Gnaeus Piso, whom the Senate despatched to Spain to get him out of the way, or Publius Autronius, the unseated consul-elect, would have had a better claim to this title of leader than Lucius Catilina, who seems only to have been known hitherto as one of Sulla's assassins, and in connection with a charge of intrigue with a Vestal virgin. The truth, however, appears to be that after the departure of Pompey for the East, and the extension of his powers by the Manilian rogation, the democratic party at Rome was without any recognised leader whatever. Caesar was coming into notice, and three years later may fairly be said to have been its most

important member; but in 66 B.C. all was confusion.
The democrats had been entrapped into assisting to
place an immense force at Pompey's disposal, and
they were now in abject terror as to how he might
use it.

It is at this conjuncture that we hear of the plots
which are described under the general head of Catiline's first conspiracy. If we will remember that the
real object of terror to all but the aristocratic party at
Rome was, not the Senate, but Pompey, that Crassus,
a personal enemy of Pompey, was at the head of the
knights or capitalists, and that Piso and Autronius,
Caesar and Catiline, were all important adherents of
a popular party which leaned, on one side on the support of the knights, on the other on that of the rabble,
this conspiracy may lose some of the mystery which
is generally attached to it. Historians have found a
considerable difficulty in the fact that the plots which
Sallust and Suetonius respectively assign to this
period are puzzlingly alike, and yet differ in important particulars. Sallust speaks of a conspiracy of
Piso, Catiline, and Autronius to murder the consuls
for B.C. 65 on the first day of the year, and seize the
reins of government. Their designs, he says, were
discovered, and they postponed their execution until
the fifth of the following month, when the precipitance
of Catiline brought about an utter failure. According
to Dion Cassius the Senate was aware of the conspiracy, but was prevented by the veto of one of the
tribunes from doing more than grant the consuls a
special guard. From Cicero we learn that Torquatus,
one of the consuls who were to have been assassinated,

subsequently supported Catiline on his trial for extortion, and declared that, although he had heard something about a conspiracy, he did not attach any belief to the report, and this incredulity, real or pretended, on the part of one of the intended victims, has led some writers, including Professor Tyrrell, to doubt Catiline's complicity in any plot prior to that of B.C. 63.   If we turn now to Suetonius, we find an account of a conspiracy, also planned to take effect about the beginning of the year, in which there is no mention at all of Catiline, but the chief parts are assigned to Caesar, then aedile, Marcus Crassus, and the two unseated consuls, Sulla and Autronius, the former of whom, if we may trust Cicero, is wrongly included among the conspirators.   The objects of this plot were to make away with certain obnoxious members of the Senate, to raise Crassus to the dictatorship, with Caesar as his Master of the Horse, and subsequently to restore the consulship to the unseated candidate ; and the fiasco in this instance was brought about, not by any undue haste in giving the concerted signal, but by the timidity of Crassus, who failed to appear at the appointed time.   The discrepancies between these two accounts are obvious, yet for the existence of the plot mentioned by Sallust we have the authority not only of that historian, but of Cicero, who more than once alludes to it, and it is further vouched for by the fact that more than one person was subsequently tried for complicity in it.   On the other hand, Suetonius adduces as evidence for his own narrative the edicts of Bibulus, a speech of the elder Curio, and the history of Tanusius Geminus, authorities too weighty to be disregarded. The obvious conclusion appears to be that there were actually two plots with very similar objects planned to take effect in the beginning of B.C. 65 ; and this conclusion is greatly strengthened by the assertion of Curio and Actorius Naso, as reported by Suetonius, that Caesar at this time was engaged in another and distinct conspiracy with the young Gnaeus Piso, whom Sallust and Cicero both represent as one of Catiline's most active associates. We should believe, then, that there were two separate plots formed at this time, in both of which Caesar and Antonius were engaged. In the one they united with the head of the equestrian order, Marcus Crassus, and planned a legitimate *coup d'état;* in the other they joined their fellow democrats Catiline and Gnaeus Piso, whom we shall probably not wrong by crediting, even in B.C. 66, with some connection with the anarchists, and, if we may believe Sallust, contemplated, besides the establishment of a military power to counterbalance that of Pompey, a more widespread and indiscriminate massacre of the nobility than Crassus would have thought needful. That two conspiracies with such similar aims should have existed side by side is undoubtedly strange, but, on the one hand, the success of Caesar's assassins shows us that if they could only have exercised secrecy and discretion there was really no need for their promoters to unite their forces ; and, on the other, though the capitalists and the anarchists might each ally themselves, for their own purposes, with Caesar and Antonius, it by no means follows that they would have been equally ready to combine directly with each other.   For the rest, the fear of what Pompey might do on his return was so entirely reasonable, that there is little difficulty in believing that the three non-aristocratical parties at Rome were simply honeycombed at this time with plots, and the Senate and Torquatus had both ample justification for ignoring the existence of intrigues, which, even after they had failed, could not have been punished without the crisis of a revolution.   Lastly, all the chief members of the conspiracies had powerful motives for action; Crassus found his in personal enmity towards Pompey, Caesar in his desire for a military command in Egypt; Antonius would wish to regain his lost consulship, Piso, his seat in the Senate, Catiline, to be freed from prosecution.   With our knowledge of the presence of such incentives to revolution, and of the abundance of material that was ever to be found ready in Rome, we should almost have been justified in postulating the existence of conspiracies at this period, even if no ancient author mentioned them. As it is, in the face of so much contemporary evidence, the attempt to disprove their reality becomes almost absurd.

The history of the two following years is chiefly remarkable for the great strides made by Caesar in the popular favour.   His munificence when aedile, his boldness in reviving the memory of the triumphs of Marius, his success in bringing Sulla's blood-stained instruments to tardy justice, would prepare us for much, but hardly for his astonishing triumph in wresting the pontificate from such a man as Q. Lutatius Catulus in March B.C. 63.   It is well not to make the mistake of imagining him in the early days of his career to have been as important a personage in the eyes of his countrymen as subsequent events make him in ours; but, after an achievement like this, it is idle to talk of any but Caesar as the champion of the popular party, and of the future dictator having first made his mark by his speech in the Senate at the close of the year. If, when he left his home, overwhelmed with debts, on the morning of that sixth of March, he felt that to fail for the pontificate would involve his ruin, when he returned that evening he must have felt that the advance he had made towards ultimate success was indeed immense. Meanwhile, however, the events of B.C. 66-65 had left him closely connected with Catiline, in whose favour Crassus also was now working. For Catiline these two years had not been so fortunate as for Caesar; his trial for extortion had been delayed until the end of 63 B.C., and though it resulted in his acquittal, unless Cicero had the power of making mountains out of, not molehills, but absolutely nothing, was attended with some loss of credit. He had also been one of those tried for the part they had taken in Sulla's murders, and, though here also, possibly through Caesar's influence, he was acquitted, the reminiscences revived must have been of a character highly inconvenient to a member of the democratic party. He was now a candidate with M. Antonius for the consulship of 63 B.C., and the pair were supported with all the influence, and, apparently, the money of Crassus and Caesar. Had they been elected, we may suppose that an agrarian law similar to that of Rullus would have been carried,

and the sons of Sulla's victims restored to their political privileges, these two measures being probably
foremost on their ostensible programme. We may
conjecture, too, that even as late as this, when
Pompey's return could not be much longer delayed, a
despairing effort would have been made to organize
a rival military power. Catiline, however, was rejected, and the influence of Marcus Tullius Cicero,
the senior of the two new consuls, was sufficient to
prevent the democratic measures from passing. The
men who were subsequently implicated in the attempt
at the end of the year, whether we like to call them
conspirators or regard them simply as " members of
a large and influential party at Rome," had began to
send emissaries to the various districts in Italy to
rouse their old partisans and to gain new ones, and it
is important here to enquire what objects they could
have had in view.

Professor Beesly, in his interesting and suggestive,
though very one-sided essay, on " Catiline as a Party
Leader,"[1] enumerates among the evils of the Senatorial rule, its misgovernment of the provinces, the exclusion of " new men " from office, and the abolition of
the system of peasant proprietorship ; and his readers
would certainly gather that these were the evils
against which the democrats were now nobly contending. A moment's consideration, however, will
show how incongruous with all we know of Catiline
are the aims here attributed to him. Was the man
who had been morally convicted of extortion while

---

[1] First published in the *Fortnightly Review*, vol. i., afterwards reprinted
in " Catiline, Clodius, and Tiberius." Chapman & Hall, 1876.

governor of Africa, to take up the cause of the distressed provinces ? Was the sneerer at Cicero as " a mere citizen-at-will," to advocate the more frequent admission to office of men whose families had hitherto been undistinguished ? Was the leader who subsequently found his best soldiers in the discontented colonists of Sulla to advocate a fresh partition of the soil of Italy, for the new proprietors to barter away their farms as their predecessors had done before them ? Mr. Beesly has surely been singularly unfortunate in the evils which he has selected for a Catiline to redress. Moreover, we may fairly ask, are the evils he mentions of a kind which the Italians, whom the conspirators tried to rouse, were likely to be interested in reforming ? They may possibly have been anxious to share in the honours of office ; if so, Cicero, the aspirate, was surely a better advocate of the " *novi homines* " than Lucius Sergius Catilina ; at all events, for the provincials the Italians had no fellow-feeling, and a proposal for a repartition of the soil could only have filled them with alarm. There had been a time when Professor Beesly's comparison of the relations of Pym, or Hampden, and the Scotch insurgents would have aptly illustrated the connection of a Roman reformer with the Italians of whose cause he was the champion, the time when Drusus made himself the mouthpiece of the men who afterwards fought Rome in the social war. Now there was but one bond of union between the conspirators at Rome and their correspondents throughout the country districts, and this was the general indebtedness. To an Italian municipality it could make little difference whether Crassus or Pompey were dictator at Rome, but it was everything to them if they could free themselves from the omnipresent money-lender. The more we study the history of the second conspiracy the plainer does it appear that it was not, as some have thought, a political revolution to overthrow the Senate, nor yet, as in B.C. 66, an attempt at a *coup d'état* to obtain a force capable of opposing Pompey. In October 63 B.C., the Senate was too weak for the democrats as a party to fear, and the time for a *coup d'état* was past, even if the country districts would have taken part in such a movement. What we have here to deal with is a purely social revolution, which had as its object neither more nor less than " *tabulae novae*," or, in plain English, the extinction of debt. Lentulus and Cethegus have been blamed for their overtures to the Allobroges, and circumstances certainly made this intrigue dangerous, but they were only doing then under the eyes of the consul what Catiline's agents for the preceding half-year had been doing in every district in Italy. The motive to which they appealed in asking the help of the Allobroges, was the only motive to which they could have appealed with any success when they were tampering with the inhabitants of the different country districts. The demand for the abolition of debts is the key-note of the manifesto of Manlius, which Sallust could not have invented entirely out of his own head. We may distrust Cicero when in a public speech he makes four out of six classes of Catiline's adherents to have been driven to join his conspiracy by the pressure of their obligations ; we have no reason whatever to distrust him when in a private letter to Atticus he alludes to his suppression of this insurrection as having given him a claim to the title of "champion of the public credit."

To justify the view here taken of the different character of the movements of 65 and 63 B.C. it remains to be pointed out that it harmonizes with all our evidence as to the behaviour throughout this period of Caesar and Crassus. We have good authority for asserting their complicity in the earlier conspiracies, which had for their object the establishment of a military counterpoise to Pompey; we see them afterwards in close political connection with Catiline and Gnaeus Piso; and we know that they were both strongly suspected of complicity in the conspiracy of 63 B.C., but that all proof of their guilt was wanting. For this suspicion, their previous intimacy with Catiline, and the rumours current about the earlier plot, provided ample grounds; the fact that no proof was forthcoming we may ascribe not only to the danger there would, now as before, have been in provoking powerful men by a prosecution, but also to the probability that they were really innocent. Caesar, it is true, was heavily indebted, but his election to the pontificate must have filled him with hope, and the veriest gambler will at least see the game on which he has staked a fortune to a conclusion before he begins another. That Crassus, the greatest money-lender in Rome, would for a moment ally himself with the men who rallied to the manifesto of Manlius is simply incredible.

THE

CONSPIRACY OF CATILINE.

EVERY man who is anxious to excel the lower animals CHAP. I. should strive with all his power not to pass his life in obscurity like the brute beasts, whom nature has made the grovelling slaves of their belly. Now our whole ability resides jointly in our mind and body. In the case of the mind it is its power of guidance, in the case of the body its obedient service that we rather use, sharing the former faculty with the gods, the latter with the brute creation. This being so, I think right to seek repute by my powers rather of intellect than of strength, and since the very life which we enjoy is short, to make the memory of us as abiding as may be. The glory of wealth and beauty is fleeting and frail, but personal merit is held in eternal honour.

Now it was long hotly contested among men whether military success was more advanced by mental ability or by bodily strength, for what we need is deliberation before we begin, and after deliberation, then well-timed action; either of itself is deficient and lacks the other's help. Thus, at the outset, CHAP. II. those who were called " kings "—for that was the first title of dominion known on earth—differed from each other, some using their intellect, others their bodily powers, for even as late as this men's lives were passed in freedom from avarice, and each was contented with his own possessions. After Cyrus, however, in Asia, and the Lacedæmonians and Athenians in Greece, began the subjugation of towns and nations, and, convinced that the greatest glory was to be found in the greatest empire, held their lust for dominion a fair pretext for war, then at last, by the actual test of results it was proved that it was intellect which was most effective in war. Were then the genius of kings and commanders as potent in peace as in war, there would be more smoothness and consistency in human affairs, nor would you see power tossed from hand to hand, and the whole world subject to change and confusion. For empire is easily retained by the very devices by which it is originally acquired. When diligence, however, has been superseded by sloth, and self-restraint and moderation by lustfulness and pride, a change of fortune accompanies that of character, and thus empire is continually being transferred to the most capable from those who are less so.

Whether they be farmers, sailors, or builders, men find that everything is obedient to merit. Many, however, the slaves of gluttony and sloth, without learning or cultivation, have passed through life as though it were a journey in a foreign land, and thus, in defiance of nature, have actually found their body a pleasure and their real vital powers a burden. Of these, for my own part, I hold the life and death to be alike, since of neither is there any record. To me, indeed, the only man who really seems to live and enjoy his vital powers is he who, in devotion to some task, seeks the fame of a brilliant exploit or virtuous accomplishment. Where the field is so wide, nature points out different paths to different persons.

It is a fine thing to serve the state by action, nor is eloquence without its glory. Men may become illustrious alike in peace and war, and many by their own acts, many by their record of the acts of others, win applause. The glory which attends the doer, and the recorder of brave deeds is certainly by no means equal. For my own part, however, I count historical narration as one of the hardest of tasks. In the first place, a full equivalent has to be found in words for the deeds narrated, and in the second the historian's censures of crimes are by many thought to be the utterances of ill-will and envy, while his record of the high virtue and glory of the good, tranquilly accepted so long as it deals with what the reader deems to be easily performable, so soon as it passes beyond this is disbelieved as mere invention.

As regards myself, my inclination originally led me, like many others, while still a youth, into public life. There I found many things against me. Modesty, temperance, and virtue had departed, and hardihood, corruption, and avarice were flourishing in their stead. My mind, a stranger to bad acquirements, contemned these qualities; nevertheless, with the weakness of my age, I was kept amid this sea of vice by perverse ambition. I presented a contrast to the evil characters of my fellows, none the less I was tormented by the same craving for the honours of office, and the same sensitiveness to popularity and unpopularity as

CHAP. IV. the rest. At last, after many miseries and perils, my mind was at peace, and I determined to pass the remainder of my days at a distance from public affairs. It was not, however, my plan to waste this honourable leisure in idleness and sloth, nor yet to spend my life in devotion to such slavish tastes as agriculture or hunting. I returned to the studies I had once begun, from which my unhappy ambition had held me back, and determined to narrate the history of the Roman people in separate essays, wherever it seemed worthy of record. I was the more inclined to this by the fact that my mind was free alike from the hopes and fears of the political partisan.

I am about, therefore, with the utmost truth I can, briefly to relate the history of the conspiracy of Catiline, for I account this affair as in the highest degree memorable for the novelty both of the crime itself and of the danger it involved. Before I begin my history, a few points concerning this man's character must be made clear.

CHAP. V. Lucius Catilina was of noble birth, of great mental and bodily vigour, but of an evil and depraved disposition. From his youth he had delighted in domestic war, murder, rapine, and civil discord, and among these he had passed his early manhood. His body could bear privation, cold, and sleeplessness, to an incredible extent. His mind was bold, crafty, and versatile, skilful alike to feign or conceal whatever he chose. As covetous as prodigal, his desires knew no bounds. Not deficient in eloquence, he had little solid wisdom. The aims of his monstrous mind were always immoderate, incredible,

and placed too high. This man, after the tyranny CHAP. V.
of Lucius Sulla, had been possessed by an overwhelm-
ing passion to control the state, nor so long as he
gained supreme power for himself did he attach any
weight to the means by which he should attain it.
His headstrong spirit was daily spurred more and
more by his want of means and his consciousness of
his crimes, each increased by the qualities I have
named. Besides this, he was urged on by the corruption of a society, plagued at once by those worst and
opposite evils, luxury and avarice.

Since occasion has reminded me of the public
morality, I seemed called upon by my subject to go
back and briefly explain the civil and military customs
of our ancestors, their mode of administering the
state, the size at which they left it, and how its
beauty and nobility were gradually exchanged for
vileness and crime.

The city of Rome, according to tradition, was CHAP. VI.
originally founded and inhabited by Trojans, who,
with Æneas, their leader, were wandering about
as exiles with no settled home. These were aided
by Aborigines, a wild race who lived free and un-
shackled, without laws and without government. It
passes belief to tell with what ease these two peoples of
unlike race and different language, and each with their
own way of life, coalesced after they came within one
stronghold. After, however, their state, improved in
population, customs, and territory, seemed to have
gained some degree of strength and prosperity, as is
usual in mortal affairs, their wealth gave rise to ill-will.
The neighbouring kings and peoples assailed them,

CHAP.
VI. few of their friends came to their aid, the rest, panic-stricken, held aloof from the danger. The Romans, however, alike active at home and in the field, made their preparations in all haste. With mutual exhortations they advanced against the enemy, and shielded with their arms their freedom, country, and kin. When their courage had repelled their own danger, they brought help to their friends and allies, and won themselves friendships by their greater readiness to give than to receive a service.

Their government was according to law, and with the name of "royalty." Chosen men, of bodies enfeebled by age, but of characters strong in wisdom, formed the council of the state. These, either from their age or from a resemblance in their duties, were called "Fathers." The royal power, which had originally conduced to the maintenance of liberty and the increase of the state, was turned at last into mere arrogance and tyranny. They then changed their constitutions, and instituted yearly magistracies and pairs of magistrates, thinking that by this way men's minds would be least able to wax wanton by license.

CHAP.
VII. It was at this conjuncture that individuals began more to distinguish themselves, and to display their talents with greater readiness. By kings the good are more liable to be suspected than the bad, and cause for alarm is always found in the merit of others. As soon, then, as the state had gained its freedom, it is incredible to relate what progress it quickly made; so great was the thirst for glory that had ensued. Now, for the first time, the young men, as soon as they were of age for service, learnt warfare by the experience of

hard labour in camp. Handsome arms and warlike CHAP.
steeds now formed their pleasures in preference to VII.
women and wine. To men like these no toil was
unwonted, no ground rugged or steep, no foe in arms
an object of fear; their courage had subdued all things.
But their greatest contests for glory were with one
another. Each was eager to strike the foe, to scale
the wall, and to be seen so engaged; this they counted
wealth, this as good repute and the highest birth.
Greedy for fame, they were liberal of money, and
wished that their glory might be unbounded, and their
wealth honourably won. I could tell of places in
which a small Roman force routed huge bodies of
the enemy, and of towns naturally strong taken by
assault, were it not that this would be too wide a
digression.

Fortune, however, is truly everywhere paramount, CHAP.
and she makes known or obscures every event accord- VIII.
ing to her own whim rather than its real value. The
performances of the Athenians, as I esteem them, were
sufficiently noble and magnificent, and yet somewhat less than fame reports. At Athens, however,
there flourished historians of genius, and, consequently,
throughout the world the exploits of the Athenians
are esteemed as of the highest order. Thus the merits
of men of action are valued in proportion to the
capabilities of men of genius to extol them in words.
Of these the Roman people have never had any great
abundance ; among them the most capable men were
always the most occupied, no one exercised his mind
apart from his body, and the best men preferred action
to narration, and to have their own services praised

CHAP.
VIII. by others rather than themselves to be another's historian.

CHAP. IX.   Thus, as I have said, virtue was practised both at home and on the field. There was the utmost concord and the least possible avarice ; the right and the good obtained among them not so much by law as by nature ; strife, discord, and enmity, they carried on with their foes; citizens contended with citizens only in virtue. In their offerings to the gods they were magnificent, in their domestic expenses sparing, to their friends loyal. Their own and their country's interests they guarded by these two devices—hardihood in war, and generous treatment when peace had ensued. Of this I can adduce a striking proof; in war, punishment was more often inflicted on those who had fought the enemy contrary to orders, or who had too slowly obeyed the signal of recall from battle, than on those who had dared to desert the standard or give way when hard pressed ; in peace, they governed rather by kindness than by fear, and when they had received an injury, preferred rather to pardon than adjudge it.

CHAP. X.   Thus by diligence and fair dealing the state was advanced ; great kings were conquered in war, wild races and vast peoples subdued by force; Carthage, the rival of the Roman Empire, perished root and branch, sea and land everywhere lay open before us, when at last fortune began to turn cruel, and throw everything into confusion. Those who had lightly borne toils and dangers, doubtful fortunes and desperate straits, found the leisure and wealth elsewhere so coveted a pitiable burden. At first the lust of

money increased, then that of power, and these, it CHAP. X.
may be said, were the sources of every evil. Avarice
subverted loyalty, uprightness, and every other good
quality, and in their stead taught men to be proud.
and cruel, to neglect the gods, and to hold all things
venal. Ambition compelled many to become deceit-
ful ; they had one thought buried in their breast,
another ready on their tongue ; their friendships and
enmities they valued not at their real worth, but at
the advantage they could bring, and they maintained
the look rather than the nature of honest men. These,
evils at first grew gradually, and were occasionally
punished ; later, when the contagion advanced like
some plague, the state was revolutionized, and the
government, from being one of the justest and best,
became cruel and unbearable. At first it was not so CHAP. XI.
much avarice as ambition which spurred men's minds,
a vice, indeed, but one akin to virtue. For glory,
distinction, and power in the state are equally desired
by good and bad, though the first strives to reach his
goal by the path of honour, the second, in the lack of
honest arts, uses the weapons of falsehood and deceit.
Avarice, on the other hand, implies a zeal for money,
an object for which no philosopher ever yearned.
Tainting the body and mind of the strong, it weakens
them as by some deadly poison ; it is always bound-
less, always insatiable ; plenty and want alike fail to
lessen it. After Lucius Sulla had seized the government by force of arms, and made a bad end to a good
beginning, robbery and plunder became universal; one
coveted a house, another an estate, the victors knew
neither limit nor sobriety, and citizens became the

object of vile and cruel outrage. To make matters worse, Sulla, to secure the loyalty of the army he had led in Asia, had treated it, in defiance of ancient usage, in a lavish and far too liberal manner. Pleasant and voluptuous quarters while at peace, had easily enervated the hardy spirit of his men. It was in Asia that a Roman army first gained habits of lustfulness and intemperance, learned to admire statues, paintings, and plate, stole them from their private or public owners, plundered shrines, and polluted everything whether sacred or common. Soldiers like these, when they gained a victory, stripped their victims bare, for, since even the wise have their temper tried by prosperity, much less could men of this abandoned

character use their success with moderation. Riches became a means of distinction and glory, power and influence followed their possession. As a result the edge of virtue was dulled, poverty was accounted a disgrace, and uprightness a kind of ill-nature. Riches made the youth a prey to luxury, avarice, and pride : at once grasping and prodigal, they valued lightly their own property, while they coveted that of others ; all modesty and purity, alike things human and things divine, everything, in short, was despised and disregarded. To one acquainted with mansions and villas built on the scale of towns, it is worth while to visit the temples erected by our ancestors, the most god-fearing of men. They, indeed, decorated the shrines of the gods with piety, and their own homes with glory, while they deprived their conquered enemies of nothing save the power of doing them harm ; but in this generation the most worthless of men in the depth

of their wickedness have deprived our allies of every- CHAP.
XII.
thing which those brave men in the hour of victory
had left them, as if the one and only use of empire
were to inflict harm. Why should I tell of things CHAP.
XIII.
which no one who has not seen them could believe, of
how often private individuals have levelled mountains
and built over seas? Such men seem to me to have
trifled with their riches in the haste with which they
ignobly abused what they might honourably have
enjoyed. But the passion for defilement, gluttony,
and all other kinds of indulgence, had kept pace with
that for wealth. Each sex alike trampled on their
modesty. Sea and land were ransacked to supply the
table. Men went to rest before they felt a desire for
sleep ; they did not wait for hunger or thirst, cold, or
weariness, but anticipated them all by luxurious
expedients. Such a life, when means had failed,
spurred youth into crime. Their minds, tainted with
bad accomplishments, could not endure to be deprived
of their sensual pleasures, and they abandoned themselves with all the more recklessness to every kind
both of gain and expense.

It was in a state of this magnitude and corruption 
that Catiline, as was indeed easily done, gathered
round him, to serve as body-guard, troops of men
stained by every vice and crime. Every gambler,
adulterer, and glutton, who, by the gratification of his
passion, had cruelly impaired his patrimony, every
one whose debts had been swollen to buy indemnity
for some shameless deed, all parricides from every
quarter, all who had committed sacrilege, who had
been tried and condemned, or whose deeds made them

CHAP.
XIV. fear a trial, all who gained a living by polluting their tongues with perjury, or their hands with their countrymen's blood, in fine, all who were harassed by crime, by need, or by the pangs of conscience—it was these who were Catiline's intimate associates; while, did anyone as yet free from guilt chance to become his friend, by daily intercourse and allurement, he was easily made a fit fellow to the rest. It was especially, however, the intimacy of young men that Catiline affected; and their pliable and unformed minds fell an easy prey to his wiles. Complying with the several forms of youthful passion, he helped some to mistresses, bought hounds and horses for others, and, in fine, spared neither his purse nor his honour to make them his faithful creatures. I am aware that there were some who held the belief that the young men who made Catiline's house their resort, behaved with too little regard for decency, but the report obtained credence rather from other considerations than from

CHAP.
XV. any direct testimony. At the very outset of his youth Catiline had engaged in many scandalous intrigues; one with a high-born maiden, another with a priestess of Vesta, and others which in like manner set law and morality at defiance. Finally he was seized with a passion for Aurelia Orestilla (a lady in whom no respectable man ever found anything to praise except her beauty), and, on her hesitating to marry him in her dislike of a grown-up stepson, killed the youth,—so it is positively believed,—and thus cleared his house for the unhallowed union. In this deed I trace one of the chief causes of Catiline's bringing his attempt to a point. His impure mind, hateful alike to gods

and men, could find rest neither awake nor asleep, so
terribly was his frenzied soul ravaged by the pangs
of conscience. His countenance grew bloodless, his
eyes haggard, his pace now hurried and now slow.
Madness was plainly stamped upon his face and expression. The young men whom, as narrated above,
he had enticed, he kept instructing in many varieties
of crime. It was from their ranks that he provided
false witnesses to facts and documents ; he bade them
think cheaply alike of honour, fortune, and danger,
and then, when he had crushed their sense of fame
and decency, his yoke became heavier. If motives
for crime were for the moment wanting, they had to
ensnare or assassinate the inoffensive as though they
had offended ; he would rather, forsooth, indulge his
wickedness and cruelty without a cause than allow
hand or brain to become sluggish by disuse. In reliance on friends and associates such as these, and
encouraged by the enormous prevalence of debt
throughout the world, and by the number of Sulla's
soldiers who had squandered their fortunes, and were
now dwelling on the memory of plunder and ancient
victories, and hoping for civil war, Catiline formed a
plan for destroying the constitution. There was no
army in Italy ; Gnaeus Pompeius was engaged 'in a
war in far distant lands ; he had great hopes of success
in his own candidature for the consulship ; the Senate
was unprepared for any emergency ; everything was
in peace and quietness, and here Catiline saw his
opportunity.

It was about the first of June in the year when
Lucius Caesar and Gaius Figulus were consuls that he

began making overtures to single individuals, encouraging some and sounding others, and expatiating on his own resources, on the lack of preparation in the government, and on the great prizes a conspiracy would gain. When he had satisfied himself on the points he desired, he summoned a meeting of all whose needs were the most pressing, and spirit the most daring. To the meeting came Publius Lentulus Sura, Publius Autronius, Lucius Cassius Longinus, Gaius Cethegus, Publius and Servius the two sons of Servius Sulla, Lucius Vargunteius, Quintus Annius, Marcus Porcius Laeca, Lucius Bestia, Quintus Curius; all of senatorial rank; with them were Marcus Fulvius Nobilior, Lucius Statilius, Publius Gabinius Capito, and Gaius Cornelius, from the equestrian order; besides many persons from the military colonies and borough towns, men of rank in their own neighbourhood. Many, moreover, of the nobility were associated in this plot, though they kept more in the background. These were spurred on rather by the hope of power than by want or any other necessity. Indeed, great numbers of young men, especially those of noble birth, were favourable to Catiline's attempt, and though, while tranquillity lasted, they had every means of living in splendour and luxury, preferred the doubtful to the certain, and war to peace. There were, too, at that crisis, some who believed that Marcus Licinius Crassus was no stranger to the conspiracy. Gaius Pompeius, his personal enemy, was at the head of a large army, and Crassus was thought to be favourable to the growth of any influence that might balance his power, in the confident belief that, should the plot

succeed, he would easily secure the chief place among CHAP. XVII.
its leaders.

A few conspirators, it must be remarked, of whom CHAP. XVIII.
Catiline was one, had before this formed a plot against
the state, of which I will give the most accurate account I can. In the consulship of Lucius Tullus and
Marcus Lepidus, Publius Autronius, and Publius
Sulla, the consuls elect, were put on their trial and
punished under the bribery laws. A little after this,
Catiline was charged with extortion, and so disqualified as a candidate for the consulship [since he could
not give in his name within the legal time]. At the
same time a certain Gnaeus Piso, a young man of
good birth but needy, ill-affected and of desperate
daring, was being urged by his poverty and evil disposition to embroil the State. With this man, Catiline
and Autronius discussed their plot about the first
week in December, and planned to murder the consuls,
Lucius Cotta and Lucius Torquatus, in the Capitol on
January 1st, to seize the insignia of office for themselves, and to send Piso with an army to hold the two
Spanish provinces. The plot was discovered, and
they again postponed their plans of murder to February 5th. On this occasion they were to contrive the
destruction not only of the consuls, but of many of
the senators, and had not Catiline, who was stationed
in front of the Senate-house, been too hasty in giving
the signal to his confederates, on that day would have
been accomplished the worst outrage of any since the
foundation of Rome. As it was, their armed supporters had not yet mustered in force, and this circumstance ruined the plot. Piso was subsequently sent as CHAP. XIX.

CHAP.
XIX. quæstor, with the powers of a prætor, to Hither-Spain. This appointment Crassus supported, as he knew Piso for a bitter enemy of Gnaeus Pompeius ; nor was the Senate unwilling to grant him a province in their eagerness to remove so abandoned a man from the sphere of politics, while many of the aristocracy looked on him in the light of a bulwark, and were already panic-stricken at the power of Pompeius. Piso, however, was murdered in his province by a troop of Spanish horse at whose head he had placed himself on a march without any other force. Some would make out that the barbarians could not submit to the injustice, arrogance, and cruelty, that marked his rule ; others, that the horsemen were old and faithful dependents of Gnaeus Pompeius, and attacked Piso with his consent. The Spaniards, they remarked, had never committed such an outrage on other occasions, but had patiently submitted to much previous tyranny. I shall leave this point as an open question, and have now said enough about the earlier conspiracy.

CHAP.
XX. When Catiline saw assembled the men whom I named a little above, although he had held many communications with each of them separately, he yet thought it would serve his purpose to address and encourage them collectively. He conducted them, therefore, to a secluded part of his house, and then, having secured the absence of any witness, spoke somewhat as follows :—

" Had I not myself tested your courage and loyalty this favourable conjuncture would have offered itself in vain. Our hopes might have been high, and power have lain ready to our hands, but it would have availed nothing. I should not now be abandoning the certain to pursue the doubtful had I only cowardly or frivolous supporters to depend on. As it is, I have learnt your valour and devotion to myself on many important occasions, and my mind has therefore dared to embark on this greatest and noblest of attempts. I am encouraged, too, by my clear perception that, whether in good or evil fortune, your interests are identical with mine ; for in this identity of hopes and fears lies the true bond of friendship.

"The plans which I have been revolving in my mind you have all separately heard ere now. For my own part, however, I find my spirit daily more on fire at the thought of what will be our lot if we fail to assert our claim to freedom. Ever since the government of the state was merged in the prerogatives and authority of a few influential men, it is to these that kings and princes have been tributary, and peoples and races have paid their dues. We, the remainder of the nation, however energetic and virtuous, whatever our birth, whether noble or base, have formed an undistinguished crowd without interest or influence, and lie at the mercy of a party to whom, were the state in a sound condition, we should be a terror. Thus all influence and power, distinction and wealth remain in their own, or their favourites' hand ; to us they have left danger and rejections, prosecutions and want. Bravest of men, what is the limit of your endurance ? Is it not better to die once for all a brave man's death than to drag out a life of misery and dishonour, as the butts of your enemies' insolence, and lose it shamefully at the end?

"But why speak of this? I call Gods and men to witness that victory is within our grasp. Our age is in its prime and our minds at their strongest, our enemies are enfeebled by years and riches. We have only to make a beginning, the course of events will do the rest. And what man, with a temper worthy of that name, can brook their possession of a surplus of wealth to squander on driving back the sea and levelling mountains, while we lack the means to procure even the necessaries of life? That they should join house to house and houses to houses, while we have nowhere a hearth to call our own? They are buying pictures and statuary and plate; are pulling down the work of yesterday to build it anew; in a word, are squandering and abusing their wealth in all possible ways; and yet, though they indulge every passion to the full, they cannot exhaust their riches. We are met by poverty at home and creditors abroad. Our fortunes are bad, our expectations still more forbidding. In fine, what have we left except the breath we draw in misery?

"Must I not then bid you awake? Before you there dawns the freedom for which you have often yearned, and now freedom, wealth, splendour, and glory rise before your eyes. Such, to the full, are the rewards which fortune has decreed to the conquerors. Your dangers and your beggary, the rich spoils which war offers, plead more powerfully with you than any words of mine. Use me as your general or your fellow-soldier; my mind and my body shall ever be

at your service. These very plans I hope, with your CHAP. XX
aid, to carry into execution as consul, unless, haply,
my mind deceives me, and you are more ready to
serve than to command."

These words were listened to by men who had every CHAP. XXI.
evil in abundance, but no good fortune, nor any hope
of it. Great, however, as the wages of revolution
appeared to them, many yet asked Catiline to explain
what would be the nature of the war, what the prizes
their arms were to seek, what help he counted on or
hoped for, and from what quarter. He proceeded to
promise them an abolition of debts, a proscription of
the rich, magistracies and priestly offices, together with
plunder, and all the gratifications enjoyed by the
victors in a war. In Hither-Spain, he continued, was
Piso ; in Mauritania, at the head of an army, Publius
Sittius Nucerinus ; both of them partners in their conspiracy. Gaius Antonius, too, was a candidate for the
consulship, and he hoped to have him as his colleague,
as a man at once intimate with himself and entangled
in the greatest difficulties. When himself consul he
should join Antonius in making the first move. He
then railed and inveighed against the whole aristocratic party ; made laudatory mention of each of his
own followers ; and reminded one of his poverty,
another of his desires, many of the danger they stood
in or the shame they had undergone, and many more
of the triumph of Sulla, in which they had found an
opportunity for plunder. At last, seeing every mind
thoroughly aroused, he bade them be zealous in support of his candidature, and dismissed the meeting.
It was asserted by some at the time that Catiline, CHAP. XXII.

CHAP.
XXII.

when, after making a speech, he was preparing to administer an oath to his accomplices, carried round in bowls a mixture of human blood and wine, and only revealed his design after all had tasted of it with such an imprecation as was customary in solemn rites. This [they maintained] he did that their mutual consciousness of such an abomination might make them more loyal to each other. Some, however, were of opinion that this story, together with many others, was invented by people who thought that the unpopularity which Cicero subsequently incurred would be diminished if the crime of his victims were recognised as peculiarly hideous. The evidence I have found for the incident is too slight to support so monstrous a charge.

CHAP.
XXIII.

Among the conspirators was a certain Quintus Curius, a man of no mean station ; he was covered, however, with shame and crime, and his infamy had caused the censors to expel him from the Senate. The man was as frivolous as bold, and could neither keep a secret nor conceal his own crimes ; in short, he was heedless alike of his words and deeds. Between him and a certain Fulvia, a woman of birth, there was a long-standing intrigue. He had lately fallen in her good graces owing to his poverty making him less lavish in his presents, when suddenly he began to boast, made her outrageous promises, and threw out at times threats of violence should she fail to be compliant ; in fine, his whole behaviour became more haughty than was his wont. On discovering the cause of Curius' strange conduct, Fulvia did not keep secret a danger so threatening to the state, but, while suppressing the name of her informant, told several persons what, and how, she had heard of Catiline's plot. This, more than anything else, roused men's zeal to confer the consulship on Marcus Tullius Cicero. Till that time many of the nobility had been in a ferment of jealousy, and had thought the consulship would be in a manner polluted if obtained by a man of no family, however distinguished. When, however, danger was imminent, jealousy and crime fell into the background.

On the poll being taken, Marcus Tullius and Gaius Antonius were declared elected. This, as was afterwards seen, was the first blow that confounded the conspirators. It did not, however, lessen the frenzy of Catiline ; on the contrary, his activity increased daily, he stored arms in suitable places throughout Italy, and conveyed money, borrowed on his own or his friends' security, to a certain Manlius at Faesulae, who afterwards took the first step in beginning the war. He is said also at this period to have gained over many men of every rank, with a number of women, who, though at the outset their beauty had provided them means to support their extravagance, now found their gains, but not their luxury, limited by advancing age, and consequently had contracted huge debts. Through them Catiline hoped to tamper with the slaves of Rome, to fire the city, and either to win over or murder their husbands.

Among these women was a certain Sempronia, who had perpetrated many crimes, often worthy of a man's daring. She was well endowed with birth and beauty and fortunate in her husband and children ; was well

CHAP.
XXV.

read in Greek and Latin literature, could sing, play, and dance more gracefully than an honest woman need, and had many of the other accomplishments of a riotous life. There was nothing she held less dear than purity and honour; indeed, it would be hard to determine if she were more careless of her wealth or her repute; so destitute was she of all modesty that more often than not, she was the first to begin an intrigue. Often ere this she had broken her engagements, forsworn her trust, and been an accomplice in murder; an extravagance which outran her resources had hurried her downwards. Her talents, however, were by no means despicable; she could write verses, bandy jests, and talk modestly, voluptuously, or pertly at will; in short, she was a woman of much pleasantry and wit.

CHAP.
XXVI.

Catiline, though he had made these preparations, was yet a candidate for the next year's consulship, hoping, should he be elected, easily to make a tool of Antonius. In the meantime he was not inactive, but was using every method of intrigue against Cicero. The latter, however, had no lack of craft and adroitness for his own protection. At the very beginning of his consulship, by dint of great promises, he had, through Fulvia, prevailed on the Quintus Curius described above, to betray to him Catiline's designs. By an agreement about the provinces he had constrained his colleague, Antonius, to desist from all disloyalty, while he secretly surrounded his own person with a body-guard of friends and dependents. The day of election came, and Catiline failed alike in his candidature and in the secret attack he had planned against the consuls in the Campus. He determined, therefore, to make open war and to go to every length, since his secret attempt had had so adverse and disgraceful an issue.

Accordingly he despatched Gaius Manlius to Faesulae and that part of Etruria, a certain Septimius of Camerinum to Picenum, Gaius Julius to Apulia, and to other quarters such persons as he thought would in each place be able to advance his ends. Meanwhile at Rome he was working at many plans at the same time, directing secret attacks on the consuls, making arrangements for a conflagration, and occupying suitable points with armed men. He himself went about armed, and bade others do the same, exhorting them always to be ready and on the watch. By day and by night he was active and wakeful, and neither sleeplessness or toil could wear him out. When nothing came of all his activity, at dead of night he again summoned the chiefs of the conspiracy to meet, this time at the house of Marcus Porcius Laeca, and there, after many complaints of their cowardice, informed them that he had despatched Manlius to head the force which he had collected for taking up arms, as well as other agents to other favourable points to begin the war. He was anxious, he said, himself to set out to the army if he could first work the destruction of Cicero, who was a great obstacle to his plans. While all the rest showed fear and hesitation, a Roman knight, named Gaius Cornelius, offered his help, and was joined by a senator, named Lucius Vargunteius. The two determined to proceed, a little later on in the same night, with an armed force

CHAP.
XXVI.

CHAP.
XXVII.

CHAP.
XXVIII.

to gain entrance to Cicero's house, as though to attend his levee, and then suddenly to take him unprepared and assassinate him in his own home. Curius, on hearing the greatness of the peril which threatened the consul, lost no time in acquainting Cicero, through Fulvia, with the plot laid against him. The assassins were turned away from the gate, and found they had planned their atrocious crime in vain.

Meanwhile, in Etruria, Manlius was tampering with a populace whose poverty, combined with their indignation at the wrong they had suffered in losing, under the tyranny of Sulla, their lands and all their property, now made them eager for revolution. With them were joined robbers of every description who greatly abounded in those parts, besides some veterans from the Sullan colonies, whose lavish indulgence of their passions had left them with nothing out of all their immense booty.

Cicero, when informed of this, was distracted by the double nature of his difficulty. On the one hand, he was unable any longer to protect the city from the conspirators' attack by such measures as he could take on his own authority; on the other, he had no certain information as to either the numbers or the designs of the army of Manlius. Under these circumstances he laid the matter before the Senate, which had now for some time been disquieted by the reports prevalent among the people. Following the course usual in dealing with any threatening emergency, the Senate made the decree: " The consuls are to take measures to protect the state from harm." This is the greatest power which the Roman constitution allows the

Senate to confer on a magistrate. It authorises him to raise an army, wage war, control in every possible way both citizens and allies, and exercise the highest military and judicial authority at home and in the field. Without this decree the consul has no powers in any of these matters except by command of the people. A few days afterwards, Lucius Saenius, a senator, read before the House a letter which he said he had received from Faesulae. It contained the news that Gaius Manlius, with a large force, had taken up arms on October 23rd. As usual in such cases, some at once began to report signs and wonders; others, to assert that meetings had been held and weapons conveyed, and that at Capua and in Apulia the slaves were rising. By a decree of the Senate, Quintus Marcus Rex was despatched to Faesulae, and Quintus Metellus Creticus to Apulia and its neighbourhood. Both these officers were waiting near the city, still retaining their commission as generals. The celebration of their triumphs had been obstructed by the underhand tactics of a clique who were accustomed to set a price on everything whether honourable or the reverse. Besides these, two praetors, Quintus Pompeius Rufus, and Quintus Metellus Celer, were sent to Capua and Picenum respectively, with powers to raise an army adequate to the needs of the time and the danger of the state. Rewards were also offered for any information as to the conspiracy against the state. These rewards were, in the case of a slave, his freedom and one hundred thousand sesterces (£850), and for a free man, a pardon for any share he might have had in the plot and double that sum. A decree was at the same

CHAP.
XXX.

time passed that the gladiatorial schools should be quartered on Capua and the other borough towns according to their means, and that, at Rome, watches should be set throughout the city under the charge

CHAP.
XXXI.

of the minor magistrates. By these measures the state was violently excited, and the appearance of the capital quite changed. The life of unrestrained pleasure and indulgence begotten of a long period of peace was suddenly replaced by universal gloom. A state of feverish anxiety ensued. No person or place was thoroughly trusted. There was neither open war nor secured peace, and each man measured the danger only by the terror in his own breast. The women, too, to whom the fear of war, now that the limits of the empire were so vast, had come as an unwonted feeling, were in great distress. They raised their hands in prayer to heaven; wept over their little children; were full of questions; and saw danger in everything; throwing aside pride and frivolity, they despaired of themselves and their country.

Despite these preparations for defence, the ruthless mind of Catiline was busy with all its former plans, and he was accused by Lucius Paulus under the Plautian law. At last, either by way of dissembling or to clear himself should he be denounced, he attended the Senate. Thereupon, the consul, Marcus Tullius, either from fear of his presence or in a burst of anger, did good service to his country by delivering a noble speech, which he afterwards wrote out and published. On his resuming his seat, Catiline, following out his determination to dissemble everything, with downcast look and in tones of entreaty began to beg the senators to form no hasty opinion of him. His birth and his conduct from his youth up justified him in cherishing the highest hopes ; it would be wrong of them to imagine that he, a patrician born, whose own and whose ancestors' public services had been so numerous, could find it his interest to destroy the state, while Marcius Tullius, a mere citizen-at-will, was engaged in its preservation. He was proceeding to further abuse when a storm of shouts and cries of " Enemy " and " Traitor " interrupted him. Furious with rage, he exclaimed, "Since I am beset and driven to destruction by my foes, I will quench in a general ruin the fire that surrounds me."

CHAP. XXXI.

With these words he dashed out of the Senate-house and hurried to his home. There his brain was soon busy. His treacherous attack on the consul was a failure, and he saw that the city was protected from incendiaries by the watches set. He thought it best, therefore, to increase his army, and to employ the time before the legions could be levied in seizing the numerous positions that might be useful for the war. At dead of night he set out with a few companions for the camp of Manlius, leaving instructions to Cethegus, Lentulus, and the others whose readiness and daring he had tested, to use every possible means of increasing the strength of their party, of pushing forward the plots against the consul, and of arranging for a massacre, a conflagration, and the other horrors of war. He promised shortly to march against the city in person, with a large army.

CHAP. XXXII.

While these events were taking place at Rome, Gaius Manlius sent deputies from his force to Marcius

CHAP. XXXIII.

CHAP.
XXXIII. Rex with a message to this effect,—"We call gods and men to witness, general, that we have taken up arms with no designs against our country nor with any wish to bring others into danger. To ensure the safety of our own persons is our only motive; for, needy wretches as we are, the violence and cruelty of usurers has robbed most of us of our country, and all of fame and fortune. Not one of us was allowed, according to ancient custom, to avail himself of that law, by which, on sacrificing his property, his person would have remained free; so pitiless were the usurers and the judge. Your ancestors often, in compassion for the commons of Rome, relieved their destitution by the decrees they proposed; and, quite recently, within our own recollection, owing to the prevalence of debt, bronze was raised for purposes of repayment to the value of silver, and this with the approval of all honest men. Often, again, the commons themselves, roused either by a lust for power, or by the insolence of magistrates, took up arms, and revolted from the Senate. We, however, ask for neither rule nor riches, though these are the cause of every war and struggle among men; we ask only for that freedom which no brave man ever abandoned while life remained. We adjure you and the Senate to take measures to relieve us, your fellow-citizens, to restore to us the protection of the law, wrested from us by judicial corruption, and not to force us to seek a course, by which, while perishing ourselves, we may wreak the completest vengeance for our blood."

CHAP.
XXXIV. To this, Quintus Marcius replied, "If you have anything to ask of the Senate, throw down your arms, and go to Rome with your petition. Such has ever been the clemency and compassion of the Senate of the Roman people that no one ever asked their help in vain."

To return to Catiline; on his way to join Manlius he sent letters to many men of consular rank, and, besides these, to all persons of any mark, informing them that beset by false accusations, and unable to make head against the cabal of his enemies, he was resigning himself to fortune, and was now on his way to exile at Massilia. This course he was taking, not because his conscience reproached him with the crimes with which he was charged, but to secure the peace of the State and to prevent any dispute about himself giving rise to sedition. To a very different effect was a letter read before the House by Quintus Catulus, which he said had been delivered to him in Catiline's name: of this letter the following is a copy,—" Lucius Catilina to Quintus Catulus— Your honour, at once so eminent and so practically proved, on which amid my great dangers it pleases me to think, encourages me to commit my affairs into your hands. I have determined, therefore, to enter on no defence as regards the fresh step I have taken, but have made up my mind, since I am conscious of no fault, to lay before you an explanation, of which, I profess, you can easily recognise the truth. Roused by the wrongs and insults I have endured, finding myself robbed of all reward for my toil and energy, and unable to gain any official position, I followed my usual bent and undertook the championship of the wretched. This I did, not because my property was insufficient to discharge my personal debts; on

CHAP.
XXXIV

CHAP.
XXXV.

CHAP.
XXXV. the contrary, the generosity of Orestilla was ready to pay off, from her own and her daughter's funds, those contracted as surety for others. No, it was the sight of unworthy men raised to the honours of office that impelled me, and the feeling that I myself was excluded on false suspicions. For these reasons I have embraced the hope, honourable in my present fortunes, of preserving what position I yet hold. I would write more, but news has just been brought that I am threatened with attack. For the present I commend Orestilla to you, and entrust her to your honour. I implore you, as you love your own children, shield her from harm. Farewell."

CHAP.
XXXVI. Catiline himself abode a few days with Gaius Flaminius at Arretium, and supplied the neighbourhood, which he had previously aroused, with arms. He then assumed the fasces and other marks of a consular commission, and marched to the camp of Manlius. When this was known at Rome, the Senate pronounced Catiline and Manlius public enemies, and fixed a day, up to which the rest of the conspirators, except those condemned on capital charges, would be held guiltless on throwing down their arms. A decree was also passed, ordering the consuls to hold a levy. Antonius was to put himself at the head of an army, and pursue Catiline with all haste; Cicero, to remain to protect the capital.

It was at this crisis that the empire of the Roman people, in my opinion, reached its most pitiable condition. From the setting to the rising sun its arms had subdued every land to obedience; at home there was peace and wealth, the

first of blessings, men esteem them, in abundance; and yet there were found citizens with minds
hardened, to undertake their own and their country's
destruction. Two decrees of the Senate had been
passed, but of all the host not one was enticed by
the reward offered to betray the conspiracy, not one
deserted the camp of Catiline, so virulent was the disease which had settled like a plague on the minds of
many citizens. Nor was disloyalty confined to those
who had been admitted to the conspiracy; it may be
said that the whole of the common people, in their
eagerness for revolution, approved the designs of
Catiline. And this seemed but natural, for it always
happens in states that the penniless envy the respectable and praise the disaffected, hate the old
order and long for the new, and in their disgust at
their own fortunes are eager for a general change.
Careless of everything, they find in riot and sedition
their meat and drink, for it is easy for the poor to
escape loss. The populace of the capital, however,
was especially impetuous, and that for many reasons.
In the first place Rome had become a sink into which
there poured all who were in any place notorious for
crime or vice, others who had shamefully squandered
their estates, and, in fine, every one whose disgraceful
conduct and actions had made him an exile from his
home. Again, there were many whose thoughts
dwelt on the triumph of Sulla; they saw some, who
had been common soldiers, now senators, and others
so rich as to live in a style of regal magnificence; each
hoped that, should he take up arms, victory would
bring him no less rewards. Besides these, many

CHAP.
XXXVII.

young men who had starved in the country on the wages of their hands, had been attracted to Rome by public or private bounties, and had learnt to prefer the ease of the capital to such thankless toil. These, and all like them, found their profit in disaster to the state, so that we need wonder the less that penniless men of bad character were filled with high hopes, and measured their country's interests by their own. Again, all those whose parents had been proscribed during Sulla's triumph, whose property had been confiscated, and their political rights impaired, were awaiting the issue of the struggle with like feelings. To these might be added all who, as being in opposition to the senatorial party, preferred a convulsion in the state to their own exclusion from power. In fine, after many years, just the old disorders had returned

CHAP.
XXXVIII.

to threaten the state. The tribunitian power had been restored in the consulship of Pompey and Crassus, and henceforth young men, made headstrong by their age and character, possessed themselves of this important office and began to rouse the mob by attacks on the Senate, next by bribery and promises to kindle their passions, and thus, finally, to attain to distinction and influence. They were strenuously opposed by many of the nobility, who made the defence of the Senate a pretext for advancing their own importance. To put the truth shortly, from the time of Sulla forward, though those who busied themselves with state affairs might allege honourable excuses, in some cases the defence of the people's rights, in others the extension of the authority of the Senate, beneath all this pretext of the public good each was secretly striving to gain power for himself. They showed no moderation, pushed hostility to an extreme, and made a bloody use of victory when won. After the despatch of Pompey to conduct the wars against the Pirates and Mithradates, the power of the commons was broken, and the influence of the oligarchy increased. They held the magistracies, the provincial appointments, and all other patronage, in their own hands ; they passed their days in prosperity, free from trouble and anxiety, and by their control of the courts terrified all who while in office treated the populace with greater mildness. As soon, however, as, amid their perilous condition, a hope of revolution was offered to the commons, the old battle-cry raised their spirits. Had Catiline come off victor, or even on equal terms, from the first battle-field, the state would, no doubt, have been prostrated by massacre and disaster, while the victorious party would only have enjoyed their success till some stronger champion snatched power and freedom from their tired and enfeebled hands. Even as it was, many persons not connected with the conspiracy, at the outbreak of the war set out to join Catiline. Among these was a certain Aulus Fulvius, a senator's son, who was dragged back when already on the way, and put to death by his father's order. At Rome, meantime, Lentulus was following out the injunction of Catiline, and tampering in person, or through his agents, with all whose character or fortunes made them, he thought, fit instruments of revolution, not confining himself to citizens, but enlisting men of every class, so long as they would be useful in war. In pursuance of this policy,

CHAP.
XXXVIII.

CHAP.
XXXIX.

CHAP.
XL.

 he entrusted a certain Publius Umbrenus with the task of seeking out the ambassadors from the Allobroges, and inducing them, if possible, to join in the war. Their great public and private indebtedness, and the warlike temperament of the Gallic race, led him to hope that they would readily join in such an enterprise. Umbrenus had previously been employed in Gaul, and was acquainted with many of the chief men in the different states. He went to work therefore at once, and on the first occasion of his seeing the ambassadors in the Forum, asked a few questions as to their public affairs, and, as if grieved for their misfortunes, began to enquire what issue they hoped for to such evils. They complained of the greed of the magistrates, accused the Senate for its failure to help them, and foreboded death as the one cure for their ills. On hearing this, he told them that if they would be men, he would show them a way of escape from the great evils they spoke of. Inspired with extravagant hopes by his words, the Allobroges implored Umbrenus to take pity on them. There was no task so hard or repellent that they would not be most eager to perform it, if it would but free their state from debt. Thereupon Umbrenus took them to the house of Decimus Brutus, which was near the Forum, and was thrown open to the conspirators by the influence of Sempronia, for Brutus at the time was absent from Rome. To lend greater weight to his words, he also summoned Gabinius, and in his presence disclosed the conspiracy, and named his accomplices, including among them, in order to inspire the ambassadors with greater courage, many persons of every rank who were perfectly innocent. At last he procured from the ambassadors a promise of their services, and dismissed them home. The Allobroges, however, wavered for a long time as to what course they should adopt. On the one side was their debt, their love of war, and the great rewards they might expect if victorious ; on the other, greater resources, an absence of risk, and a certain and immediate reward instead of uncertain hope. Thus they examined both sides of the question ; but the fortune of the republic at last prevailed. They betrayed the whole affair, just as they had heard it, to Quintus Fabius Sanga, whose patronage their state mostly employed. Cicero, informed by Sanga of the plot, instructed the ambassadors to make a great show of zeal for the conspiracy, to visit the rest of the intriguers, make them ample promises, and use every exertion for their complete exposure.

Almost simultaneously, there were risings in Hither and Farther Gaul, as also in Picenum, Bruttium, and Apulia. The agents whom Catiline had previously despatched on every side were, with a rashness that approached insanity, pushing on all their plans at once. Their midnight councils, their transport of arms and weapons, their general hurry and bustle had caused more fear than actual danger. Many of these agents had been brought to trial by the praetor, Quintus Metellus Celer, in accordance with a resolution of the Senate, and by him thrown into prison, and Gaius Murena had pursued the same course in Farther Gaul, where he held command as a legate.

Meanwhile at Rome, Lentulus, with the other heads

CHAP.
XLIII. of the conspiracy, had equipped what seemed to them a large force, and determined that, on the arrival of Catiline and his army at Faesulae, Lucius Bestia, a tribune of the commons, should hold a public meeting, complain of the steps taken by Cicero, and throw the odium of having caused a most terrible war on that excellent consul. Taking this as their signal, the rank and file of their supporters were on the following night to carry out their respective tasks. Report said that these were distributed in the following manner :— Statilius and Gabinius, with a large force, were to set fire simultaneously to twelve suitable points in the town ; the confusion thus caused would gain them easier access to the consul, and to the others at whom they aimed ; Cethegus was to beset Cicero's door and attack him by force; others of the conspirators had other victims ; and the young men, most of them of noble birth, were to murder their parents, and in the general panic that the simultaneous massacre and fire would occasion, a sally was to be made to join Catiline. While these preparations and arrangements were being made, Cethegus was continually complaining of the cowardice of his associates. He declared that by their hesitation and delay they had wasted splendid chances ; in such a crisis it was action that was needed, not deliberation, and he himself, he protested, were he joined by only a few others, would attack the Senate house, while the rest played the coward. Naturally bold and impetuous, he was ever ready to strike a blow, and was convinced that prompt action offered the highest advantages.

CHAP.
XLIV. To return to the Allobroges ; in obedience to Cicero's

injunction, they procured a meeting through Gabinius
with the rest of the conspirators, and demanded from
Lentulus, Cethegus, Statilius, and also Cassius, an
oath which they might bear, duly attested, to their
countrymen.   Without this it would be a difficult
task to make them join in so serious an attempt. The
rest did as they were asked without any suspicion, but
Cassius promised to go shortly to Gaul in person, and,
indeed, left the city on that journey some little time
before the ambassadors.   On the departure of the
latter, Lentulus sent with them a certain Titus Volturcius of Crotona, so that previous to their return
home they might strengthen the bonds of their alliance
by exchanging assurances with Catiline.   He further
entrusted Volturcius with a letter to Catiline, of which
I give a copy :—" Who I am you will learn from the
bearer.   Consider the danger of your position, and
remember that you are a brave man.   Think what
your plans demand ; seek help from all, even from
the lowest."   Besides this letter he sent a verbal
message asking, now that he had been declared a
public enemy by the Senate, what he had to gain by
refusing the help of slaves ?   The preparation he had
ordered in the capital had been made ; there must be
no delay on his part in advancing nearer to Rome.
When matters had gone thus far, on the night agreed
on for their departure, Cicero, whose emissaries had
informed him of everything, gave orders to the praetors, Lucius Valerius Flaccus, and Gaius Pomptinus,—
to plant an ambush by the Mulvian bridge, and seize
the Allobroges, with their retinue.   He explained
clearly the object on which they were sent, and em-

CHAP
XLIV.

CHAP.
XLV.

CHAP.
XLV. powered them to manage the details as need might arise. The praetors, men used to war, quietly stationed their guards, and secretly occupied the bridge, according to their instructions. The ambassadors, with Volturcius, had no sooner arrived at the place than a simultaneous shout arose from either side. The Gauls quickly recognised the design, and promptly surrendered to the praetors. Volturcius at first encouraged the rest to resistance, and defended himself with his sword against his numerous assailants; finding, however, that he was deserted by the ambassadors, after many entreaties to Pomptinus on the score of their acquaintance to secure his safety, he at last, in great fear and trembling for his life, surrendered to the praetors as though to declared enemies.

CHAP. XLVI. On the successful execution of the design a full account was quickly conveyed to the consul, whose mind was filled at once with anxiety and rejoicing, with joy at the news that by the disclosure of the plot, the state was saved from its danger; but with deep anxiety, in his hesitation as to what must be done with citizens of such rank detected in so great a crime. To punish them, he thought, would bring trouble on himself, while to allow them to escape might ruin the state. Summoning all his resolution, he ordered Lentulus, Cethegus, Statilius, and Gabinius, to be called before him, and with them a certain Caeparius of Tarracina, who was preparing to set out for Apulia, there to rouse the slaves. The rest appeared without delay; Caeparius, who had left his house a little before, had learnt the discovery of the plot, and escaped from the city. Lentulus, as praetor, the consul himself conducted, holding him by the hand, the rest under guard he ordered to come to the temple of Concord. Thither he had summoned the Senate, and in a crowded assembly of its members he now introduced Volturcius with the ambassadors, while he ordered the praetor Flaccus to bring the despatch box, with the letters which he had received from the ambassadors. Volturcius was then examined on the subject of his journey, the letter, and finally as to his purpose and motive. At first he made pretences, and tried to conceal all knowledge of the conspiracy; afterwards, when bidden to speak with a guarantee from the state of his safety, he betrayed everything just as it had taken place, and informed the Senate that, as he himself had only been admitted to the conspiracy by Gabinius and Caeparius a few days before, he knew no more than the ambassadors. He could only say that he had been used to hear from Gabinius that Publius Autronius, Servius Sulla, Lucius Varguntius, and many others were among its members. The confession of the Gauls was to the same effect, and when Lentulus pretended ignorance, they convicted him not only by the letter but by the words he had often used. "The Sibylline books," he had said, "prophesied that three Cornelii should rule Rome; Cinna and Sulla had already done so, and he himself was the third to whom fate assigned the government of the city; moreover, this was the twentieth year from that in which the Capitol had been burnt, and augurs had frequently declared on the strength of prodigies that it should be rendered bloody by a civil war." All the prisoners had previously acknowledged

CHAP.
XLVI.

CHAP.
XLVII.

CHAP.
XLVII.

their seals; and, accordingly, after the letters had been read, the Senate made a decree that Lentulus on laying down his office, as well as the rest, should be kept in "free" or private custody. Accordingly they were delivered to the following guardians:—Lentulus, to Publius Lentulus Spinther, at that time an aedile; Cethegus, to Quintus Cornificius; Statilius, to Gaius Caesar; Gabinius, to Marcus Crassus; and Caeparius (who had been pursued and just brought back), to a senator named Gnaeus Terentius.

CHAP.
XLVIII.

Meanwhile the commons, who, at first, in their eagerness for a revolution, were too favourable to the idea of war, now that the nature of the conspiracy was laid bare, experienced a revulsion of feeling. They cursed the designs of Catiline, exalted Cicero to heaven, and were as full of joy and gladness as though they had escaped from slavery. Any other outrage of war would rather have given them plunder than have done them harm, but a conflagration they thought a ruthless and extravagant measure, and one fraught with misery to themselves, whose whole wealth consisted in articles of daily use and personal clothing.

On the following day there was brought before the Senate a certain Lucius Tarquinius, who was said to have been pursued and captured on his way to join Catiline. He offered, if granted a public guarantee, to give information about the plot, and was ordered by the consul to make a full confession of all he knew. He told the Senate a tale very similar to that of Volturcius, about preparations for firing the city, a massacre of the respectable classes, and the approach of the enemy, but added that he himself had been sent by Marcus Crassus with a message to Catiline "not to let the seizure of Lentulus, Cethegus, and others of the conspirators alarm him, but to make it an additional reason for a rapid advance on Rome, by which the spirits of the rest would be revived and the prisoners more easily rescued from danger." On the mention, however, of Crassus, a man of birth, of enormous wealth, and the very greatest influence, some thought the story unworthy of belief, others again deemed it true, yet were of the opinion that at such a crisis a man of his importance should rather be conciliated than provoked, and as most of the senators were, in their private affairs, at the mercy of Crassus, all united in a cry that the witness was no honest one, and demanded that a motion should be made on the subject. On the motion therefore of Cicero, and in a crowded house, the Senate resolved that, "Whereas the witness of Tarquinius appears dishonest, he is to be kept in custody, and to be granted no further privilege of audience until such time as he confess at whose instigation he fabricated so grievous a charge." It was thought at the time by some that the information was contrived by Publius Autronius, in order that Crassus by the accusation might be made to share the peril of the rest, and these then gain the protection of his power. Others asserted that Tarquinius was set on by Cicero to prevent Crassus, according to his wont, taking the sedition under his patronage, and so embroiling the state. At a later period I personally heard Crassus declare that Cicero had actually put this insult upon him.

CHAP.
XLIX.

At the same conjuncture Quintus Catulus and Gaius Piso failed, either by bribery or influence, to induce Cicero to have Gaius Caesar dishonestly accused by means of the Allobroges or some other informer. Both these nobles were at bitter enmity with Caesar; Piso he had assailed when on his trial for malversation, on the score of having unjustly punished a certain Transpadane; Catulus hated him on account of their contest for the Pontificate, in that, at the close of his life and after filling the highest offices, he had been beaten by such a mere youth as Caesar. The state of the latter's affairs also favoured the accusation, as his extraordinary profusion and the splendour of his public entertainments had sunk him heavily in debt. Unable to induce the consul to commit such a crime, they applied themselves to individual intrigues, and, by coining falsehoods, which they declared they had heard from Volturcius or the Allobroges, raised much odium against Caesar. So successful, indeed, were they, that some Roman knights, who were on guard under arms round the Temple of Concord, were carried away either by the greatness of the danger, or their own excitable character, and, on Caesar's leaving the Senate, threatened him with their swords, in order to show their zeal for the constitution.

CHAP.
L.

While the Senate was engaged with this business, and in decreeing rewards to the ambassadors of the Allobroges, and to Titus Volturcius, as informers whose witness had been verified, the freedmen and a few of the dependents of Lentulus went different ways about the city, trying to rouse the artisans and slaves in the streets to rescue him; while others sought out the popular mob captains, who had been wont to sell their services in disturbing the state. Cethegus, moreover, employed messengers to entreat the slaves and freedmen of his household, men picked and trained [in the school of audacity], to come in an armed body and break into the house where he lay. The consul, on learning of these designs, posted guards wherever occasion demanded, and having summoned the Senate, put the question how they would deal with the men in custody. It should be mentioned that, shortly before this, the Senate in a crowded house had pronounced their conduct treasonable. On the present occasion, Decimus Junius Silanus, who as consul elect was the first called upon to give his opinion as to what was to be done with the actual prisoners, and besides them with Lucius Cassius, Publius Furius, Publius Umbrenus, and Quintus Annius, in the event of their capture, at first gave his vote for their punishment; afterwards, however, he was so influenced by the speech of Gaius Caesar that he declared that on a division he would side with Tiberius Nero, who had proposed that the question should be adjourned till the guards round the Senate house had been increased. The speech of Caesar, when it came to him to be asked his opinion by the consul, was to the following effect:—

"All men, Senators, who deliberate on doubtful matters should be equally free from hate and friendship, from anger and compassion. When these obstruct the view, the mind does not easily discern the truth; nor has any one ever harmonized the dictates of passion and interest. When the intellect is alert

 it is strong ; but if passion gains a footing it becomes
a tyrant, and the reason is reduced to impotence. I
have no lack of examples of kings and peoples who,
under the sway of anger or compassion have erred in
their counsels. I prefer, however, to remind you of
some occasions on which our own ancestors preserved
a due and orderly course of action though it conflicted
with their passions. In the Macedonian war, which
we carried on with King Perseus, the great and
splendid State of Rhodes, which had prospered by the
help of the Roman people, proved disloyal and hostile
to us. When the war was finished and the conduct
of the Rhodians came to be considered, our ancestors,
to avoid giving any pretext for an assertion that they
went to war not to avenge an injury, but for the sake
of wealth, allowed them to go unpunished. Similarly
in all our Punic wars, though the Carthaginians
often committed many outrages in times both of
peace and of truce, our ancestors availed themselves
of no opportunity to do the like, but took in consideration rather what was worthy of themselves than what
might fairly be inflicted on their enemy.

A like occasion has now arisen, and you, Senators,
must be on your guard lest the crime of Publius Lentulus and his fellows weigh heavier with you than your
own dignity, and lead you to a resolution that will
better satisfy your wrath than your repute. If, indeed,
the object of our search is some penalty adequate to
the offence, then I approve of our abandoning all precedent in our measures; but if the enormity of the
crime taxes our ingenuity too heavily for this, I am
of opinion that we should confine ourselves to such

punishments as are by law provided. Most of those who have spoken before me have in studied and noble language bewailed the misfortune of the republic, have dilated on the horrors of war and the fate of the vanquished, and have reminded you of how maids are ravished, children torn from their parents' arms, matrons placed at the mercy of the conquerors' passions, temples and houses plundered, fire and slaughter carried everywhere, and whole towns filled with arms and corpses, blood and mourning. But at what, I ask, was all this eloquence aimed? To stir you to detestation of the conspiracy? As if the man whom the horrible reality has not moved could be roused by any eloquence! That is not human nature, nor are men ever wont to underestimate their own injuries; rather, in many cases they have been known to take too serious a view of them. Extravagance of behaviour, Senators, takes a different hue in different stations. Men of low rank pass their life in obscurity, and their faults of passion are known to few, for their notoriety never rises above their fortunes. Those, on the other hand, who are the heirs of a great sovereignty, and live in a high position, have their doings known to all the world. The higher their fortunes the greater the restrictions upon them; they must know nothing of favour or disfavour, and least of all of anger; for what in others is called anger, in rulers receives the name of pride and cruelty. And, though, for my own part, I think any and every punishment inadequate to the crimes of the prisoners, yet most people only remember the end of an incident, and, in the case of the wicked, often forget their misdeeds in talking of

 their punishment, if that has been somewhat unusually
severe.

"I feel sure that the proposal of that brave and
active citizen, Decimus Silanus, was made in all zeal
for the state, and that in a matter of such importance
he would allow himself to be influenced neither by
hatred nor partiality. My knowledge of his character
and self-restraint convinces me of this. But his motion strikes me, I will not say as cruel—for what
proposal could be cruel when aimed at men like
these ?—but as foreign to the spirit of our state. It
must certainly have been either panic or a strong
sense of wrong that moved you, Silanus, a consul
elect, to propose an unprecedented form of punishment. To speak of terror were needless, especially
when, by the activity of our illustrious consul, we have
such numerous guards under arms. As to the actual
punishment you propose, I might observe, what is
indeed the case, that to men in grief and misery
death comes as a relief, not as a pain, that it annuls all
the ills that flesh is heir to, and that beyond it neither
trouble nor joy find place. But what I wish to ask
you is, Why did you not add to your motion that the
condemned should first be punished with the scourge ?
Was it because it is forbidden by the Porcian law ?
If so, there are other laws which forbid condemned
citizens to be deprived of life, and offer the alternative
of exile. Did you omit it, then, because scourging is
a heavier punishment than death ? Yet what sentence
can be harsh or too severe for men convicted of so
atrocious a crime ? Again, if you thought scourging the lighter punishment, how can it be proper to

fear the law in the smaller matter after neglecting it in the greater?

"It may be asked, Who will take exception to any, decree against traitors? I answer, time, the events of a day, and fortune whose caprice rules the world. Whatever the prisoners' fate, it will have been well deserved ; but you, Senators, must consider the precedent which you are establishing./ Every bad precedent has arisen out of a measure in itself good ; but, when power has fallen to unskilful or less worthy hands, the precedent is no longer applied to fit and deserving subjects, but to unfit and undeserving. The Lacedaemonians, when they had crushed the Athenians, imposed on them an oligarchy of thirty members. This government began by executing, without trial, those whose guilt or unpopularity was greatest ; the people rejoiced, and justified their action./ As the spirit of license gradually increased, they killed good and bad alike in mere wantonness, while they filled the rest of the citizens with terror./ Thus the state paid for its foolish rejoicing the heavy price of slavery. In our own times the victorious Sulla, amid universal approval, ordered the execution of Damasippus and his fellows, who had fattened on the public disasters. The men were stained with crime and treason, their seditious spirit had embroiled the state, and it was agreed that their death was richly deserved.. Nevertheless, that action was the inauguration of a great massacre. Did a man covet a house or villa, nay, even a piece of pottery or of raiment, he used all his exertions to include its owner in the list of the proscribed. Those who had rejoiced at the death of

Damasippus were soon themselves dragged to execution, and the massacre only ceased when Sulla had glutted all his followers with wealth. I do not fear any such conduct on the part of Marcus Tullius, nor at the present crisis ; but a large state contains many and diverse characters. At a future time, and under another consul, entrusted, in his turn, with an army, some false charge may be believed true, and when the consul has followed this precedent, and, at the decree of the Senate, drawn his sword, who will there be to check or restrain him ?

"Senators, our ancestors never showed themselves wanting in either wisdom or courage, nor did they allow their pride to prevent them imitating the customs of foreign nations, so long as they were good. Most of their armour and weapons of warfare they adopted from the Samnites, and the emblems of their magistracies from the Etruscans ; in fine, they zealously copied in their own administration all that seemed serviceable among their allies or enemies. They preferred, I may say, to imitate rather than to envy the good. Now, it was at this period of imitation that they adopted the [Greek] custom of scourging citizens and inflicting capital punishment on convicted criminals. With the growth, however, of the state, and the greater violence of party strife, which resulted from the increase of population, it was found that innocent persons were made victims and that other like abuses were becoming common. To meet this danger, the Porcian and other laws were provided, by which convicted persons were allowed to retire into exile. This, Senators, I think a most weighty reason against our adopting any resolution for which there is no precedent. I cannot but think that the men, who, with the small resources at their command, won so great an empire, were endowed with greater courage and wisdom than are we who find a difficulty even in keeping what they so nobly won.

" Am I then in favour of dismissing our prisoners, to swell the army of Catiline? Far from it. My proposal is that their goods be confiscated, and that their persons be imprisoned in such borough towns as are best able to support the charge, and that no one hereafter make any motion with reference to them in the Senate, or bring their case before the people, on pain of the Senate's adjudging his action treasonable and prejudicial to the State."

On the close of Caesar's speech, all the senators merely gave their votes for the different motions, some for the one, some for the other, until it came to Marcus Porcius Cato. He, when asked his opinion, delivered himself as follows :—

" When I turn, Senators, from surveying the dangers of our position, and reflect on the opinions of certain previous speakers, the impression I receive is very different. These speakers appear to have discussed the punishment of the men who have raised war against their country and parents, their altars and hearths. Our position warns us rather to guard against their attack than to consider their sentence. Other crimes you may be content to avenge when they have actually been committed ; against this, if you fail to prevent it, you will in vain invoke the law,

CHAP.
LI.

CHAP.
LII.

for when a city is once stormed the conquered have no further resources. I profess, though, I should remember that in you I am appealing to men who ever valued their houses and villas, their statues and paintings more highly than they did the state. If you would keep these cherished possessions, of whatever kind—if you would have leisure to indulge in your pleasures—now at last awake and take an active part in the work of government. This is no question of tribute or of the wrongs done to our allies ; it is our liberty and our lives that are at stake.

"Many a time, Senators, have I spoken at length in this house. Often have I complained of the self-indulgence and avarice of our citizens. By so doing I have made many enemies ; but as I never had to excuse any such sin to my own conscience, I could scarcely be so tender to another's vices as to pardon his ill deeds. You made slight account of this advice, but the stability of the state was not shaken ; its resources could bear the strain of your neglect. The question, however, now at stake is not whether our lives shall be moral or immoral, nor as to the size or splendour of the empire of the Roman people ; it is whether this empire, just as it is, shall remain our own, or fall, with ourselves, a prey to our enemies. Here some one reminds me of clemency and compassion. Why, long ere this we have ceased to call things by their right names. To be lavish of the goods of others is now called generosity, and to be daring in the commission of crime courage. This fashion has brought the state to the brink of ruin ; but even granting, since morality is come to this, that men may be generous with the fortunes of our allies, and compassionate in dealing with plunderers of the exchequer, at least let them hesitate to squander our blood, and, in sparing a few villains, work the ruin of all honest men.

"Gaius Caesar has just addressed to you an eloquent and polished disquisition on life and death. He disbelieves, I suppose, those traditions about the dead which assign to the bad a path different from that of the good, and lead them to noisome and savage abodes full of horrors and terrors. Holding this opinion, he has moved that the property of the prisoners be confiscated, and they themselves kept in confinement in the borough towns. He evidently fears that, should they remain at Rome, they may be rescued either by their accomplices or by a hired mob. As if bad and abandoned men were to be found only in the capital, and not throughout Italy, or boldness were not more powerful where the means of repelling it are less! His proposal is thus plainly idle, if he really apprehends danger from the prisoners, while if, amid such general alarm, he alone is fearless, there is the more reason why we others should be cautious. In making your decision, then, on Publius Lentulus and his associates, be assured that you are at the same time deciding the fate of the army of Catiline and of all the conspirators. The more vigorous your measures, the more will their courage be shaken. If they see you hesitating, but for a moment, you will have the whole pack marching valiantly against you.

"Think not that it was by arms that our ancestors raised the state from insignificance to grandeur. If that were so, it would now be at its noblest beneath our sway, for our force of allies and citizens, not to mention that of arms and horses, is far greater than was theirs. The sources, however, of their greatness were very different from these, and we have none of them. Such were their energy at home, the justice of their rule abroad, and the unbiassed mind, the slave neither of sin nor of lust, which they brought to their councils. For these we have substituted self-indulgence and avarice, a bankrupt state and private millionaires. Our praise is of riches; idleness our pursuit. Good and bad can no longer be distinguished ; intrigue wins all the prizes which merit deserves, and who can wonder at it ? Each of you frames his policy to serve his individual ends ; in your homes you worship pleasure, in the Senate money or influence; and so, when an attack comes, the state is found with none to defend her.

"However, I will say no more of this. Citizens of the highest rank have conspired to destroy their country ; to aid them in the war they summon the Gauls, a people most hostile to the name of Rome; the leader of our enemies with his army is at our doors. Can you still be hesitating how to treat enemies caught within your walls ? You are to pity them, I suppose. The young men have been led into a mistake, and you are to dismiss them, armed though they be. Look to it that this clemency and mercy do not turn to your own misery, if once they take up arms. The state of affairs is indeed unpromising, but perhaps you do not fear it ? Say rather that you are in the greatest terror, but that in your sloth and irresolution you hesitate and wait one for another, full, of course, of a pious trust in the eternal gods who have so often upheld this state amid the greatest dangers. I tell you that the help of heaven is not won by vows and womanish prayers; but that by vigilance, by action, by wise counsels, a happy issue is attained. Abandon yourself to sloth and cowardice, and you may invoke the gods, but it will be in vain; they are angered and adverse. In the days of our forefathers, Titus Manlius Torquatus, during the Gallic war, ordered his son to be executed for having fought the enemy against orders. That noble youth atoned by his death for his untempered valour, and are you hesitating as to your sentence on these ruthless traitors? Of course the rest of their lives stand in contrast to this one crime! Respect then the rank of Lentulus, if ever he respected his modesty, his honour, or any god or man. Pardon the youth of Cethegus, if this be not the second time he has made war on his country. What am I to say of Gabinius, of Statilius, of Caeparius? If it had not been for their utter heedlessness they could never, I suppose, have entertained such designs upon the state! To conclude, Senators, I profess that, if we could safely make a mistake, I would readily suffer you to be convinced of your error by the course of events, since you despise my words. We are, however, actually beset on every side. Catiline, with his army, is at our throats; we have other enemies within the walls and in the very heart of the city; we can make no preparation and come to no determination without its being known; all these are so many reasons for greater despatch.

"I therefore move that ' inasmuch as the criminal

designs of traitorous citizens have placed the state in the greatest danger, and inasmuch as the prisoners by the information of Titus Volturcius and the ambassadors of the Allobroges, stand convicted of having planned a massacre, a conflagration, and other disgraceful and cruel atrocities, against their fellow-citizens and their country; that, therefore, punishment be inflicted according to ancient custom, on those who have confessed their guilt, as though they had been convicted of capital offences.'"

On Cato resuming his seat, all the men of consular rank, together with many other members of the Senate, commended his proposal, and praised his courage to the skies. Reproaching each other for what they now called their timidity, they accounted Cato a great and brilliant statesman, and a decree of the Senate was passed in the words of his resolution.

I have read and heard much of the noble deeds of the Roman people in peace and in war, on land and on sea ; and chance has disposed me to consider what circumstance it was that had done most to support it in its gigantic task. I was aware that on many occasions it had confronted large bodies of the enemy with but a handful of troops. I knew of the wars which Rome, with her scanty resources, had waged against wealthy kings. I knew, too, that she had often had to bear the rude attack of fortune ; and that in eloquence the Greek, in warlike renown the Gaul, had outstripped her children. After much reflection, however, I arrived at the conclusion that it was the pre-eminent merit of a few of our citizens that had accomplished all; that this was the power that had enabled poverty to subdue wealth, a handful to rout a host. When, however, the state was corrupted by luxury and indolence, the republic, in its turn, by its very greatness, lent strength to its blundering generals and magistrates; while, as if the vigour of their fathers had perished, at many periods there was not a single man in Rome of conspicuous merit. In my own time, however, there have been two men of surpassing merit, though different character—Marcus Cato and Gaius Caesar. As my subject has brought them into notice, it is not my design to pass them over without disclosing their respective natures and characters, so far as my ability will allow me. *[CHAP. LIII.]*

In birth, age, and eloquence, Caesar and Cato were nearly equal; and they were well matched in the loftiness of their aims, and in the renown which, each in his own way, they attained. Caesar was esteemed for his kind offices and munificence; Cato for the strict uprightness of his life. The former was distinguished by his clemency and compassion; sternness added dignity to the latter. Caesar won renown by his readiness to give, to help, and to pardon; Cato by never offering a bribe. The one was the refuge of the wretched; the other, the destruction of the bad. The former was praised for his affability; the latter for his consistency. In fine Caesar had formed the resolve to work, to be ever on the watch, to promote his friends' interest even to the detriment of his own, and to refuse nothing which was worth the giving. He aimed at a high command, an army, a war in some new field where his talents might be displayed. Cato, on the other hand, made *[CHAP. LIV.]*

CHAP.
LIV.

temperance, dignity, and, above all, austerity of behaviour, his pursuit. He did not vie in wealth with the wealthy, nor in intrigue with the intriguer, but in courage with the man of action, in honour with the scrupulous, in self-restraint with the upright. He preferred to be good rather than to seem so; and thus, the less he pursued renown, the more it attended him.

CHAP.
LV.

When, as I related, the Senate had passed Cato's resolution, the consul, thinking it better to forestall the coming night, lest the interval should be used for any revolutionary movement, ordered the officers to make the necessary preparations for the execution. After posting guards at various points he personally conducted Lentulus to the prison, while the praetors did the same to the rest. In the prison there is a place, called the Tullianum, which, after a slight ascent to the left, you find sunk about twelve feet in the ground. It is guarded on every side by walls, and above it is an arched roof of stone ; desolation, darkness, and stench give it a loathsome and dreadful appearance. To this place Lentulus was conducted, and there strangled by the appointed executioners. A patrician of the illustrious house of the Cornelii, and a man who had held the office of consul at Rome, he met an end worthy of his character and his crimes. On Cethegus, Statilius, Gabinius, and Caeparius, the same punishment was inflicted.

CHAP.
LVI.

While this was happening at Rome, Catiline, from the whole force made up of his own contingent and of the original army of Manlius, organized two legions, and filled up the cohorts in proportion to the number of his men. Afterwards, as volunteers or members of the conspiracy arrived in the camp they were drafted in equal numbers into the several divisions ; and in a short time he had raised his legions to their proper strength, although at first he had not more than two thousand men. Not more than a quarter, however, of his whole force was equipped with weapons of war. The rest, as chance had armed them, carried hunting spears or javelins, and, in some cases, pointed stakes. On the approach of Antonius with his army, Catiline moved to and fro among the mountains, frequently changed his quarters, turning now towards Rome, now towards Gaul, and offered the enemy no chance of fighting ; for he hoped, should his accomplices at Rome succeed in their plans, soon to be at the head of large forces. Meanwhile he rejected the slave bands, which at the outset rallied round him in large numbers. He trusted to the strength of the con-spiracy, and at the same time thought it prejudicial to his designs to appear to have made the cause of citizens one with that of runaway slaves. On the arrival at the camp of the news that at Rome the plot was discovered, and that Lentulus, Cethegus, and the others whom I have named above, had been executed, many, who had been attracted by the hope of plunder or desire for revolution, now deserted. The rest Cati-line led by forced marches over rugged mountains to the district of Pistoria, intending to retreat secretly by cross roads into Transalpine Gaul. Quintus Me-tellus Celer, however, was stationed in Picenum with three legions, and surmised that Catiline, in his present difficulty, would be adopting the very course I have described. Learning the latter's route from deserters,

CHAP.
LVI.

CHAP.
LVII.

he hastily advanced and pitched his camp at the very foot of the mountains which Catiline would have to descend on his hasty march towards Gaul. Antonius also was close upon him; his army was large, but it was aided by the more level character of its road, and he could thus follow in pursuit. Catiline now saw himself hemmed in between the mountains and the forces of the enemy; in the capital he had been defeated; and he had no hope either of escape or refuge. He thought best, therefore, in so perilous a case, to try the fortune of war, and determined to come to an instant engagement with Antonius. Accordingly, he called his troops around him, and spoke as follows :—

"Soldiers, I have long discovered that words cannot inspire courage, and that no speech of a general can give a flagging army energy, or the timid courage. Just so much daring, natural or acquired, as resides in each man's breast, does he display in war. The man insensible to the call of glory and danger you will harangue in vain; his cowardice stops his ears. Nevertheless I have called you together to give you a few words of advice and at the same time to disclose the motive of my resolution.

"I make certain, soldiers, that you know of the disastrous consequences, to himself and to us, of the cowardice and indolence of Lentulus, and how, while awaiting reinforcements from the capital, I have been prevented from marching towards Gaul. You know, too, as well as I do, our present position. Two hostile armies close our path, the one on the side of Rome, the other of Gaul. Want of corn and other necessaries forbid us to remain longer in our present quarters, desire it though we may. In whatever direction we determine to march, we must cut our way with our swords. I exhort you, therefore, to keep a brave and ready heart, and, when you enter battle, to remember that in your own right hands lie wealth, honour, and fame, as well as your freedom and the possession of your country. If we conquer, our safety will be secured; we shall have provisions in plenty, and the gates of boroughs and colonies will be thrown open to us. If we give way in fear, we shall have all these against us. No place nor friend will protect the man who has failed to protect himself with his own arms. Moreover, soldiers, we and our enemies will be fighting under motives of very different force. For us the contest is for country, for freedom and for life, while our enemies can have little interest in fighting to maintain the supremacy of a narrow class.

"Let these thoughts inspire you with hardihood; advance to the fight, mindful of your ancient valour. You might, though to your deep disgrace, have passed your lives in exile. Some of you might, after the confiscation of your goods, have lingered in Rome, on the watch for a stranger's bounty. Such courses seemed shameful and unbearable to men of spirit, and so you have chosen to follow the one that has led you here. If you would now quit it you must use your daring, for it is at the discretion of the victor that war is changed for peace. To hope for safety in flight, when your backs, unprotected by armour, are turned to the enemy, is indeed folly. In a battle it is always the greatest cowards who run the greatest risks, while courage is as a wall of defence.

Chap. LVIII. "When I look on you, soldiers, and count up your achievements, I am possessed with high hope of victory. Your resolution, your age, and your courage, and above all the inevitable nature of the encounter, which often makes even the timid brave, exhort me to this; and the narrowness of the position prevents our being surrounded by the host of the enemy. If, however, fortune shows herself jealous of your valour, see that you do not fall unavenged, nor prefer by a surrender to be butchered like sheep rather than to fight like men, and leave your enemies a bloody victory that shall cost them dear."

Chap. LIX. At the end of this speech, after a trifling delay, he ordered the signal to sound, and led his troops, in orderly array, down to the level ground. He then sent away the horses of all who owned them, in order that the soldiers might be encouraged by the sense that their danger was shared by all alike. He himself, on foot, then drew up his army with due regard to the nature of the ground and his own numbers. The plain lay between mountains on the left, and a rugged line of rocks on the right; here he posted eight cohorts to form the front, while the other divisions, with their standards, were stationed in closer order as a reserve. From these cohorts he withdrew all the picked and veteran centurions, with the bravest and best armed of the common soldiers, and added them to the front. He ordered Gaius Manlius to take the command on the right, and a certain man of Faesulae on the left. He himself, with his own freed-men and some soldiers' servants, took up his station by his eagle; one, it was said, which Gaius Marius used in his army in the Cimbrian war.

On the other side Gaius Antonius was prevented by lameness from taking part in the battle, and entrusted his army to his lieutenant, Marcus Petreius. By him the veteran cohorts which he had levied to suppress the revolt were posted in front, and the rest of the army behind them as a reserve. Petreius himself reviewed his army on horseback, accosting the soldiers by name, encouraging them, and entreating them to remember that they were fighting against half-armed brigands for their country and children, their altars and homes. He was an experienced soldier, and, during a career of more than thirty years in the army, in which he filled the offices of tribune, praefect, legate, and praetor with great distinction, had gained a knowledge of many of his men and their brave deeds ; and by reference to these he now kindled their spirits.

When he had satisfied himself on every point, Petreius sounded the signal and ordered the cohorts to advance slowly, and the same movement was made by the enemy. On reaching a distance at which the light troops could engage, the two armies raised a great shout and charged each other, standard to standard. Dropping their javelins, they fought with swords. The veterans, remembering their ancient valour, pressed on to engage at close quarters ; their opponents fiercely withstood them, and the conflict raged with the greatest fury. Meanwhile Catiline, with his light troops, was busy in the front. He relieved the hard-pressed, called up fresh men to fill

CHAP.
LX.

the places of the wounded, had an eye for every need, often fought himself, and often struck down his man. In fine, he played the part at once of an active soldier and a skilful general. Petreius, on seeing Catiline making such vigorous and unexpected exertions, led the cohort of his guards against the enemies' centre. Their ranks were now in confusion, and they could only offer a straggling resistance; he cut them down and proceeded to attack the survivors on either flank. Manlius and the Faesulan fell fighting in the front rank, and Catiline saw that his troops were routed, and only himself and a few others left. He remembered his race and the rank he had once held, and, rushing into the thickest of the foe, fought on till he was pierced with wounds.

CHAP.
LXI.

It was only after the battle was decided, that it could be fully seen with what daring and resolution Catiline's army had been inspired. Almost the exact position which each had taken up while living he now in death covered with his body. A few of those in the centre, who had been dislodged by the praetor's body guard, had fallen less closely together in the different places where they had made a stand; but all bore their wounds in front. Catiline, however, was found at a distance from his own men among the enemy's dead. He continued to breathe for a short time, and retained on his countenance that savage courage which had marked him in life. I should not forget to mention that out of all that host not a single free-born man was made prisoner, either in the battle or the rout; so unsparing had all been alike of their own and their enemies' lives. Nor was the victory of the national army either happy or bloodless ; its bravest soldiers had perished in the fight, or came out of it badly wounded. Many, too, who had come from the camp out of curiosity, or for the sake of plunder, in turning over the bodies of the enemy, found some a friend, others those bound to them by the ties of hospitality or blood, while others recognised the features of an enemy. Thus throughout the whole army grief and gladness, sorrow and rejoicing, held divided sway.

NOTES TO CATILINE.

CHAP. IV.

I determined to narrate the history of the Roman people in separate essays wherever it seemed worthy of record (statui res gestas populi Romani carptim, ut quaeque memoria digna videbantur perscribere).

Besides the "Catiline" and "Jugurtha," we have fragments of a history, written by Sallust, in five books. This work is usually supposed to have embraced the period from B.C. 78 to B.C. 66. Mr. Long, however, thinks that there is evidence of the treatment by Sallust of an earlier period, and considers it a probable conjecture that he wrote, in all, four other essays besides the "Catiline" and "Jugurtha": the first on the twelve years which preceded the death of Sulla, the second on the attempt of Lepidus, the third on the war of Sertorius, and the last on that against Mithridates, and that these were subsequently, though at a very early period, arranged by some grammarian into the form of a connected history in five books. This theory is certainly more conformable to the determination expressed in the text, than that which would make the "Jugurtha" and "Catiline" the only two works which Sallust published in the form of essays.

Lucius Catilina was of noble birth, of great mental and bodily vigour, but of an evil and depraved disposition. (Lucius Catilina, nobili genere natus, fuit magna vi et animi et corporis, sed ingenio malo pravoque.)

CHAP. V.

Lucius Sergius Catilina was praetor in B.C. 68, and was, therefore, born in, or a little before, the year B.C. 108, for forty was the lowest age at which the praetorship could be held, and most men of any mark obtained the office as soon as they were eligible for it. The Sergii, of whom his family was a branch, were one of the oldest houses in Rome; and his grandfather, M. Sergius Silus, had served as a legatus in the Macedonian war, while his great-grandfather of the same name held the praetorship in B.C. 167. His birth was, therefore, decidedly noble ; his bodily vigour was allowed, even by Cicero, to be extraordinary ; the opinions of historians as to his mental capacity differ according to the view which they take of his enterprise. As to his disposition, it may be well here to contrast with the uniformly lurid description of Sallust, the less monotonous portrait of him which Cicero drew when he wished to justify his client, Caelius, for at one time associating with the conspirator. "Catiline," he says, "as I think you must remember, showed in very many ways, not indeed the certain marks, but the form and outline of the highest virtue. He was the friend of many worthless creatures, and, withal, professed himself devoted to men of the highest character. While in his nature dwelt many lustful passions, he had also certain qualities which spurred him to exertion and perseverance. If the vices of a sensual temper burnt within him, his zeal was also great for military service. Indeed, I do not think that there ever existed on earth so strange a being, such a fusion of natural longings and desires, so different, so opposite, so inconsistent. Who, at one period, could have been happier in 'the friendships of more illustrious men? Who more closely intimate with baser objects? At one time what citizen could have been a member of a nobler party? Who a more bitter foe to this state? In sensuality, who deeper stained? In toils, who more enduring? Who in greed more covetous? In generosity more lavish? These, judges, were the wonderful qualities united in this man; he bound many to him in the bonds of friendship, and gave his services in their cause; he would share his possessions with all men, and would assist any of his friends in their difficulties with his money, his influence, his personal exertions, and, if need were, with reckless crime. He could turn and guide his own nature as occasion required, twisting it and bending it this way and that. With the stern he could bear himself soberly, with the lax gaily, seriously among the aged, pleasantly among the young, with the vicious recklessly, with the libertine riotously. And so this changeable and versatile spirit, at the very time when he had gathered round him every wicked and abandoned person from every land, still held fast many good men and true by a certain show of virtue that was not his. Never, indeed, could the man have conceived that unholy desire of destroying this government had not so monstrous a tale of vices had some basis of

good nature and forbearance on which to rest. Even CHAP.
VI.
I myself was at one time almost deceived by him. I
took him for a loyal citizen, eager for the acquaintance
of all good men, and for a true and trusty friend. My
eyes detected his misdoings before I had a thought
of them ; the proof was in my hands before my
suspicions were aroused."—(" Pro Caelio," chap. 5
and 6.)

As soon as the state had gained its freedom, it is CHAP.
VII.
*incredible to relate what progress it quickly made. (Sed
civitas incredibile memoratu est adepta libertate quan-
tum brevi creverit.)*

In three places in this book Sallust undoubtedly
quotes from Thucydides : in chap. 3, as to envy as a
cause of incredulity (Thuc. ii. 35) ; in chap. 20, as to
community of interests being the true bond of friendship ; and in chap. 52, as to the exchange of names
between the virtues and vices in a low state of public
morality (Thuc. iii. 82). In the present passage I
think there can be little doubt that he had in his mind
the chapter in Herodotus (v. 78), when that historian
traces the sudden rise of Athens into greatness to the
successful establishment of the democracy. If this is
so, we have here a striking instance of the thoroughly
artificial character of Sallust's introduction, which
takes up, it may be noted, a sixth part of the whole
book. The remark in Herodotus is a sound historical criticism ; Sallust saw that there was a general
resemblance between the expulsion of the Peisistra-
tidae and of Tarquinius Superbus, and at once made
the remark apply to Roman history. The establish-

E

CHAP.
VII.

ment, however, of the republic at Rome (B.C. 509) was followed by no such outburst as at Athens; on the contrary, the succeeding two centuries of its history are chiefly memorable for the struggle between the patricians and plebeians, and during that time Rome was once, if not twice, captured by its enemies, and was only one among the many Italian states. The remark of Herodotus thus becomes meaningless when transferred from Athenian to Roman history, and that Sallust did so transfer it is a proof that all he aimed at in this introduction was to produce a piece of " fine writing."

CHAP.
XIV.

In fine, all who were harassed by crime, by need, or by the pangs of conscience, it was these who were Catiline's intimate associates (postremo omnes, quos flagitium, egestas, conscius animus exagitabat, hi Catilinae proxumi familiaresque erant).

In the speech which Cicero addressed to the people on the day after Catiline's departure from Rome, he enumerated six classes of Catiline's fellow-conspirators. The first of these classes he represented as made up of rich spendthrifts who simply wanted to avoid paying their debts; the second of ambitious politicians whose pecuniary embarrassments at present shut them out of any official career; the third of ruined Sullan colonists; the fourth of the hopelessly insolvent; the fifth of parricides and criminals of every description; and the last of the bodyguard of dissolute dandies who were especially closely attached to Catiline, and who, for all their elegance and delicacy, had learnt not only how to sing, and dance, and play the lover, but to poison and assassinate as well (Cat. ii. 8-10). On the previous day, in the Senate, quite in the spirit of this chapter of Sallust, he had asserted that for many years there had been no crime committed in Rome for which Catiline was not responsible (Cat. i. 7). Cicero himself, however, in the passage from the "Pro Caelio," quoted in a previous note, shows that Catiline had other and more respectable associates than these desperadoes, and we know that Caesar and Crassus supported him in his canvass in 64. As regards this chapter, as Mr. Long remarks (Hist. iii. p. 227), Sallust's absurd assertion that Catiline forced his wretched instruments still to cheat and murder for sake of practice though all other motives were absent, shows how largely the historian's account of the character of the conspirators was drawn from his imagination.

CHAP.
XIV.

At the very outset of his youth, Catiline had engaged in many scandalous intrigues, one with a high-born maiden, another with a priestess of Vesta, and others which in like manner set law and morality at defiance. Finally, he was seized with a passion for Aurelia Orestilla, and by killing his own son, so it is positively believed, cleared his house for the unhallowed union. (Jam primum adolescens Catilina multa nefanda stupra fecerat, cum virgine nobili, cum sacerdote Vestae, alia hujuscemodi contra jus fasque. Postremo captus amore Aureliae Orestillae, pro certo creditur necato filio vacuam domum scelestis nuptiis fecisse.)

CHAP.
XV.

Unsavoury as the subject is, it is necessary briefly to examine the charges which have been brought against the private character of Catiline, because, even with the low state of morality at this time prevalent in Rome, there must have been some line drawn between the respectable statesman and the political adventurer, and Catiline's private life is important as helping us to decide in which of these two classes he himself ought to be ranked. The accusations which are brought against him may be summarized as follows :—

(1) That during the tyranny of Sulla he had been placed at the head of some Gallic auxiliaries, and had murdered a number of Roman knights, among others his brother-in-law Quintus Caecilius, an inoffensive man who had never taken any part in politics. To this story, which comes to us on the authority of the two Ciceros, Plutarch adds that his victim's name was not on the list of the proscribed, and was only placed there by Catiline's influence after the murder had been committed.

(2) That during the same period he had publicly, and amid circumstances of the greatest atrocity, murdered Marcus Marius Gratidianus, a praetor much beloved by the people, and had carried his bleeding head to Sulla, through the streets of Rome. This charge also is made by Quintus, and reiterated by Marcus Cicero.

(3) That he had committed adultery with a Vestal virgin (Sallust xv. 2), who is identified by the commentator Asconius with Cicero's sister-in-law, Fabia.

(4) That when his manifest guilt had caused him to be charged with extortion in his province of Africa, he had procured his acquittal by bribery so profuse as

to render him as needy at the end of the trial as some
of the jurymen had been at the beginning.

Besides these definite accusations, there are a host
of vague charges which need not be examined at any
length. Plutarch and the two Ciceros between them
make him guilty of several varieties of incest, and, as
a matter of course, in the case of one whose name had
been mentioned in such connections, the Ciceros accuse
him of the nameless vice, at this time so prevalent at
Rome, but with which Sallust refuses distinctly to
charge him. Cicero does not mention the accusation
of murdering his own son which Sallust brings against
Catiline in the present passages ; he speaks, however,
in the first Invective of his murder of some woman,
and some commentators have thought that this crime,
as well as that in connection with his son, was committed in order to pave the way for the marriage with
Aurelia Orestilla, and that they both occurred in the
interval between the speech In Toga Candida and the
first Invective. That Catiline should have busied
himself in these ghastly love affairs at such a time, or
that his enemies should have allowed the two murders
to pass unnoticed, is highly improbable. The whole
of these vague charges, indeed, may safely be dismissed as the outcome of party malice ; they only
serve to furnish us with evidence that Catiline was
thought a man at whom the filthiest mud might be
thrown with some chance of its sticking.

When we come to examine the other charges, the
result is not very different. Cicero in one place speaks
of Catiline as having been brought to trial on two occasions, by which he has been thought to mean on two

only ; but our other authorities make it probable that, besides the accusation on the charge of sedition in B.C. 63, of which nothing came, he was formally accused three times ; and these three trials cover the whole of the definite charges which we possess against him. The earliest of these trials is placed by Orosius in the year B.C. 73, when Catiline and the Vestal Fabia were accused of unlawful intercourse. They were both acquitted, and the Ciceros, who had their family reason for not challenging the verdict in *this* case, simply point to the charge as a proof of the taint which invariably attended Catiline's presence. The next trial took place when Caesar was the head of the commission "*de sicariis*," and was bringing many of the Sullan murderers to justice. Lucius Lucceius accused Catiline, whether of the exact offences recorded under the first and second head or not we cannot tell ; anyhow, the verdict was again for his acquittal. The fact that Caesar was the judge may be taken to account for this, but, as both Professor Beesly and Mr. Long remark, the innocence of a man who has been tried and acquitted ought at least to be held an open question. The charge against Catiline of murdering Marius Gratidianus does indeed involve a most extraordinary dilemma ; if he was guilty, we cannot understand how he could ever have gained the favour of the Roman mob ; if innocent, how Cicero could have dared to bring such a charge against him. The student must take his choice of difficulties. As regards the last of the definite accusations, the prevalence of the crime of extortion among the governors of provinces, at once makes it likely that Catiline was guilty of it, and that, whether guilty or innocent, his enemies would bring it against him on his return to Rome. The fact, however, that the Africans had previously complained of his conduct to the Senate, and the references to the trial in Cicero's letters, at a time when he was quite unprejudiced against Catiline, and actually thought of undertaking his defence, makes it almost certain that he was guilty. Neither this, nor the fact of his having procured his acquittal by bribes, the profuseness of which is startling in the case of a man always represented as overwhelmed with debts, would lower his estimation with the Roman political world. We have thus against him nothing but a number of vague accusations, together with three or four more serious charges of which he was formally acquitted, though by no very respectable tribunals. Evidently we have here no sufficient materials for evoking the bloodthirsty and lascivious stage villain which Catiline has so often been made to appear. On the other hand, we cannot help feeling that the accusations which were brought against him were something very different from the fifty charges on which Cato Major was tried during the course of his life. There is only too much truth in Professor Beesly's remark, that "if Cicero had been their contemporary, with his theories on '*Mendaciuncula*,' the Gracchi would have been handed down to us stained with every vice that humanity most shudders at!" Let us struggle, however, to avoid prejudice and exaggeration as much as we may, it is hard to rid ourselves of the impression, which even Mr. Beesly seems in some measure to share, that Catiline ranked among the disreputable and not among the respectable politicians of Rome. This is the minimum value to which the consistent assertions of all our authorities can be reduced ; and this, it may be added, is quite enough to decide the aspect in which we should regard the conspiracy. If Catiline had come down to us with the character of a Drusus, it might be possible to credit him with lofty aims, even though it were difficult to see what those aims could have been, and there were not a single remarkable action recorded in his life. As it is, there is nothing in history to make us alter the verdict which the conspirator pronounced upon himself when he declared that he was one who would bring about his country's ruin in order to avoid his own.

To this meeting came Publius and Servius Sulla. (Eo convenere P. et Servius Sullae.)

This Publius Sulla is not the same as the Publius Cornelius Sulla, the consul-elect for B.C. 66, as is proved by a passage in Cicero's defence of the latter, in which he speaks of this Publius as a man whose cause no one would undertake. Cicero's speech, however, was actually in defence of his client's innocence of the very charge which some have thought that Sallust here brings against him. Cornelius Sulla had shared the fate of Publius Autronius in being unseated on petition, and it was thought likely that he had shared his colleague's guilt in connection with both the first and second conspiracy. Hortensius defended him on the former charge, Cicero on the latter ; and by their efforts he was acquitted.

Gnaeus Pompeius, his personal enemy, was at the head of a large army. (Gn. Pompeius invisus ipsi magnum exercitum ductabat.) CHAP. XVII.

The question of the complicity of Crassus in the conspiracy is dealt with in the Introduction. There can be no doubt that Sallust has here touched on the one motive which could induce him to mix himself in such concerns. His enmity towards Pompey dated from the close of the Servile War, B.C. 71, when the latter, as he was returning from Spain, cut to pieces some straggling companies of the main body which Crassus had defeated, and on the score of this achievement, arrogated to himself the credit of having finished the war. Cicero's subsequent support of Pompey in this unjust claim was one cause of the ill-feeling which Crassus till shortly before his departure for Syria entertained towards him.

A few conspirators, of whom Catiline was one, had before this formed a plot against the state. (Sed antea item conjuravere pauci contra rempublicam, in quibus Catilina fuit.) CHAP. XVIII

It may be well here to quote some of our other authorities as to the mysterious conspiracy of B.C. 65, the nature of which is discussed in the Introduction to this book. The account given by Dion Cassius is substantially the same as Sallust's; he adds, however, some important details. "Publius Paetus," he says, "and Cornelius Sulla (a nephew of the Dictator), on being convicted of bribery after their election as consuls, made a conspiracy to murder their accusers, Lucius Cotta and Lucius Torquatus, finding an additional incentive in the fact that these had been chosen to supersede them.   In this attempt they were joined, among others, by Gnaeus Piso and Lucius Catilina, the latter a desperate man who had himself stood for the consulship, and was hence a malcontent.   Their efforts, however, came to nothing, as the plot was prematurely betrayed, and a guard was granted by the Senate to Cotta and Torquatus.*   A resolution also would have been passed against the conspirators, had not one of the tribunes vetoed it.   Piso's spirit, however, was not quelled, and the Senate, alarmed lest he should disturb the state, despatched him to Spain under the pretext of assigning him a command. There he committed some injustice, and was murdered by the Spaniards."   (Hist. xxxvi. 27.)   In the sentence asterisked, it should be mentioned, the reading is very doubtful.

The references to the plot in Cicero are as follows : —In the speech "In Toga Candida," delivered in B.C. 64, he says, " I pass over that impious attempt of yours, that day which so nearly brought bitterness and sorrow to the Roman people, when, with Gnaeus Piso, and none other, as your accomplice, you designed to massacre the Optimates."   Again, in the first Invective, delivered November 8th, B.C. 63, he says, " Can this light give you pleasure, Catiline ; the air of this clime be sweet to breathe, when you know that there is no one here present who is ignorant that on the last day of the consulship of Lepidus and Tullus (December 31st, B.C. 66), you stood in the Comitium with your weapons about you, and that you had hired a band of men to murder the consuls and the leading men in the state ?" (Chap. 6.) In the " Pro Murena," spoken in the early part of 62, the first conspiracy is again briefly alluded to—" Everything which has been agitated throughout these three years, from the time when, as you know, Lucius Catilina and Gnaeus Piso formed their plot to massacre the Senate, is now breaking out." (Chap. 38.) Lastly there are two passages in the " Pro Sulla," which may be quoted. In the first of these Cicero says, " You make frequent extracts from the letter which I wrote to Gnaeus Pompeius on the subject of my own performances and of public affairs in general. From this letter you seek to find some accusation against Publius Sulla, and when I write that the incredible frenzy which had been plotted two years before had broken out in my consulship, you cite me as thus proving that Sulla had a share in the former conspiracy. As if I, of all people, imagined that Piso, Catiline, Varguntius, and Autronius could have done no deed of impious daring without the help of Publius Sulla!" (" Pro Sulla," chap. 24.) Finally, we come to the second passage, in which Cicero is defending himself and others of his party from the charge of inconsistency in pleading for anyone accused of complicity with Catiline. One of Sulla's prosecutors was a son of the consul Torquatus, who had returned at the second election for B.C. 65 ; Cicero thus retorts on him—" Even your own father, Torquatus, when Catiline, a bad man, but then his suppliant, and who, whatever his recklessness, had once been his friend, was accused of extortion, appeared to plead for him. This he did after information had been laid before him as to that first conspiracy, but he declared that though he had heard something about it, he did not believe the report. If you remind me that your father did not support Catiline on his second trial, while the others did, I answer that, if he subsequently learnt anything of which during his consulship he was ignorant, you certainly cannot blame those who heard nothing more. If, on the other hand, it was the original information which weighed with him, I may fairly ask why it should have been more worthy of attention when stale than when fresh?" ("Pro Sulla," chap. 29.)

If the quotations above given, joined with the chapter in Sallust, had been our only authorities for the conspiracy of B.C. 65, no difficulty could have arisen. Suetonius, however, in his life of Julius Caesar, gives another history which is at once so like and so unlike that of Sallust as to cause considerable confusion. The translation here given is that of Thomson with a few alterations. Caesar, it should be premised, while acting as Quaestor in Farther Spain, is supposed to have been excited by a dream. "Quitting the province, therefore, before the usual time, he visited the Latin colonies, then taken up with petitioning for the franchise, and would have excited them to some bold step, had not the consul met his intrigues by detaining for some time the legions levied for Cilicia. Nothing daunted, he soon after engaged in a greater attempt in the capital itself. For a few days before he entered upon the aedileship he incurred the suspicion of engaging in a conspiracy with Marcus Crassus, a man of consular rank, and Publius Sulla and Lucius Autronius, who had been convicted of bribery after being chosen consuls. The plan of the conspirators was to fall upon the Senate in the beginning of the year, and murder such persons as they should have agreed on. Crassus was then to assume the dictatorship, Caesar to be appointed master of the horse, and when the state had been ordered at their pleasure, the consulship was to be restored to Sulla and Autronius. Mention is made of this plot by Tanusius Geminus in his history, by Marcus Bibulus, in his edicts, and by Curio the elder in his orations. Cicero likewise seems to hint at it in a letter to Axius, when he says that Caesar had in his consulship secured to himself that arbitrary power to which he had aspired when aedile. Tanusius adds that Crassus, from remorse or fear, did not appear upon the day appointed for the massacre, and that therefore Caesar on his part withheld the signal which he was to have given. The agreement, according to Curio, was that he should slip his toga from his shoulder. We have the authority of the same Curio and of M. Actorius Naso for Caesar's having been likewise concerned in another conspiracy with young Gnaeus Piso, to whom, upon a suspicion of some mischief being meditated in the city, the province of Spain was decreed out of course. The arrangement was that Piso abroad and Caesar in Rome should unite in a revolutionary rising with the help of the Ambiani and Transpadanus. The death of Piso made the execution of either part of the plot impossible."—(Suetonius, " Julius Caesar," 8-9).

CHAP.
XVIII. For an attempt to reconcile these accounts, the reader is referred to the Introduction to this book.

CHAP.
XVIII. *A little while after this, Catiline was charged with extortion, and so disqualified as a candidate for the consulship* [*since he could not give in his name within the legal time*]. *Post paullo Catilina, pecuniarum repetundarum reus, prohibitus erat consulatum petere* [*quod intra legitumos dies profiteri nequiverat*].

Sallust, as a rule, is very careless in his chronology; if he is accurate here we must suppose that Catiline wished to offer himself as a candidate for one of the consulships vacated by Autronius and Sulla, and was thus the rival, not of them, but of Cotta and Torquatus. His coalition with Autronius in the intrigues of 65, renders this all the more probable. The way in which he was prevented from going to the poll is further explained by Cicero, according to whom the consul, L. Volcatius, after consultation with the leading men of the state, refused to receive his name on the ground of the accusation under which he was lying. The "legal time" referred to in the bracketed passage was the seventeen days previous to the election, and Professor Beesly conjectures that the charge of extortion was trumped up by the aristocrats on purpose to disqualify Catiline. Unfortunately, however, for this view, the Provincials had previously sent a deputation to complain to the Senate of their governor's conduct. The trial did not come on till after the consular election for the next year also, and thus Catiline was prevented, even if he had wished to do so, from standing

for the consulship for B.C. 64. When it at length took
place, by the collusion of the prosecutor, Publius
Clodius, and the corruption of the jury, Catiline was
acquitted. Cicero at one time had thought of defending him to secure his help in the consular election for
63 ; the speech, " In Toga Candida," however, makes
it almost certain that he did not carry out his
intention.

CHAP. XVIII.

*The horsemen were old and faithful dependents of
Gnaeus Pompeius, and attacked Piso with his consent.
(Alii autem equites illos Gn. Pompeii veteres fidosque
clientis voluntate ejus Pisonem aggressos.)*

CHAP. XIX.

Pompey had held command in Spain from 76 to 71,
during which time he was engaged against Sertorius.
Throughout his life Spain continued one of the chief
strongholds of his power, and after his death his sons
were able to raise an army there with which they
fought Caesar at the battle of Munda, B.C. 45.

*In Mauritania, at the head of an army, Publius
Sittius Nucerinus. (In Mauritania cum exercitu P.
Sittium Nucerinum.)*

CHAP. XXI.

P. Sittius Nucerinus was a Roman soldier of fortune
who had gone to Spain B.C. 64, and in the following
year crossed over to Mauritania, and took service in
the armies of the different African kings. In B.C. 62
Cicero defended him in his absence on a charge of
complicity with Catiline, but in the following year his
possessions in Italy were sold to pay his creditors,
and he never returned to Rome. In B.C. 46, when
Caesar landed in Africa, Nucerinus rendered him

CHAP.
XXI.

material assistance by invading the kingdom of Juba. At the end of the war he was rewarded by Caesar with a grant of territory in Western Numidia, but was shortly afterward assassinated.

CHAP.
XXI.

Gaius Antonius, too, was a candidate for the consulship, and he hoped to have him as his colleague, as a man at once intimate with himself, and entangled in the greatest difficulties. (Petere consulatum G. Antonium, quem sibi collegam fore speraret, hominem et familiarem et omnibus necessitudinibus circumventum.)

Gaius Antonius had served under Sulla in Greece in B.C. 83, and, at the head of some squadrons of cavalry, plundered the people of Achaia. For this, in B.C. 76, he was accused by Caesar and condemned, and it was on this occasion that he complained to the tribunes of having, before a jury of his fellow-countrymen, "no fair play against the Greeks." In B.C. 70 he was removed from the Senate by the censors Gellius and Lentulus on the score of his condemnation and of his generally lawless behaviour. He was soon afterwards readmitted to the Senate, and was praetor in B.C. 66, and in this office as well as the consulship had Cicero for his colleague. As to his behaviour during the year B.C. 63, our evidence is doubtful. Dion Cassius represents him as ill-affected up to time of Catiline's flight from Rome, and the conspirator, as Sallust says, very likely had reason to trust him until his own rejection for the consulship in 62. On the other hand, Cicero would hardly have entrusted him with the command of one of the armies against Catiline had he suspected his loyalty, and

Antonius, when tried on this and other charges in
B.C. 59, was acquitted.

*It was asserted by some that Catiline carried round
in bowls a mixture of human blood and wine. (Fuere
qui dicerent, Catilinam humani corporis sanguinem
vino permixtum in pateris circumtulisse).*

This foolish story appears in a grosser form in
Plutarch and Dion Cassius, both of whom probably
obtained it from Cicero's last account of his consulship
in Greece, the περὶ ὑπατείας. According to these
writers, a boy was slain at the meeting, and the conspirators all partook of his flesh.

*Some, however, were of opinion that this story, together
with many others, was invented by people who thought
that the unpopularity which Cicero subsequently incurred
would be diminished if the crime of his victims were
recognised as peculiarly hideous. (Nonnulli ficta et haec
et multa praeterea existumabant ab iis, qui Ciceronis
invidiam quae postea orta est, leniri credebant atrocitate
sceleris eorum qui poenas dederant.)*

This is one of the shrewd remarks in which Sallust
shows himself as a practical statesman instead of, as
in his introductory chapters, as a pedant, anxious to
drag in a sermon on some literary text. There can
be no doubt that both during and after the conspiracy
it was Cicero's interest to exaggerate the atrocity of
its aims, and it is equally certain that he did so
exaggerate, and with all the power of a great orator.
Dion Cassius informs us that until the news that
Manlius had taken up arms in Etruria reached Rome,

Cicero's story was generally thought to be a malicious accusation, and both the first and second Invectives make it abundantly clear that, as late as November 8th and 9th, there were still many people who refused to believe in the existence of any conspiracy at all. Before any measures could be taken against the partisans of Catiline, Cicero had first to rouse popular indignation against them. After the suppression of the revolt, his motives to blacken the characters of its leaders were even greater. Cato and Catulus might declare that he had saved their country, and the Senate and respectable classes might echo their cry, but with the democratic party and all the rabble of Rome Cicero was distinctly unpopular, and even his friends were gradually alienated from him by his intolerable self-laudation. When he laid down office, a Tribune, Metellus Neps, forbade him, as a man who had murdered his countrymen, to make the usual address to the people. When he defended Sulla, he had to defend himself as well against the insinuations of Torquatus, that he was aiming at " kingly power." In giving Atticus an account of the trial of Clodius (February B.C. 61), he uses the phrase, " My swelling unpopularity has been reduced by bleeding " (Att. I. 16, II.), and years afterwards (February 49) he expresses a dread that Caesar may attack him more fiercely than others, hoping thereby to gain popularity (Att. VIII. 3-5). Undoubtedly by his conduct in his consulship Cicero lost the favour of the lower classes of the city, and in Rome at this time the power of the mob was greater, probably, than at any other.

This, more than anything else, had roused men's zeal to confer the consulship on Marcus Tullius Cicero. Till that time many of the nobility had been in a ferment of jealousy. (Ea res in primis studia hominum accendit ad consulatum mandandum M. Tullio Ciceroni. Namque antea pleraque nobilitas invidia aestuabat.)

Professor Tyrrell, in his excellent introduction to "The Correspondence of Cicero," has rendered a most important service to English historical scholarship by his vigorous protest against the aspersions which have been cast on the great orator's political consistency. Dion Cassius, that most malignant of historians, seems to have been the first to make the accusation, and in our own times Professor Mommsen almost adopts his language when he introduces the "*pater patriae*" to his readers as the "notorious political trimmer, M. Tullius Cicero." Mr. Beesly goes even farther, and plainly asserts "up to this time" (*i.e.* his canvass for the consulship), "Cicero had courted the revolutionary party. But he now sold himself to the nobles and began to earn his wages by denouncing revolutionary measures, and the leader of that party, Catiline," and proceeds to talk of "the earliest efforts of his venal tongue." Now this language is simply unjustifiable. As Professor Tyrrell shows, and as, in any other connection, every historical writer is ready to admit, for an enterprising young man at Rome the surest road to office lay through success at the bar. To obtain reputation as an advocate, Cicero was ready to beard Sulla in his defence of Roscius, to rouse popular indignation against Verres, and to defend Fonteius, who was probably equally

CHAP.
XXIII. guilty, on a precisely similar charge. His speech
in favour of the Lex Manilia may be explained
partly by his devotion to Pompey, and partly by his
intimate connection with the Roman knights who
were eager for Pompey's appointment. It is not true
to say that down to the time of his consulship Cicero
had courted the democrats; he had simply accepted
every brief which he thought might win him distinction, and so help to smoothe away the difficulties
which the fact of his being a " *novus homo* " placed in
his career. Cicero's political life really begins with
his consulship, and from that time forward, except for
a moment when embittered by the conduct of the
nobility after his return from exile, he devoted himself
to the vain but not dishonourable attempt of maintaining the authority of the Senate by inducing the
moneyed classes to throw in their cause with that
of the nobility.

CHAP.
XXVI. *By an agreement about the provinces he had constrained his colleague Antonius to desist from all
disloyalty. (Ad hoc collegam suum Antonium pactione
provinciae perpulerat, ne contra rempublicam sentiret.)*

Cicero, in his speech "In Toga Candida," had
thundered against Antonius with almost as much
vehemence as against Catiline. He now, however,
tried to win him over by agreeing that Antonius, at
the expiration of the consulship, should have the
governorship of Macedonia, the province which he
wished. Cicero always represents himself as actuated
in this bargain by an unselfish spirit of patriotism; it
is not certain, however, that his conduct was so disin-

terested as he would make out. There are mysterious references in his letter to an advance of money which he expected from a certain Teucris, and this Teucris seems to have been none other than Antonius. The latter, while plundering the Macedonians, openly gave out that he was earning money for Cicero; but such evidence as this is not worth much. We are equally unable to draw any conclusion from the fact that Cicero defended and procured the acquittal of Antonius in his trial for extortion in B.C. 59; he would have been expected to have done as much for his colleague in any case. On the whole the evidence is not conclusive, but there is not much in Cicero's character that need make us think he would scorn the Themistoclean policy of making his own profit, while advancing the public good.

CHAP.
XXVI.

Besides some veterans from the Sullan colonies (non-nullos ex Sullanis colonis).

CHAP.
XXVIII.

In fulfilment of promises to his soldiers and to provide his new constitution with a standing garrison in Italy, Sulla had assigned as many as 120,000 allotments of land to his veterans, chiefly in Etruria. Instead, however, of giving stability to his arrangements, these colonists, who had lost all taste for agricultural pursuits, proved a constant source of danger to the state, and it was of them that the army of Manlius was now chiefly composed.

The Senate made the decree " The consuls are to take measures to protect the Senate from harm." (Itaque Senatus decrevit, darent operam consules, ne quid respublica detrimenti caperet.)

CHAP.
XXIX.

CHAP.
XXIX.   Sallust shows here more than his usual carelessness
with regard to chronology. The meeting at Laeca's
house took place on November 6th, and Cicero, speaking on the 8th, refers to the decree as having been
passed for twenty days. In the same speech he prides
himself on a prophecy, made on October 21st, that
Manlius would take up arms on the 27th of the same
month. Asconius, therefore, is probably right when
he says that Cicero used, twenty as a round number
for eighteen, and the decree was most likely passed
on the day of his prophecy, on October 21st. Anyhow Sallust is wrong in placing it after the meeting
in Laeca's house and the receipt of the message from
Etruria announcing Manlius' revolt.

CHAP.
XXX.   *The celebration of their triumphs had been obstructed
by the underhand tactics of a clique (impediti, ne trium-
pharent, calumnia paucorum).*

Q. Marcius Rex had earned his triumph in Cilicia,
Q. Metellus in Crete.   Both generals had been placed
under Pompey by the provisions of the Manilian law,
and their right to a triumph for their previous services
could now be disputed on the ground that they were
not in possession of an independent command.

CHAP.
XXX.   *A decree was at the same time passed that the gladiatorial schools should be quartered on Capua and the
other borough towns. (Itemque decrevere, uti gladiatoriae
familiae Capuam et in cetera municipia distribuerentur.)*

The popularity of the gladiatorial games had led
to the formation of huge *familiae* or training schools
throughout Italy, and a great many of these were

established in or near Capua. The revolt of Spartacus
had demonstrated the fighting power of these wretched
men, and they were now frequently employed by the
party leaders to raise or suppress riots in the streets
of Rome. After the murder of Caesar a force of
gladiators owned by Decimus Brutus was very useful
as a protection to the assassins. At the present crisis,
according to Cicero, the gladiators were all on the side
of Catiline.

CHAP.
XXX.

*He was accused by Lucius Paulus under the Plautian
law (ipse lege Plautia interrogatus erat ab L. Paullo).*

CHAP.
XXXI.

The *Lex Plautia de Vi* is supposed to have been
passed in B.C. 89, and to have been aimed against all
plotters against the public peace. When thus accused
Catiline offered to place himself under the surveillance
of several of the chief men of Rome, including Cicero.
On their all declining to receive him, he took up his
abode with a certain M. Marcellus or M. Metellus,
whom Dion Cassius confuses with the praetor, Q.
Metellus Celer, who was one of those who had refused
to receive Catiline, and by this time was acting against
him in Picenum.

*Thereupon the consul, Marcus Tullius, did good
service to the state by delivering a noble speech which he
afterwards wrote out and published. (Tum M. Tullius
consul orationem habuit luculentam atque utilem rei-
publicae quam postea scriptam edidit.)*

CHAP.
XXXI.

This speech has been handed down to us as Cicero's
first " Invective " against Catiline. The consul had
probably no evidence against Catiline such as would

CHAP.
XXXI.

have ensured his condemnation by a Roman jury, and even if he had he could not in this way have procured his capital punishment.   Public feeling was not as yet ripe for such measures as he afterwards took against the other conspirators, and his object in this speech was to drive Catiline to the camp of Manlius, and so to open rebellion.   This object he effected by disclosing his acquaintance with the details of the conspiracy, while he endeavoured to frighten Catiline by his claim to be able to put him to death on his own authority. On the next day, November 1st, he addressed to the people the second "Invective," in which he rejoiced over Catiline's flight, and further roused popular indignation against him and his fellow-conspirators.   The words, *quam postea scriptam edidit,* point to the extensive alterations which Cicero made in his speeches prior to their publication, the alterations which so detract from their value as historical documents.

CHAP.
XXXI.

Marcus Tullius, a mere citizen-at-will. (M. Tullius inquilinus civis urbis Romae.)

Inquilinus, literally translated, is a "lodger."   Cicero was a native, not of Rome, but of Arpinum ; and his family did not remove to the capital until he was at least four or five years of age.

CHAP.
XXXI.

I will quench in a general ruin the fire that surrounds me. (Incendium meum ruina restinguam.)

Sallust's melodramatic picture of Catiline's last exit from the Senate is rather spoilt by the fact that Cicero (" Pro Muraena," c. 25) reports these words as spoken some time before the twenty-first of October.   It is

possible that the orator made a slip as to the date, but
it is more likely that Sallust thought the sentence a
good one to put into Catiline's mouth at such a
moment. If this is so, those who think that Catiline
left Rome on November 8th, simply because it
was convenient to him, have their case materially
strengthened. Dion Cassius (xxxvii. 33), it may be
mentioned, represents him as glad of such an excuse
for departure.

CHAP.
XXXI.

*Your ancestors often, in compassion for the commons
of Rome, relieved their destitution by the decrees they
proposed; and quite recently bronze was raised for
purposes of repayment to the value of silver. (Saepe
majores vestrum miseriti plebis Romanae, decretis suis
inopiae ejus opitulati sunt, ac novissume . . . . argen-
tum aere solutum est.)*

CHAP.
XXXIII.

By the *Lex Poetilia Papiria*, passed B.C. 326, imprisonment for debt had been abolished. Towards
the close, however, of the republic, economic difficulties
assumed proportions such as they had never attained
before. In B.C. 89, a crisis was brought about by the
occurrence of the social war, and the troubles in Asia.
The debtors raked up an obsolete law against usury,
and claimed from their creditors fourfold the amount
of the illegal interest which they had exacted from
them. This claim was allowed by the praetor, Asellio,
but his compliance cost him his life, as he was torn to
pieces by a mob of creditors in front of the Temple of
Concord. The measure to which Manlius here refers
was the result of a compromise between the contending
parties.

CHAP.
XXXIV.

Of this letter the following is a copy (earum exemplum infra scriptum est).

The following chapter contains, according to Professor Beesly, "a simple and dignified letter, which, as the Emperor Napoleon says, offers a striking contrast to the passion of Cicero." In his introduction to Cicero's speeches Mr. Long writes, " The historian says that the letter is genuine, and it looks like the genuine production of a villain and hypocrite who does not know what to say ;" and again in his history (iii. 295), " This foolish, incoherent epistle, if it is genuine, shows that the man had little sense." Mr. Long is the most impartial of historians, and Professor Beesly rejects by anticipation the charge of maintaining a paradox ; it shows with what difficulties this chapter of history is beset when such widely different judgments can be formed on a single letter.

CHAP.
XXXVII.

Young men who had starved in the country on the labour of their hands, had been attracted to Rome by public or private bounties. (Juventus, quae in agris manuum mercede inopiam toleraverat, privatis atque publicis largitionibus excita.)

Since the time of the last Carthaginian war, the free cultivators of the soil had been replaced, all over Italy, by the slaves of large proprietors. The Gracchi had for a time stayed this tendency by granting allotments of public land to the poorer burgesses, and these efforts were continued down to the time of Catiline's conspiracy. They were never, however, really successful for any length of time, as the small farms were always gradually absorbed by the estates of the capitalists. Their owners then flocked to Rome to swell the rich man's train of clients, and to get their share at the public distributions of corn, in which only residents in the capital were allowed to participate.

All those whose parents had been proscribed during Sulla's triumph, whose property had been confiscated and their political rights impaired. (*Quorum victoria Sullae parentes proscripti, bona erepta, jus libertatis imminutum erat.*)

According to Valerius Maximus, the number of Sulla's victims was no less than 4700, and by a *lex Cornelia* the children of these, in addition to the loss of their patrimony, were excluded from all offices of the state. The young men were now agitating to be restored to their full political rights, and a bill with this object was brought forward during the year 63. It was defeated, however, and mainly by Cicero's exertions. The consul did not deny its substantial justice, but he contended that, at so disturbed a period, it was inexpedient to put power into the hands of men who would naturally be eager for revenge.

Others so rich as to live in a style of regal magnifi-cence. (*Alios ita divites, ut regio victu atque cultu aetatem agerent.*)

When the estates of the proscribed were put up for sale, no one dared to bid against the favourites of Sulla ; thus one of his freedmen purchased a property worth £60,000 for £20, and another became possessed

CHAP.
XXXVII. of an estate worth £90,000. It was in this way that Marcus Crassus laid the foundations of his enormous wealth.

CHAP.
XXXVIII. *The tribunician power had been restored in the consulship of Pompey and Crassus. (Postquam Gn. Pompeio et M. Crasso consulibus tribunicia potestas restituta est.)*

Sulla, during his dictatorship, had diminished the importance of the tribunate in three ways. He fettered the right of intercession by the imposition of a heavy fine in all cases of its abuse, made the exercise of the right of access to the people dependent on the pleasure of the Senate, though as to this point there are some doubts, and lastly made the holding of the tribunate a disqualification for any higher office. Efforts to repeal his legislation on this subject were made in 76 and 74, but unsuccessfully, and it continued unaltered down to the consulship of Pompey and Crassus, when the tribunes were restored to all their former power. There can be no doubt that Sallust is right in what he says as to the dangerous character of this office when in the hands of ambitious men. Whatever a tribune proposed to a so-called public meeting was sure to be carried unanimously, and the safety of the state was dependent on such check as the ten holders of this office might exercise upon each other.

CHAP.
XXXIX. *After the despatch of Pompey to conduct the wars against the pirates and Mithridates, the power of the commons was broken and the influence of the oligarchy*

increased. (Postquam Gn. Pompeius ad bellum mariti-
mum atque Mithridaticum missus est, plebis opes im-
minutae, paucorum potentia crevat.)

This is a most extraordinary statement of Sallust and is very difficult to account for. The bill of Gabinius by which Pompey had been given such large powers against the pirates had been passed in 67, and that of Manilius, by which these powers were further extended for the war against Mithridates, in the following year. Since then the democrats had been harassing the Senate in every possible way. Caesar, for instance, in the year 65 had revived the memory of Marius, and in 64, as president of the commission regarding murder, caused many of Sulla's executioners to be brought before him and condemned. The bills of Gabinius and Manilius did not increase, but crushed the power of the Senate ; they were, however, a real blow to the democrats, notwithstanding that their temporary alliance with Pompey compelled them to give them an unwilling support. They distrusted their too powerful ally, and dreaded lest on his return from the East he should imitate the behaviour of Sulla. Hence their desire to obtain for one of their leaders a counterbalancing command in Egypt, and hence, also, the mysterious intrigues of January and February, 65.

Their great public and private indebtedness led him to hope that they would readily join in his enterprise. (Existumans publice privatimque aere alieno oppressos, facile eos ad tale consilium adduci posse.)

The Roman " negotiatores " employed such capital

CHAP.
XL.

as could not be invested in Italy in loans to foreign princes and provincial towns, at the most usurious rates of interest, sometimes as much as 48 per cent. The towns had to borrow from them to comply with the exactions of the governors and tax-farmers, and from the moment that the loan was completed, the town was wholly at the mercy of its creditor. In a case which happens to be mentioned in a letter of Cicero, the agent of the philosophic assassin, Marcus Brutus, starved to death five of the municipal senators of the town of Salamis in Cyprus, in order to obtain payment of one of these loans at 48 per cent. A Lex Gabinia was passed to make such loans illegal, but its provisions were never enforced, and the scandal continued until the reorganization of the provincial system under the empire.

CHAP.
XLI.

They betrayed the whole affair to Quintus Fabius Sanga, whose patronage their state mostly employed. (*Itaque Q. Fabio Sangae, cujus patrocinio civitas plurimum utebatur, rem omnem aperiunt.*)

It was customary for the different provinces to place themselves under the protection of some influential Roman, who stood to them in the same relation in which, in the earlier days of Rome, the patron had stood to his client. Provincials who were under the protection of a powerful patron—the Spaniards, for instance, under that of the elder Cato—felt themselves sure of redress for any ill-treatment they might suffer from Roman officials ; and a member of a provincial town would look to its patron for assistance in any business he might have at Rome. The patronate was in some cases hereditary, and often the first patron was the general who had completed the subjugation of the province.

Many of these agents had been brought to trial by the praetor Q. Metellus Celer, and by him thrown into prison, and Gaius Murena had pursued the same course in Further Gaul. (Ex eo numero compluris Q. Metellus Celer praetor, causa cognita, in vincula conjecerat; item in ulteriore Gallia G. Murena.)

This is one of the passages which should be noted as showing how widely the ramification of the conspiracy extended. Q. Metellus Celer was one of the bulwarks of the aristocratic party; it was he who saved the life of Rabirius by striking the flag on the Janiculum, and as consul elect in 61, and consul the following year, he was foremost in opposition to both Caesar and Pompey. In spite of Cicero's having secured the province of Cisalpine Gaul to Metellus in B.C. 62, a coolness arose between them owing to the attitude which the latter assumed when his brother Nepes attacked Cicero on his laying down his office. The breach however was subsequently healed, and Metellus did his best to frustrate the designs of Cicero's enemy Clodius, although the latter was his own brother-in-law. His death occurred suddenly in B.C. 59. Gaius Licinius Murena, who was now pro-praetor in Gallia Transalpina, was elected to the consulship for B.C. 62, and was successfully defended by Cicero and Hortensius when charged with bribery. He was one of those who voted for the sentence of death on December 5th, B.C. 63; after his consulship nothing further is known of him.

CHAP.
XLIII. *Taking this as their signal, the rank and file of their supporters were on the following night to carry out their respective tasks. (Eo signo proxuma nocte cetera multitudo conjurationis suum quisque negotium exsequeretur.)*

According to Cicero, the plot was to be carried out at the beginning of the Saturnalia, on December 19th. There is considerable room, however, for doubt whether any such extraordinary programme was ever really framed.

CHAP.
XLIV. *The Allobroges demanded from Lentulus, Cethegus, and Statilius, an oath which they might bear duly attested to their countrymen. (Allobroges ab Lentulo, Cethego, Statilio . . . postulant jusjurandum, quod signatum ad civis perferant.)*

Cicero, in his third speech against Catiline, gives an account of the scene in the Senate when the letters of the conspirators were opened. "First," he says, "we showed his seal to Cethegus; he acknowledged it. We then broke the thread, and read it. It was written in his own hand to the Senate and people of the Allobroges, and its purport was that he, on his part, would perform what he had promised their ambassadors, and that he begged that they, on theirs, would carry out the assurance which their ambassadors had given him." The letter of Lentulus seems to have been to the same effect. The particular service which the conspirators asked from the Allobroges, according to Cicero, was the supply of a body of cavalry.

CHAP.
XLV.

On the night agreed on for their departure, Cicero gave orders to the praetors Lucius Valerius Flaccus and Gaius Pomptinus to plant an ambush by the Mulvian bridge and seize the Allobroges with their retinue. (Constituta nocte, qua proficiscerentur, Cicero L. Valerio Flacco et G. Pomptinio praetoribus imperat, ut in ponte Mulvio per insidias Allobrogum comitatus deprehendant.)

From Cicero we learn that the two praetors posted their men in the villas on each side of the river, and sallied out thence to attack the Allobroges. Flaccus was governor of Asia in the succeeding year, and on his return was successfully defended by Cicero and Hortensius on his trial for extortion. Pomptinus was assigned the province of Gallia Narbonensis, and in B.C. 61 inflicted a defeat on the Allobroges, who, in spite of the rewards voted to their ambassadors, had apparently obtained from the Senate no redress of their grievances, and were at this time in revolt. For this victory Pomptinus demanded a triumph, for which he had to wait till B.C. 54. In B.C. 51 he accompanied Cicero as legate to Cilicia, and remained with him for a year.

CHAP.
XLVII.

The Senate made a decree that Lentulus on laying down his office, as well as the rest, should be kept in "free" or private custody. (Senatus decernit, uti abdicato magistratu Lentulus, itemque ceteri in liberis custodiis habeantur.)

The Senate had no power of depriving a magistrate of office, and though the people twice claimed the right to depose a refractory tribune, such a claim was

Chap. XLVII.

distinctly unconstitutional. On the other hand, a magistrate could not be tried for any offence during his term of office, and Lentulus could thus, if he had chosen, have increased Cicero's difficulties by refusing to resign. The free custody in which the conspirators were kept would allow them to do what they pleased so long as they remained under their guardian's watch. To leave the guardian's house, like Dion Cassius supposes Catiline to have done, when he placed himself under "*libera custodia*" on being accused under the Plautian law, would be a serious breach of faith on the part of the prisoner, and would only be possible if allowed by the carelessness or complicity of the custodian. In the present case, historians have noticed that for fear of such connivance on their part, Caesar and Crassus were only entrusted with the two least important prisoners.

Chap. XLVIII.

Others asserted that Tarquinius was set on by Cicero to prevent Crassus, according to his wont, taking the seditious under his patronage, and so embroiling the state. (Alii Tarquinium a Ciceroni immissum aiebant, ne Crassus more suo suscepto malorum patrocinio rempublicam conturbaret.)

Whatever Cicero's real opinion as to the complicity of Caesar and Crassus in Catiline's designs, he took care to conceal it. Caesar, when accused by Vettius, appealed to him for confirmation of his statement that he had voluntarily informed him of some particulars of the conspiracy (Suetonius, "Julius Caesar," 14), and apparently the confirmation was given. According to Plutarch, the orator, in his περὶ ὑπατείας, acknowledged a similar service on the part of Crassus, but nevertheless Crassus suspected his conduct. Plutarch also informs us that in a speech published after the deaths of Caesar and Crassus Cicero openly accused them both of complicity in the plot, but he does not name the speech, and there is no such passage in any extant oration. In a letter to Atticus, written in B.C. 49 (Ad Att. x. 8. 8), Cicero says that he must not give way to those against whom the Senate gave him powers to preserve the state from harm, and Mr. Tyrrell refers this to the decree passed October 21st, B.C. 63, and finds in it a distinct assertion of Caesar's guilt. Mr. Watson, however, and I think rightly, makes the passage allude to the extraordinary powers conferred on all who held the imperium, of whom Cicero was one, on January 1st, B.C. 49. There is also a sentence quoted by Suetonius from a letter of Cicero to Axius, in which he speaks of Caesar's "attaining in his consulship the kingly power at which he had aimed when aedile," but this may well refer not to any complicity in the first plot, but to the efforts Caesar made to gain popularity by the extravagance of his entertainments.

At the same conjuncture Quintus Catulus and Gaius Piso failed, either by bribery or influence, to induce Cicero to have Gaius Caesar dishonestly accused by means of the Allobroges or some other informer. (Sed eisdem temporibus Q. Catulus et G. Piso neque pretio neque gratia Ciceronem impellere quievere uti per Allobroges aut alium indicem G. Caesar falso nominaretur.)

It is rather characteristic of Professor Beesly's

method of dealing with the history of the conspiracy that he quotes this sentence without giving his readers any warning of Sallust's Caesarian sympathies. Catulus and Piso would doubtless have been glad to have had Caesar accused, if there had been any chance of a conviction, which, to all appearance, there was not ; but even if they had made any dishonourable proposals to Cicero, Sallust could by no possibility have known of them. I cannot but think that this is another instance of our author assuming the functions of the historical novelist, just as he does elsewhere in his account of the motives of Catiline for entering on the conspiracy. The following is a translation (Thomson's) of the chapter in Suetonius which narrates the fate of two subsequent accusers of Caesar :—

" Caesar now fell into a fresh danger, being named among the accomplices of Catiline, both before Novius the quaestor by the informer Lucius Vettius, and in the Senate by Quintus Curius, to whom a reward had been voted for having been the first to disclose the designs of the conspirators. Curius affirmed that he had received his information from Catiline ; Vettius even engaged to produce against him a document which he had given to the latter in his own handwriting. Thinking this to be past bearing, Caesar, with an appeal to Cicero for confirmation, declared that he had voluntarily disclosed some particulars of the conspiracy, prevented Curius from receiving his expected reward, and obliged Vettius to give pledges for his behaviour. He also caused the goods of the latter to be distrained, and, after seeing him roughly

used, and almost torn to pieces in an assembly of the
people at the Rostra, threw him into prison.   Thither,
too, he sent Novius the quaestor for having presumed
to take an information against a magistrate of higher
authority."   (Suetonius, " Julius Caesar," 17.)

Both these nobles were at bitter enmity with Caesar
(uterque cum illo gravis inimicitias exercebant).

Quintus Lutatius Catulus was the leader of the
aristocratic party at Rome.   As consul B.C. 78, he opposed his colleague Lepidus in his attempt to subvert
the Sullan constitution, and as censor in B.C. 65 he
prevented Marcus Crassus from making Egypt tributary to Rome.   In the debate in the Senate on the
punishment of the conspirators Catulus threw his
influence on the side of those who voted for the
penalty of death, and he was the first to hail Cicero
by the title of "parens patriae."   His enmity with
Caesar was a long-standing one, as in B.C. 65 he had
accused him in the Senate for his restoration of the
statues of Marius.   His defeat by Caesar in the election for the Pontificate took place on March 6th, B.C.
63, and the first proposition which the latter brought
forward in his praetorship the following year was one
to deprive him of the honour of completing the
restoration of the Capitol.   Catulus, however, succeeded in repelling this attack, and died in B.C. 60,
before Caesar had acquired further power of annoyance.

Gaius Calpurnius Piso, Caesar's other enemy, was
of the same political party as Catulus, and, as consul
in B.C. 67, had joined the latter in his endeavour

CHAP.
XLIX.

to defeat the Gabinian law. During the two following years he acted as governor of Gallia Narbonensis, and on his return was defended by Cicero in B.C. 63, when accused of extortion and of the unjust execution of a Transpadane Gaul. This latter charge was promoted by Caesar, who had taken the Transpadanes under his protection. According to Suetonius, he had recently visited them for the sake of extending his influence, though we can hardly follow the historian in believing that his intrigues were so dangerous as to necessitate the detention of a force intended for Cilicia to restrain them. Caesar subsequently founded a colony at Comum, for which he procured the Latin citizenship, and the conduct of G. Marcellus, consul for B.C. 50, in scourging one of its magistrates, was regarded as an insult to him personally. The full citizenship was subsequently conferred upon the Transpadanes by their patron by one of the laws which he passed during his first dictatorship of eleven days in B.C. 49. Of Piso after his trial, nothing further is known ; he must have died before the beginning of the civil war.

So successful, indeed, were they that some Roman knights who were on guard, under arms, round the temple of Concord, on Caesar's leaving the Senate, threatened him with their swords. (Usque eo ut nonnulli equites Romani qui praesidi caussa cum telis erant circum aedem Concordiae, egredienti ex Senatu Caesari gladio minitarentur.)

According to Suetonius, Caesar persisted in his opposition after the speech of Cato, and the knights threatened him while still in the house. Plutarch, however, gives the same account of the incident as Sallust, and adds that Caesar was only protected by the devotion of Curio, who sheltered him with his toga, and that the knights, when minded to kill him, looked to Cicero for a nod of consent, which the latter was afterwards blamed for withholding. Plutarch also contradicts the improbable statement of Suetonius that Caesar was so frightened by the attack of the knights that "he not only gave up his opposition, but absented himself from the House for the remainder of the year." He informs us, on the contrary, that "a few days afterwards Caesar entered the Senate and endeavoured to clear himself of the suspicions under which he lay. His defence, however, was received with indignation and reproaches ; and, as the sitting was unusually prolonged, the people beset the House, and with violent outcries demanded Caesar, absolutely insisting on his being dismissed." (Plut. " Julius Caesar," Langhorne's translation.)

While the Senate was engaged with this business . . . the freedmen of Lentulus went different ways about the city, trying to rouse the artizans and slaves in the streets to rescue him. (Dum hacc in Senatu aguntur . . . . liberti Lentuli divorsis itineribus opifices atque servitia in vicis ad eum eripiundum sollicitabant.)

The business here referred to was transacted on December 4th, and Cicero on the following day, in his speech to the Senate, referred to the attempt of Lentulus' freedmen with great contempt. Appian, however, (ii. 5,) represents the dependants of the

CHAP.
L. accused as raising a riot while Cicero was delivering this very speech, so great as to cause him to leave the temple in order to quell it. On his return, according to Appian, he pressed his resolution more vigorously, a phrase which is unfortunate for those who fix on the exact place in the speech where the interruption took place, and make its occurrence account for the resigned tone of the conclusion. Cicero either himself thought sufficiently seriously of the power of the rioters, or was anxious enough to make others do so, to take elaborate precautions against them. Besides posting the guard of knights round the temple of Concord, and watches at other points in the city, he required all the citizens on the morning of December 5th, to take an oath before the praetor, and give in their names for service if need should arise. It is important to note this, because the large means at the disposal of the Government, and the loyalty shown by all the respectable classes, tend to weaken the argument that the execution of the prisoners was justified by the urgent necessity for their removal beyond the reach of rescue.

CHAP.
L. *On the present occasion Decimus Junius Silanus, who, as consul elect, was the first called upon to give his opinion . . . . at first, gave his vote for their punishment. (Tum D. Junius Silanus, primis sententiam rogatus, quod eo tempore consul designatus erat . . . . supplicium sumundum decreverat.)*

In a letter to Atticus, written B.C. 45, on the occasion of the publication by Marcus Brutus of a treatise in honour of Cato, Cicero gives the following list of men of consular rank who spoke in favour of the severer penalty on this occasion—Catulus, Servilius, the Luculli, Curio, Torquatus, Lepidus, Gellius, Volcatius, Figulus, Cotta, Lucius Caesar, Gaius Piso, Manlius Glabrio, and Silanus and Murena, the consuls elect. Consuls elect were not, strictly speaking, consulars, and this alone would account for the position of the names of Silanus and Murena, even if we could suppose that Cicero after the lapse of so many years, was trying to give the speakers in the order in which they spoke. There is thus no need to see here, as some have done, a contradiction between our two authorities.

As regards the subsequent change of opinion on the part of Silanus, Sallust's narrative conveys the impression that Tiberius Nero brought forward a distinct motion, and that Silanus thereupon abandoned his own in its favour. Suetonius, however, tells us that "Silanus thought proper to qualify his decision (because it was not very honourable to change it), by a softening interpretation, as if his opinion had been understood in a harsher sense than he had intended." It is noticeable that in Silanus' motion, the words "*More majorum*," do not occur, and that thus it would easily lend itself to be explained away; and the theory that he did not withdraw, but emasculated his motion, also furnishes a reason why Cato proposed a fresh resolution about which there could be no mistake, instead of simply declaring his support of that previously moved. The proposal credited to Tiberius Nero, it may be remarked, and not that of Caesar himself, was the legitimate outcome of the latter's speech. If the conspirators could be suffered to live without detriment to the state,

CHAP.
L.
there was no justification whatever for asking the Senate to violate the law by sentencing them to perpetual imprisonment, when the delay of a few months, at most, would enable them to be legally tried. This, however, is what Caesar actually proposed to do.

CHAP.
LI.
Now it was at this period of imitation that they adopted the [Greek] custom of scourging citizens and inflicting capital punishment on convicted criminals. (Sed eodem illo tempore, [Graeciae morem imitati], verberibus animadvortebant in civis, de condemnatis summum supplicium sumebant.)

Punishment by scourging was a genuine Roman custom, and Caesar is certainly wrong in attributing it to a Greek source. If we accept Dietsch's proposal to expunge the words " Graeciae morem imitati," we must suppose Caesar to mean that the Romans were slower in abolishing capital punishment than in adopting other reforms, and that they were finally convinced of the evil at the time of the Porcian law.

CHAP.
LI.
Was it because it is forbidden by the Porcian law? If so, there are other laws which forbid condemned citizens to be deprived of life, and offer the alternative of exile. (An, quia lex Porcia vetat? At aliae leges item condemnatis civibus non animam eripi, sed exilium permitti jubent.)

The Porcian law, enacted B.C. 97, deprived the magistrates of the power of inflicting the punishment by death or scourging upon any Roman citizen, and a subsequent law of Gaius Gracchus forbade the appointment by the Senate of extraordinary commissions

of high treason, such as that which, under Publius Popil-
lius, had inflicted such bloody sentences on his brother's
adherents.   In the present year, the trial of Rabirius,
who was accused of having committed murder while
suppressing the insurrection of Saturninus under the
Senate's order, had practically decided in the negative
the question whether that body could invest the
consuls with absolute power of life and death.   The
circumstances of the two cases were, indeed, very
similar.   If Saturninus had been killed while fighting
in the streets, his slayer would have been able to claim
the protection of the Senate's decree ; his death, how-
ever, took place after all resistance had ceased, and
after he himself had personally surrendered to Marius.
The emergency, it was contended, had thus ceased, and
the ordinary law had resumed its reign.   In the same
way in the present case, if the conspirators had met their
death while trying to fire the city, the slayers would
doubtless have been held guiltless ; but after they had
been apprehended and securely lodged, there was no
need, it may be said, for any but the ordinary provisions
of the law to be enforced.   If Cicero, indeed, had been
a courageous man, he might have contended that the
existence of Catiline at the head of an armed force in
Etruria, and of the bands of Lentulus within the city,
constituted a continued danger to the state, and thus
distinguished the case altogether from that of Rabirius
and Saturninus.   Had he put the conspirators to death
on his own authority, his unpopularity might have
come all the same, but he would at least have had
something to plead in his favour.   As it was, by putting
to the Senate, and executing an illegal vote, he incurred

CHAP.
LI.

the very responsibility which he was anxious to shun.
The solitary plea which he could allege in his defence,
that the conspirators as accomplices of Catiline and
Manlius who had been declared 'hostes' by the
Senate, were 'hostes' themselves, and not citizens at
all, is a paltry quibble which could not even be sus-
tained in law, as neither the Senate, nor apparently
the people itself, had the power of disfranchising a
Roman citizen.

CHAP.
LI.

*My proposal is that their goods be confiscated and their
persons imprisoned in such borough towns as are best able
to support the charge.* (*Sed ita censeo, publicandas
eorum pecunias, ipsos in vinculis habendos per municipia
quae maxume opibus valent.*)

According to Cicero, Caesar's resolution made the
towns responsible in heavy fines for the safe keeping
of the prisoners, and this the consul regarded as a distinct hardship. Some historians have interpreted
Caesar's proposal as though it were similar in effect
to that of Nero, and would have allowed the prisoners
ultimately to be brought to trial. The latter half of
the resolution, however, leaves no room for doubt that
Caesar, sincerely or insincerely, proposed to the Senate
to inflict life-long imprisonment on these men who
had never been properly tried; a punishment which
would have been to the full as illegal as that which
was actually carried out, while it was impossible to
plead the necessity of the time as an excuse for such
illegality long after the crisis was past. Caesar's proposal for confiscating the conspirators' goods was at
first accepted, but afterwards allowed to drop on his

representing that it would be unfair to adopt the
severe, while they rejected the merciful part of his
resolution.

*On the close of Caesar's speech, all the senators merely
gave their votes for the different motions, some for one,
some for another, until it came to Marcus Porcius Cato.
He, when asked his opinion, delivered himself as follows.
(Postquam Caesar dicendi finem fecit, ceteri verbo alius
alii varie assentiebantur: at M. Porcius Cato, rogatus
sententiam, hujuscemodi orationem habuit.)*

It is remarkable that Sallust in his account of this
debate omits all mention of the speech which Cicero,
whether we possess it in the fourth oration against
Catiline or not, certainly delivered on this occasion.
In that speech Cicero alludes only to the motions of
Silanus and Caesar, and it is therefore probable that
he spoke not only before Cato, but before Tiberius
Nero also. His speech is described by Plutarch as
adding no small weight to the proposition of Caesar,
but, as we have it, it rather shows a desire for the conspirators' death, which the speaker was too timid to
distinctly urge. Cicero, however, (ad Att. xii. 21)
claims the credit of not only putting the motion for
capital punishment to the vote, but for having himself
supported it. The resolution, he says, was only passed
in the terms which Cato proposed, because the speech
of the latter was marked by more vigour than those
of the previous speakers. It should be noticed, too,
that Plutarch makes Catulus and not Cato the first
senator to have spoken in favour of the punishment
of death after Caesar's speech. This statement, how-

ever, he contradicts in his life of Cato, and it seems
unlikely that a man of Catulus' weight should have
postponed the expression of his opinion for so long.
The fact that Cicero in his letters to Atticus places
Catulus first among the men of consular rank who
voted for the extreme penalty, does not help us to
decide at what period of the debate he actually spoke,
for, as above remarked, we have no reason to suppose
that Cicero adhered to any particular order in his list
of names.   Anyhow, the impression conveyed by the
text that all the senators from Caesar to Cato simply
gave their vote without making any formal address, is
certainly a wrong one.

As regards the speech which Sallust puts into the
mouth of Cato, Mr. Long accepts it as giving the sub-
stance of what Cato really said.   Plutarch, however,
writes as if he had Cato's speech, which was taken
down at the time by shorthand writers, actually before
him ; and his version agrees much better with the
account given by Suetonius and with what we know of
Cato's character, than does that of Sallust.   According
to Plutarch, Cato, after reproaching Silanus for his
timidity, made a straightforward attack on Caesar for
trying to subvert the government in the name of
humanity, and broadly hinted his belief in his complicity in the plot.   Of this attack there is no trace in
the speech as recorded by Sallust, and it is not difficult .
to suppose that the vanity which made Roman historians firmly believe that they could improve on any
speech actually delivered, was in this case reinforced
by the Caesarian sympathies of our author.

He himself took up his station by his eagle, one, it was said, which Gaius Marius used in his. army in the Cimbrian War.   (Ipse propter aquilam assistit, quam bello Cimbrico C. Marius in exercitu habuisse dicebatur.)

Gaius Marius was the first to introduce the eagle into the Roman army.   The possession by Catiline of this particular standard seems to have been well known in Rome before his departure.   Cicero alludes to it more than once in his speeches; he charges Catiline with erecting a kind of altar to it in his house, and mentions his taking it with him at the time of his quitting the city.

CHAP LIX.

THE JUGURTHINE WAR.

H

INTRODUCTION
TO THE JUGURTHINE WAR.

SALLUST has himself informed us of the reasons which induced him to write the history of a period so painful in many respects to a patriotic Roman as that of the war with Jugurtha. It attracted him, he tells us, in the first place, "as a great and severe contest waged with varying success;" and, in the second, as "the occasion of resistance being for the first time made to the pride of the nobility," which resistance he regards as the prelude to all the civil wars which afterwards exhausted Italy and the whole Roman world. The interest of his narration is, therefore, twofold, both military and political, and his success in bringing it home to his readers is by no means equal in the different parts of his work. In its military aspect the war with Jugurtha is really of little importance. Some hundred and twenty or thirty years later, in the reign of Tiberius, another Numidian arose, who gave the Romans almost as much trouble as Jugurtha. Tacfarinas, like Jugurtha, had become acquainted with the Roman discipline; like him, he was always (with one trifling exception) defeated in pitched battles; like him, by surprises and petty skirmishes he wore out the enemy whom he could not meet with success in the field. Two Roman generals triumphed for bringing the war to a supposed conclusion, but each time, after an interval, Tacfarinas renewed it with as much and as little success as before; and, as in the case of Jugurtha, it was only brought to a final end by his death, after the contest had been carried on for seven years (A.D. 17-24). Tacitus gives us the history of this war in some seven chapters (Annals ii. 52 ; iii. 21, 73, 74 ; iv. 23-25), and it may fairly be said that the knowledge we receive from these is quite as satisfactory as that which Sallust's prolix narration affords us of the conflict with Jugurtha. The materials, indeed, for writing a good military history of any war in Africa did not exist, and we, therefore, cannot blame Sallust for his failure. If he had had an accurate map of Numidia to refer to as he wrote, and the accounts of eye-witnesses to supply him with details of the several campaigns, there is no reason to doubt that he would have produced an excellent and thoroughly intelligible history of the war. The vivid description which he gives of the battle of the Muthul, where he had the account of one of the Roman officers, Publius Rutilius Rufus, to guide him, is a sufficient proof of his ability to deal with good materials when he possessed them. As it is, in the absence of all information as to the geography of the country, and with a chronology which seldom ex- tends beyond such references as " after a few days," or " in the course of the same campaign," it is impossible to extract from the account of Sallust any clear idea of the details of the war. We have, indeed, certain sieges and battles assigned to the several campaigns, but the links connecting them are mostly wanting, and their place is inadequately supplied by repeated assertions that each new tactic of Metellus or Marius reduced Jugurtha to frenzy and despair, and then, after a while, had to be abandoned by the Roman general as ineffectual. Even in the case of the operations which he describes at length, it is often impossible to help feeling that the historian is drawing largely on his imagination, or, which comes to the same thing, is filling in some bare outline of fact, which he found in his authorities, from the commonplace book of Roman military description.

If we turn now to the chapters in which he deals with the politics of the capital, we shall find much more reason to be grateful to Sallust for his history of this period. It is true that his love of fine writing and his pompous affectation of a virtue which he did not possess, seriously detract from the value of his work ; the recurrence, too, of .tags like " pauci quis omnia, honesta atque inhonesta, vendere mos erat," gives an annoying impression of pedantry and unreality to much that he says. Despite these drawbacks, however, Sallust often speaks of the relation of parties in Rome with all the weight of a practical and clear-headed politician, and, for one who lived in the thick of the very struggle of which he narrates the beginning, is singularly broad and comprehensive in his views. The period with which he deals is full of instruction. Gaius Gracchus had been murdered in B.C. 121, and from that time down to the end of the Jugurthine war Senate and democrats alike did nothing but demonstrate at once their power and their impotence. The

Senate could recall Popilius, uphold Opimius, at least for a time, and prevent any further divisions of the domain land by converting as much of it as still remained in private hands at first into perpetual leaseholds, and afterwards into full freeholds. As was shown, however, by the prosecutions of B.C. 110, and again in B.C. 105, and by the election of Marius to the consulship, it became utterly powerless as soon as the mob asserted its will. It could not even defend its successful general, Metellus, from a most unjust attack, or prevent the whole credit of terminating the war, which was really due to Metellus and Sulla, falling to the democratic leader, Marius. It is significant, indeed, that at this crisis of their fate the aristocracy of Rome could find no better commander than M. Aemilius Scaurus, a man who, except by some village triumphs in the Alps, had never in his life distinguished himself, whose morality was no higher than that of his fellows, and who, when the storm came, was quite ready to surrender his party so long as he could save himself. On the other hand, the democrats were not much better ; they could assert their power by persecuting the nobility on the occasion of any disaster to the state, but they were destitute of any worthy policy which they could unite to pursue. Their narrowness of view and anarchist tendencies alienated from them the two allies by whose help they might have obtained a peaceful triumph over the Senate. The Italians they had made their enemies by threatening to encroach on the domain lands held by the allied towns, and by the disfavour with which they regarded any proposals for a liberal concession of the full Roman franchise. As for the equites or capitalists, the disturbances in the streets of Rome had sufficed to estrange them from the party by whose help they had secured the control of the law courts. These two great powers were content to stand aside and allow the nobles and democrats to decide their battles by themselves, and, as a result, the nobles were enabled to maintain their monopoly of all the chief offices and prizes of the state, while the mob continued supreme in the streets of Rome. Such a condition of affairs could not continue for ever, and the Jugurthine war ushered in the military regime by which it was to be superseded. Not only was it in this war that both Sulla and Marius made their name, but the change was effected by which the future generals in the civil war were provided with armies suitable to their purposes. Hitherto, levies had always been made from the respectable class of citizens, men who had some interest in the welfare of the state, and who looked on war as an evil to be brought to an end as soon as possible. Marius, when starting for Numidia, recruited his army from among the "capite censi," who had no stake in the country, but now adopted arms as their profession, and looked to their general for reward. Armies composed of men like these murdered their commanders if they had become unpopular; if popular, they would follow them to death, but, henceforth, obedience was neither rendered nor refused out of any consideration of duty towards the state. This was the kind of force of which a Caesar could make use.

THE JUGURTHINE WAR.

CHAP. I. IT is the unfounded complaint of mankind that they are naturally weak and short-lived, and that it is chance, not merit, that rules their destiny. So far is this from the truth, that consideration will show that nothing surpasses or excels our nature, and that it is rather energy that is lacking to it than power or length of days. It is mind that is the guide and commander of life in mortal men. Where this advances to glory along the path of virtue, its powers, resources, and renown are ample without the help of fortune; for uprightness, activity, and other good qualities, fortune can neither give nor take away. Where, on the other hand, it has become the slave of low passions and has succumbed to sloth and bodily pleasures, a short submission to the fatal influence of lust suffices to fritter away strength, opportunities, and intellect, in idleness, and then the weakness of our nature receives the blame, and the doers charge circumstances with the defect that lies in themselves. Were men but as anxious in an honourable cause as they are zealous in the pursuit of matters of no concern or profit, and often even attended with danger [and ill effects], they would be as much the masters as the slaves of destiny, and would attain to such a pitch of

greatness as would make them, as far as mortal men
may be, undying in their glory. | Men are made up of
body and soul ; hence all their fortunes and passions
follow in some cases the character of their body, in
others that of their mind.   Beauty of person and
greatness of wealth, with bodily strength, and all other
blessings of this kind, are soon spent, but the noble
achievements of genius are as eternal as the soul itself.
Moreover, in the case of blessings of body or of fortune,
as is the beginning so is the end.   They no sooner are
risen than they begin to fall, and decay from the
moment of their prime.   The mind is pure and eternal ; itself ungoverned, as the guide of man, it moves
and governs all things.   Hence we may be the more
astonished at the degradation of those who surrender
themselves to bodily pleasures, and spend their life in
luxury and sloth, while they allow the intellect, the
best and noblest factor in man's nature, to become
inert from indolence and neglect ; and this, too, when
the qualities of mind by which the highest renown
may be won, are so many and diverse.

Of these pursuits, however, magistracies and military commands, or in fact any share in the public administration, seem to me at the present time far from
desirable, since the honours of office are refused to
merit, while those who attain them either by knavery
or force gain nothing in security nor yet in distinction.
To govern country or parents by force, even where
such rule is possible, and is used for the correction of
crime, is yet a grievous matter, especially when every
revolution is the sure forerunner of massacres, banish-
ments, and the other horrors of war.   On the other

CHAP.
III.

hand, to labour without result, and seek no other reward for toil than unpopularity, is the height of madness, except, perhaps, for those who are mastered by a disgraceful and fatal impulse to sacrifice their own honour and freedom to the power of a clique.

CHAP.
IV.

Among the tasks that occupy the intellect, historical narration holds a prominent and useful place. As its merits have been often extolled, I think it best to leave them unmentioned, and thus escape any imputation of arrogantly exalting myself by praise of my own pursuit. And yet I have no doubt that there will be some who, because I have determined to pass my life at a distance from public affairs, will apply the name of indolence to my long and useful task. At any rate, the men to whom it seems the height of energy to court the mob, and buy favour by their public entertainments, will do so. These I would ask to remember the character of the men who were unsuccessful as candidates at the times when I obtained my several offices, and the class who subsequently gained admittance to the Senate; if they do this they will certainly consider that my change of determination was dictated by sound reason rather than by sloth, and that more profit is likely to accrue to the state from my leisure than from the activity of others. I have often heard that Quintus Maximus, Publius Scipio, and, besides these, other illustrious citizens of our state, were wont to remark that as they gazed upon the effigies of their ancestors their spirits were strongly stirred to the practice of virtue. It was not the wax or outward form, they said, that possessed this power, but the memory of gallant deeds that kindled a fire in the breasts of brave men that cannot be quenched until their own merit has rivalled their ancestors' fame and renown. As matters now are, is there a single man who does not prefer to vie with his ancestors in wealth and expenditure rather than in probity and energy? Even the men of no family, who formerly when they won a victory over the nobility, won it by superior merit, now struggle into honours and commands by intrigue and violence, rather than by any honourable qualities, and seem to think that the prætorship, consulship, and other high offices, possess an intrinsic renown and splendour, instead of being only esteemed according to the merits of their occupants. I have wandered, however, too far afield in my sorrow and shame at my country's degradation; I now return to my task.

I am about to write a history of the war which the Roman people carried on with Jugurtha, king of the Numidians, in the first place because it was a great and severe contest, waged with varying success; and in the second, because resistance was then for the first time made to the pride of the nobility, and this struggle threw all things, both human and divine, into confusion, and reached such a pitch of fury that amid the passions of her citizens war and devastation made an end of Italy. But, before I set forth how these things began, I will touch on a few points of earlier history, that my whole narrative may be clearer and more open to the view.

In the second Punic war, in which the Carthaginian general Hannibal had inflicted the severest blow that the resources of Italy had received since the Roman power became supreme, Massinissa, king of the Numidians, was admitted to our friendship by Publius Scipio, whose merits subsequently gained him the title "Africanus." He achieved many brilliant military successes, and after the conquest of the Carthaginians, and the capture of Sufax, whose rule was powerful in Africa, and of wide extent, was rewarded by the Roman people with a gift of all the cities and lands which they had conquered. Thus favoured, Massinissa ever remained our loyal and honourable friend, and at last his authority and his life came to a common conclusion.

After Massinissa's death, his son Micipsa, whose brothers, Mastanabal and Gulussa, had been removed by disease, succeeded to the throne. He had two sons of his own, Adherbal and Hiempsal, and also reared in the palace, on equal terms with his own children, Jugurtha, his brother Mastanabal's natural son, who, on account of his birth, had been left by Massinissa in a private position.

Powerful in frame, and of handsome appearance, but especially remarkable for mental ability, Jugurtha, on arriving at manhood, did not abandon himself to the seductions of luxury and sloth, but took part in the national pursuits of riding and marksmanship, vied with his fellows in the race, and, while surpassing all in glory, at the same time won every heart. He passed much of his time in hunting, and was the first, or among the first, to wound the lion and other prey; yet, while thus prominent in action, he was the last to talk about himself. Jugurtha's behaviour at first delighted Micipsa, who thought that his merit would

add lustre to his own rule.   When, however, he marked
his nephew in the prime of life ever rising in importance, while his own existence was now near its close,
and his children were still young, he was greatly
disquieted, and turned over in his mind many reme-
dies.   He was terrified as he thought of man's innate
lust for power and rashness in indulging his heart's
desire, and reflected, besides, how his own and his
children's age offered the favourable chance which
leads even unambitious men astray in the hope of
gain.   He saw, too, that the affection of the Numidians was kindled towards Jugurtha, and he was
distracted by the fear that to make away with a man
of such distinction might occasion riots or even war.
Beset by these difficulties, he saw that a man who
had so won the favour of his countrymen could not be
crushed either by violence or craft, and since Jugurtha was ready of hand and eager for military renown,
he determined to expose him to danger, and in this
way to see if fortune would help him.

In pursuance of this plan, Micipsa, on sending to
Spain a contingent of Numidian foot and horse to the
help of the Roman people in the Numantine war,
placed Jugurtha in command of this force, in the hope
he would meet his death, either in some display of his
own courage or by the fierceness of the enemy.   The
issue, however, of his plans was very different to what
he had expected.   Jugurtha, such was the energy and
activity of his nature, had no sooner acquainted himself with the character of Publius Scipio, who was
at that time in command of the Roman troops, and
with the quality of the enemy, than, by dint of exer-

tion and forethought, by the most unassuming obedience, and by the frequency with which he exposed himself to risk, he had quickly won such distinction as to be the darling of our soldiers and the greatest terror of the Numantines. He achieved, indeed, that most difficult task of uniting vigour in battle with a sound discretion, though the one in its foresight so often breeds terror, and the other in its boldness too rash a hardihood. The general was thus led to employ Jugurtha in nearly every task of difficulty; he ranked him among his friends, and daily became more attached to him as a man whose advice and enterprise were ever attended with success. Jugurtha had also a generous temper, and a tact by which he at once united many of the Romans to himself on terms of intimacy.

Just at this time there were in our army many men, some of illustrious, some of undistinguished descent, with whom riches weighed more than virtue and honour. By their intrigues at Rome, and their influence over the allies, they had attained prominence rather than distinction, and now began to incite the aspiring spirit of Jugurtha by promises that, on the death of King Micipsa, he should have sole possession of the kingdom of Numidia. His own merit, they told him, was of the highest order, and at Rome there was nothing that could not be bought. At last Numantia was destroyed, and Publius Scipio determined to dismiss the contingents of the allies and return home. After awarding the most distinguished presents and praises to Jugurtha in a public assembly, he took him apart to his own quarters, and there privately advised him to seek the friendship of the Roman people rather publicly than through individuals, and to avoid the habit of bribing anybody. It was a dangerous matter, he said, to buy from the few the favour which rested with the many. If he would be content to persevere in the exercise of his talents, glory and dominion would come to him of themselves : should he hasten too eagerly to power, his own money would ensure his ruin. After this speech Scipio dismissed him with a letter for Micipsa. Its purport was as follows :—" In the Numantine war the merits of Jugurtha have been pre-eminent; at this I am sure you will rejoice. To me his services have so endeared him that I shall use every effort to recommend him as strongly to the Roman Senate and people. Receive my congratulations, as our friendship demands. In Jugurtha you have a kinsman worthy alike of yourself and of his grandfather Massinissa." The king, on finding the reports he had heard thus confirmed by the general's letter, was impressed both by the merits of Jugurtha and the favour which he had won. He now changed his purpose, and endeavoured to win him by active kindness, adopted him at once, and in his will appointed him his heir on an equal footing with his own sons.

A few years passed, and then, worn out by illness and old age, Micipsa perceived that his end was at hand. In the presence of his friends and kinsmen, as well as of his sons Adherbal and Hiempsal, he is said to have addressed Jugurtha somewhat as follows :—

" As a child, Jugurtha, you lost your father and were left without hopes or fortune. I received you into the royal family under the belief that my kindness would make me as dear to you as though you had been my son, and the result has not disappointed me. To pass over your other great and noble exploits, quite lately on your return from Numantia, the glory you had won shed fresh lustre on myself and my kingdom, and your merits drew our ties of friendship with Rome still nearer. You have renewed the fame of our line in Spain; and, lastly, have achieved the hardest of tasks— you have conquered envy by your renown. Nature is bringing my life to an end, and now, by this right hand, by the honour of a king, I warn and adjure you to hold dear these boys who are your kinsmen by descent, your brothers by my favour. Do not choose the novel friendship of strangers instead of maintaining the established alliance of blood. The bulwarks of empire are not armies or treasures, but friends, and friendship can neither be compelled by force nor won by money, but only by service and loyalty. And has friendship a closer tie than that of brother to brother; can you hope to find loyalty in a stranger if you turn traitor to your kin? My part is done in assigning my kingdom to you and them. If you act uprightly it will be strong, if treacherous, you will find it weak. By harmony, fortunes grow from small to great; by discord the greatest melt to nothing. It becomes you, Jugurtha, rather than these boys, as their superior in years and wisdom, to guard against any ill result; for in every contest the stronger, even when attacked, is made by his greater power to seem the aggressor. For you, Adherbal and Hiempsal, I bid you respect and esteem the great qualities of Jugurtha. Make his virtues your model. and strive that I may not seem

more fortunate in the son of my adoption than in
those I have begotten."

Jugurtha was aware of the hollowness of the
king's words, and the views that occupied his own
thoughts were very different.   He made, however, a
kind reply as the occasion demanded.   A few days
afterwards Micipsa died.

After burying him with all the splendour of a
royal funeral, the princes met together for a discussion among themselves of matters in general.
Hiempsal, the youngest, was of a headstrong disposition, and had long looked down on Jugurtha
for his low descent on his mother's side.   On this
occasion he took his seat on the right of Adherbal to
prevent Jugurtha holding the middle place, which the
Numidians consider the seat of honour.   His brother
importuned him to give way to superior age, and at
last, though with great reluctance, he crossed over to
the other side.   A discussion ensued on many points
of administration, and Jugurtha, among other proposals,
suggested that it would be well to cancel all the edicts
and decrees of the previous five years, on the ground
that during that period Micipsa had been so weakened
by age as to have little mental power.   On this
Hiempsal replied that he was of the same opinion
himself, for it was only within the last three years that
Jugurtha, by his adoption, had been admitted to
authority.   This remark sank deeper into Jugurtha's
breast than anyone thought at the time.   Thenceforth,
distracted by anger and fear, he intrigued, planned,
and indeed devoted his whole attention to plots for
treacherously seizing Hiempsal.   These schemes pro-

gressed but slowly; this, however, did nothing to soften his savage spirit, and he determined to carry out his design by any means that offered.

At that first meeting between the princes which I have mentioned, they had determined, as a safeguard against disputes, to divide the treasures and to settle the limits of their several dominions. A date was fixed for each of these measures, but the division of·the money was to be made first. Meanwhile the princes retired to different places in the neighbourhood of the treasury, and it so happened that Hiempsal, who was in the town of Thermida, occupied the house of a man who had acted as Jugurtha's nearest attendant, and had always been esteemed and favoured by him. Finding this instrument offered him by chance, Jugurtha loaded him with promises, and induced him on pretence of visiting his own property to go to his house and procure copies of the keys to the gates, as the true ones were always delivered to Hiempsal; for the rest, he said, that on a fitting opportunity he would come in person with a strong body of followers. The Numidian soon executed his orders, and, according to his instructions, admitted Jugurtha's soldiers by night. They burst into the house and searched for the king in every direction, killing some of his attendants as they slept and others as they ran out to meet them, ransacking every recess, breaking bars and bolts, and with their noise and tumult causing a general confusion. In the midst of this, Hiempsal was found hiding in the hut of a female slave, whither at the outset he had fled in his fright and ignorance of the place. The

Numidians, according to their orders, conveyed his head to Jugurtha.

The news of so great an outrage was quickly spread throughout Africa, and fear came upon Adherbal and upon all who had lived under the rule of Micipsa. The Numidians separated into two parties, the larger of which followed Adherbal, while the more warlike joined his rival. Jugurtha armed as large forces as he could, won over the cities to his government, in some cases by force, in others with their own consent, and prepared to assert his rule over all Numidia. Meantime Adherbal had despatched an embassy to Rome to inform the Senate of his brother's murder and his own position, but, trusting in the numbers of his troops, was also preparing for open war. He was soon defeated in a pitched battle, and fled from the field into the Roman province, and subsequently to Rome itself. Jugurtha had attained his end ; and now that he had gained possession of all Numidia, had leisure to reflect on the nature of his conduct. He feared the Roman people, and had no other hope of defence against their anger than was afforded by the cupidity of the nobles and his own wealth. In the course, therefore, of a few days, he despatched ambassadors to Rome with a large sum in silver and gold, and instructions that after loading his early friends with presents they should proceed to gain him new ones, and, in fine, should be zealous in enlisting every ally whom money could procure. The ambassadors reached Rome, and, in accordance with their instructions, sent large presents to the king's old friends, and to others whose influence was at that time powerful in the Senate, and

CHAP. XIII.

thus produced such a change of feeling as raised Jugurtha from the greatest unpopularity into the favour and good-will of the nobility. Some of these incited by the hope, others by the actual receipt of a payment, strove by canvassing individual senators to prevent any really serious steps being taken against him. As soon, therefore, as the ambassadors felt sufficiently assured, a day was fixed, and the Senate gave a hearing to both parties. I have been informed that on this occasion Adherbal spoke to the following effect :—

CHAP. XIV.

"Senators, my father Micipsa charged me on his deathbed to account only the administration of the kingdom of Numidia as my own, the real authority and supremacy as belonging to you. At the same time he bade me strive both in peace and war to serve the Roman people to the utmost of my power, and to regard you in the place of relations and kin. If I did this, your friendship, he told me, would serve instead of armies and treasures as the safeguard of my kingdom. I was acting in obedience to my father's commands when Jugurtha, the blackest villain on the face of the earth, in defiance of your government, drove me, the grandson of Massinissa, and, by my very descent, the friend and ally of the Roman people, from my kingdom and all my possessions.

"Senators, since I was fated to reach this depth of distress, I could wish that I was able to claim your help on the strength of personal, not of ancestral services ; if possible, that the Roman people should have owed me, for benefits received, a requital I had no need to ask; or, at least, that if I needed your

services, I might have received them as my due.   But
unaided innocence is poorly secured from danger; the
character of Jugurtha it was not mine to shape; and
so, Senators, I fly to you for refuge, to whom it is the
bitterest part of my fate that I must be a burden
before I can be a help.

"All other kings were admitted to your friendship
after being conquered in war, or sought your alliance
when their own fate was in the balance.   My family
formed its friendship with the Roman people in the
Carthaginian war, when we could hope to find in you
no more than a loyal though luckless ally.   Of these
old confederates I am the descendant, and I bid you
not to allow me, the grandson of Massinissa, to ask
your help in vain.

"Had I no other plea to support my request than
my pitiable fortunes, that I, who but yesterday was a
king, rich in ancestry, in renown, and in resources,
am now overcast with misery and become a needy
suppliant for foreign help, it would yet accord with
the dignity of the Roman people to prevent the wrong
and to refuse to allow any man to increase his kingdom by crime.   But the realm from which I am ousted
is that which the Roman people granted to my ancestors, that from which my father and grandfather
united with you in expelling Sufax and the Carthaginians.   It is the gift of the Senate of which I have
been robbed; it is you who are contemned in the
wrong I suffer.

"Miserable man that I am!   Has your kindness,
Micipsa my father, resulted in this, that the man
whom you made the equal of your children, and

joint heir of your kingdom—that he, of all others, is to be the destroyer of your race? Is our family never to be in peace? Must our lot be always one of blood, of battle, and of flight? While the power of Carthage was unbroken, we suffered every cruelty as our natural due. The enemy was close at hand; you, our allies, were far away; our only hope lay in our swords. That plague-spot was rooted out of Africa, and we were enjoying the delights of peace, as men who had no enemies, except those whom you might haply bid us regard as such, when, of a sudden, Jugurtha came upon us, overweening and reckless. In a burst of insolence and crime he murdered my brother, his own cousin, and then began by seizing the kingdom as the reward of his guilt. When he found that the same device failed to put me in his power, he drove me, when prepared for anything rather than violence and war, into exile, as you see, in your dominions, far from country and home. He has heaped want and misery upon me, and has rendered me anywhere safer than in my own kingdom. Senators, I placed my faith in a maxim which I once heard my father deliver, that those who diligently cherished your friendship took to themselves, it was true, many a toil, but enjoyed in return an unequalled safety. That side of the agreement which it lay with our family to perform we have carried out; we have fought by your side in all your wars; it lies with you, Senators, to secure our safety in time of peace.

"My father left behind him two sons, my brother and myself, and thought that his kindness would unite Jugurtha to us as a third. Of my co-heirs, the one has been murdered, and I myself have hardly escaped the wicked hands of the other. What am I to do? Whither in my misfortune were it best for me to fly? Every support of my family has perished. My father has paid the inevitable debt to nature. My brother, who little deserved such a fate, has been foully slain by his cousin. All my family, connected with me by blood or by marriage, have been overwhelmed by some form of destruction. Of those made prisoners by Jugurtha, some have been sent to the cross, others thrown to wild beasts, and the few who are still allowed to breathe are immured in darkness, and, amid sorrow and lamentation, drag out a life more bitter than death.

"Had I still all the supporters whom I have lost, or who have deserted me for the enemy, yet, were any sudden calamity to befall me, I should still invoke the aid of your House, for the greatness of your dominion makes right and wrong throughout the earth your care. But being, as I am, an outcast from my country and my home, alone, and lacking every appurtenance of my rank, whither shall I go, to whom shall I take my prayer? To the races and beings whose enmity my family has earned by its friendship for you? Is there any land I can approach where my ancestors have not left memorials in numbers of their hostility? Is there any that can have compassion upon me, who has been at any time an enemy of Rome?

" Finally, Senators, Massinissa laid down for us this rule, that we should seek the friendship of no people save the Roman, form no fresh alliances or engagements. In your friendship, he said, we should find protection sufficient for every need ; and, should the fortunes of your empire change, it was our duty to share your fall. By your valour, and the favour of heaven, you are great and wealthy. All things are favourable, all nations obedient to you, and so it is the easier for you to make the sufferings of your allies your care.

"One thing and one only do I fear, and this is lest some be led astray by a private friendship for Jugurtha, which they have not yet had time to prove. I hear that his envoys are using every exertion, and are canvassing and importuning you, man by man, to come to no decision against the accused in his absence, and before the case has been investigated, and asserting that I come here with a lying tale, and playing the part of an exile when at liberty to remain in my kingdom. Would that I may see that man whose unhallowed deed has hurled me to this depth of distress playing this part that now is mine. Would that either you or the immortal gods may begin to take some thought for the affairs of men! When that is so, he who is now so confident, so brilliantly successful, in his crimes, will be racked with every ill, and pay the heavy penalty of his disloyalty to my father, his murder of my brother, and the misery that he has occasioned me.

"Brother, dear to my heart, your life was torn from you before its time by the hand that should have been the last to do the deed, yet I count your lot a cause for gladness rather than for grief. With your life you did not lose a kingdom but flight, exile, beggary, and all the miseries that are crushing me. Less fortunate

than you, I have been hurled from my ancestral throne
into all these ills, and stand here, to show what human
fortune is.   I know not what course to take ; can I,
helpless myself, attempt to avenge your wrongs, or
take thought for my kingdom when my power of life
and death depends on foreign help ?   Would that
death offered an honourable release from my troubles,
and that I could escape well-merited contempt if,
wearied out by misfortune, I submitted to wrong.   As
it is, I have no pleasure in life, and cannot die without
disgrace.

"Senators, by your own selves, by your children
and parents, by the dignity of the Roman people, I
demand your help in my misery.   Take arms against
wrong-doing, refuse to allow that kingdom of Numidia,
which is your own, to languish amid crime, and the
blood of our family."

After the king had made an end of speaking, the
ambassadors of Jugurtha, in reliance rather on their
bribes than on the goodness of their cause, made a
brief reply.   Hiempsal, they said, had been killed by
the Numidians for his own cruelty ; as for Adherbal,
he had made war without provocation, and, now that
he was beaten, was complaining because he had failed
to inflict a wrong.   All that Jugurtha sought from the
Senate was that they should think of him as the man
he had proved himself at Numantia, and refuse to
prefer the words of an enemy to the evidence of his
own deeds.   Each party then quitted the House, and
the Senate proceeded to discuss the question.   The
patrons of the ambassadors, reinforced by a large
section of the Senate, made light of the assertions of

CHAP.
XIV.

CHAP.
XV.

CHAP.
XV.

Adherbal, extolled Jugurtha's services, and strove by personal influence, by eloquence, and by every means in their power, to shield the crime and wickedness of a stranger as though it were their own honour that was at stake. On the other side a few, who valued right and justice more dearly than wealth, gave as their opinion that help should be rendered to Adherbal, and the death of Hiempsal sternly punished. Of these the most conspicuous was Marcus Aemilius Scaurus, a man of high birth, an energetic partisan, greedy for power, office, and wealth, and an adept in concealing his personal vices. Perceiving the notorious and shameless character of the king's bribery, he feared lest such scandalous excess might rouse indignation, as in such a case often happens, and, therefore,

CHAP.
XVI.

restrained his usual greed. Success, nevertheless, fell to the party in the Senate which let profit and personal influence outweigh the interests of truth. A decree was passed ordering that the kingdom which Micipsa had held should be divided between Jugurtha and Adherbal by ten commissioners. At the head of this commission was Lucius Opimius, a man of distinction, and at that time of great influence in the Senate, owing to the stern use which he had made as consul of the victory of the nobility at the time when Gaius Gracchus and Marcus Fulvius Flaccus were murdered. At Rome, Jugurtha had counted him as one of his enemies; nevertheless, he received him with laboured respect, and by large gifts and promises succeeded in making him prefer his advantage to reputation and honour, and even to his own true interests. Approaching the other commissioners in the same way, Jugurtha gained the majority of them: it was only a few who held their honour dearer than money. In the division, the part of Numidia bordering on Mauritania, the richest in soil and population, was assigned to Jugurtha; the remainder, to which its abundance of harbours and public buildings gave the appearance rather than the reality of higher value, Adherbal received as his share.

· My subject seems to require that I should briefly explain the position of Africa, and touch upon the races with which we have been at war or in alliance. Of the regions and tribes which, on account of the heat, ruggedness, or desert nature of the country, have been less often visited, I could hardly, did I wish it, give any certain account; the rest I shall deal with as briefly as possible.

In dividing the earth most writers have made Africa a third continent ; a few hold that only Asia and Europe can be reckoned as such, and that Africa forms a part of Europe. It is bounded on the west by the strait that unites our sea with the ocean; on the east, by a shelving plain, called by the inhabitants Catabathmos. The sea is stormy and harbourless ; the soil productive and good for pasture, but wanting in timber, while both rainfall and springs are scanty. The natives are healthy, nimble, and inured to toil ; except the victims of wild beasts and the sword, few succumb to any disease but old age. It must be added that the number of dangerous animals is large. As to who were the original inhabitants of Africa, and who subsequently arrived, or how the races intermingled, I know that my account differs from the received opin-

CHAP.
XVII.

ion. I shall, however, briefly present it as it was interpreted to me from the Punic books said to have belonged to King Hiempsal, and as the inhabitants of the country believe the events to have taken place. For the truth of the version my informants must be responsible.

CHAP.
XVIII.

The original inhabitants of Africa were Gaetulians and Libyans, savage and barbarous peoples, living on the flesh of wild beasts, or, like cattle, on the grass of the field. They were controlled by no customs or laws, nor by any chief; wandering aimlessly about, they occupied such quarters as night compelled. But after Hercules, for so the Africans believe, died in Spain, his leaderless army, which was made up of various races, dispersed itself abroad, as his followers sought to win themselves dominions on this side or that. Of its troops, the Medes, Persians, and Armenians crossed in ships to Africa, and settled on the lands nearest to our own sea. The Persians took up their abode nearest to the ocean; they turned the hulls of their boats upside down, and used them as huts, for there was no timber in their land, and no means of obtaining it by purchase or barter from Spain, as the wide sea and their ignorance of the language made commerce impossible. Gradually the Persians, by intermarriage, absorbed the Gaetulians, and, as in their frequent search for suitable lands they had wandered widely from place to place, took the name of Nomads. To this very day the dwellings of the Numidian country people, which they call *mapalia*, are of an oblong shape and curving roofs which resemble the keels of boats. The Medes and Armenians were reinforced by

Libyans, a people who lay closer to the African sea, CHAP. XVIII.
while the Gaetulians lived more directly beneath the
sun, near to the zone of intensest heat. The combined nation early possessed towns, for, as they were
but divided by a strait from Spain, they had formed
the practice of mutual barter. Their name was in
course of time perverted by the Libyans, who, in their
barbarous speech called them Mauri instead of Medes.
The power of the Persians rapidly increased, and
subsequently a part of them, under the name of Numidians, separated from the parent stock, on account
of their growing numbers, and settled on the territory round Carthage which is now called Numidia.
Thenceforth, each in reliance on the others' support,
by the terror of their arms they forced their neighbours to submit to their rule, and won for themselves
glory and renown. This was more especially the case
with those whose territory extended to our sea. For
the Libyans are less warlike than the Gaetulians. At
last the greater part of the coast of Africa was occupied by the Numidians, and the conquered were all
merged in the race and name of their lords.

At a later date, the Phoenicians, some wishing to CHAP. XIX.
win dominions, others to lessen the home-population,
urged the commons and such others as were eager
for change to emigrate, and founded Hippo, Hadru-
metum, Leptis, and other cities along the coast.
These quickly rose to importance and served, in some
cases as a defence, in others as an ornament to their
parent states. As to Carthage, I think it better to be
silent than to give an inadequate account, for time
warns me to hasten to another subject.

After the Catabathmos, which divides Egypt from Africa, the first place, as you follow the coast, is Cyrene, a colony of Thera ; next to this come the two Syrtes, and between them Leptis ; then " the altars of the Philaeni " the boundary of the Carthaginians on the side of Egypt, and after this other Punic cities. The rest of the land, as far as Mauritania, is held by the Numidians ; Mauritania lies nearest to Spain. To the south of Numidia I learned that the Gaetuli lived, some in huts, others wandering about in a more barbarous state ; beyond these are the Ethiopians, and beyond them again, lands dried up by the burning heat of the sun. In the Jugurthine war most of the Punic towns, and the lands which the Carthaginians had owned just before their fall were governed by the Roman people through magistrates. A great part of the Gaetulians, and the Numidians, as far as the river Mulucha, were under Jugurtha ; while the ruler over all the Mauritanians was King Bocchus, who knew nothing of the Roman people save their name, and had hitherto been brought beneath our notice neither in peace or war. The foregoing account of Africa and its peoples will suffice for our needs.

When the kingdom had been divided, the commissioners left Africa, and Jugurtha found himself, in spite of his fears, in possession of the reward of his crime. He now took the maxim which he had heard from his friends at Numantia, " that at Rome all things might be bought," for an assured truth, and, excited by the promises of the men whom he had recently glutted with his gifts, turned his thoughts towards the kingdom of Adherbal. He himself was

of an active and warlike nature ; the man he assailed
was quiet and peace-loving, of a gentle disposition,
which laid him open to injury, and one who rather felt
than inspired fear. He therefore suddenly marched into
Adherbal's territory with a large force, seized many
prisoners, with cattle and other booty, burnt buildings,
made cavalry raids on many places, and then retreated with his whole force into his own kingdom,
in the belief that indignation would make his victim
avenge his wrongs by arms, and that such a step
would give rise to war. Adherbal, however, feeling
himself no match for Jugurtha in arms, and placing
more reliance on the friendship of the Roman people
than on his Numidian subjects, sent ambassadors to
Jugurtha to complain of this aggression ; and, although
the answer they brought back was insulting, determined to endure anything rather than embark on a
war, since his former attempt had ended so unfavour-
ably. This availed nothing to lessen the greed of
Jugurtha, for he was already, in imagination, possessor
of the whole kingdom. Not as before with a band of
marauders, but at the head of an army duly equipped,
he began open war, undisguisedly seeking dominion
over all Numidia. On his march he laid waste cities
and fields, carried off booty, and threw fresh heart into
his own men, fresh fear into the enemy. Adherbal
now understood that matters had reached such a pass
that he must either abandon his kingdom or defend it
by arms. Under the pressure of necessity, he mustered his forces, and advanced against Jugurtha.
And now the army of either king took up a position
near the town of Cirta, not far from the sea ; but, as it

CHAP.
XX.

CHAP.
XXI.

was late in the day, battle was not given. When, however, the night was far advanced, in the darkness that still prevailed, the soldiers of Jugurtha, at a given signal, fell upon the enemy's camp, and scattered and routed its defenders, who were but half awake or in the act of seizing their arms. Adherbal, with a few horsemen, made his escape to Cirta, and had not there been a number of Roman citizens in the place, who stopped the Numidian pursuers from entering the wall, a single day would have seen the beginning and the end of the war between the two kings. As it was, Jugurtha blockaded the town, and set about reducing it by means of mantlets, towers, and engines of every kind, using the greatest haste in forestalling the ambassadors whom he had heard that Adherbal had sent to Rome before the battle took place.

When the Senate received news of their war, it despatched three young men to Africa, to go to both kings and acquaint them, in the name of the Roman Senate and people, that it was their will and determination that they should lay down their arms [and decide their disputes by arbitration instead of war]. Such a course, they were to say, would be worthy both of their advisers and of themselves. The commissioners speeded on their journey to Africa, all the more because, while they were making their preparations for departure, news was received in Rome of the battle and the siege of Cirta, though the report dealt lightly with the facts. After listening to their address, Jugurtha replied that nothing carried more weight with or was dearer to him than the authority of the Senate; from his early manhood, he said, he had used

every effort to win the approval of the good ; it was
his merit, and not any cunning devices, that had recommended him to the noble Scipio ; these same
qualities, and not any lack of children of his own, had
caused Micipsa to adopt him into the royal family ;
for the rest, the more proofs he had given of his devotion and energy, the less was he inclined to submit to
wrong ; Adherbal had conspired to take his life, and,
on discovering the plot, he had taken up arms against
his guilt ; the Roman people would be acting neither
rightly nor for their own interests if they hindered his
exercise of the law of nations ; lastly, he was intending shortly to send ambassadors to Rome to explain
the whole state of affairs.   After this, they separated.
Adherbal the commissioners had no means of addressing.

CHAP.
XXII.

Jugurtha, as soon as he judged that they had left
Africa, finding it impossible, on account of its situation, to take Cirta by storm, threw a rampart and trench
round its walls, raised and garrisoned towers, and,
while assailing the town night and day by attacks
both open and disguised, held out to the guardians of
its walls now promises and now threats, roused his
men to courage by his exhortations, and, in fine,
showed himself bent on making every possible provision.   Meantime Adherbal perceived that his fortunes
were desperate, his enemy implacable, himself without
hope of help, and that, from lack of the requisite
means, the war could not be prolonged.   He therefore chose the two most enterprising of his fellow-
fugitives to Cirta, and, by large promises and pitiful
allusions to his own plight, encouraged them to make

CHAP.
XXIII.

their way by night through the enemy's lines to the nearest point on the coast, and thence to Rome.

In a few days the Numidians carried out his orders, and Adherbal's letter was read in the Senate. Its purport was as follows :—

"It is through no fault of mine, Senators, that I send so often to you to implore your help. I am compelled to do so by the violence of Jugurtha, who has been seized with such a passion for my destruction that, unmindful alike of yourselves and of the immortal gods, he prefers my blood to all else beside. Hence it is that I, the friend and ally of the Roman people, have now been besieged for more than four months, and that neither the services of my father Micipsa, nor your decrees, avail me aught. I am pressed by sword and famine ; by which the harder I cannot say. My previous fortune dissuades me from writing more about Jugurtha ; I have already discovered how little the wretched are believed. It may be, however, that I am right in my conviction that my foe is aiming at a higher mark than myself, and that he does not expect to retain at once your friendship and my kingdom ; which of the two he holds of more importance is obvious enough. He began by murdering Hiempsal, my brother, and then ousted me from my ancestral kingdom. These wrongs, I admit, were personal to myself and did not touch you. But now he is in armed possession of a kingdom which belongs to you, and is keeping me, whom you made ruler over the Numidians, a close prisoner. How little weight he attaches to the words of your commissioners my danger may serve to show. What means, then, of moving him is there,

other than the might of Rome? For myself, I could
wish that the words I am now writing and those in
which I once made my complaint in the Senate, told
an idle story rather than that they should be confirmed
at the cost of my own misery. But as I was born to
give Jugurtha scope for the display of his wickedness, I crave no relief from death or hardship, I only
seek to be saved from the tyranny of an enemy and
bodily torture. Make what provision you will for the
kingdom of Numidia, for it is your own, but rescue me
from this unhallowed grasp; this I entreat of you by
the dignity of your empire, by the loyalty of your
friendship, and by whatever memory of my ancestor,
Massinissa, still lingers among you."

On the reading of this letter, some proposed the
despatch of an army to Africa for the immediate
rescue of Adherbal, and that meanwhile they should
discuss Jugurtha's conduct in disobeying the commission. Every effort, however, was used by the king's
old partisans to prevent such a decree being passed;
and, as generally happens, the public good was over-
ruled by private interest. Commissioners, however,
were sent to Africa of a more advanced age, of noble
birth, and who had filled high offices of state; among
their number was the Marcus Scaurus of whom I
spoke above, a man who had been consul and at that
time was leader of the Senate. The matter was exciting odium, and the prayers of the Numidians were
urgent; the ambassadors, therefore, embarked on the
third day, and, after a quick passage to Utica, sent a
despatch to Jugurtha commanding his immediate
attendance in the province, and announcing their

CHAP.
XXV.

commission to him from the Senate. Jugurtha, on hearing that men of distinction, whose influence in Rome he knew by report, had come to bar his proceedings, was at first greatly disturbed, and wavered between the impulses of fear and passion. He was afraid of the anger of the Senate should he fail to obey the commissioners, while the vehemence of his desire blindly hurried him along to complete his crime. The result in his covetous nature was the victory of the evil course. Encircling Cirta with his army, he strained every nerve to force his way into the town, and was filled with hope that, could he divide the strength of the enemy by assault or stratagem, victory would fall to his lot. His efforts failed, and he could not attain his object of seizing Adherbal before meeting the commissioners. Fearful, therefore, lest further delay should anger Scaurus (of whom he was most afraid), he entered the province attended by a few horsemen. But though serious threats were uttered in the name of the Senate if he did not raise the siege, after much parleying the commissioners departed without having effected anything.

CHAP.
XXVI.

When this news reached Cirta, the Italians, whose courage was defending its walls, confident that the greatness of the Roman people would secure their safety on a surrender, advised Adherbal to deliver up himself and the town to Jugurtha, only bargaining for his life, and leaving everything else to the care of the Senate. Adherbal judged any course preferable to reliance on the word of Jugurtha, yet saw that, should he resist, his advisers had power to compel, and therefore made the surrender. Jugurtha's first act was to torture and put him to death. Next he made an indiscriminate massacre of all the adult Numidians and the traders, as they came in contact with his troops.

When this was known in Rome, and the matter began to be discussed in the Senate, the old supporters of the king attempted, by wasting time over questions and quarrels, and by the exercise of private influence, to soften the enormity of the offence. Indeed, had not Gaius Memmius—a tribune elect, an active man and an enemy to the power of the nobility—apprised the people that their object was to enable a few partisans to gain Jugurtha pardon for his crime, by the delay of the inquiry, all public feeling against the king would have subsided, such was the power of his wealth and influence. The Senate, however, conscious of its guilt, feared the people, and, in accordance with the Sempronian law, Numidia and Italy were assigned to the consuls of the next year as their provinces. The consuls elected were Publius Scipio Nasica, and Lucius [Calpurnius] Bestia ; Calpurnius received Numidia, and Scipio Italy. An army was then levied for service in Africa, and pay and what else was needed for the conduct of the war voted.

Jugurtha received the news of all this with great surprise, so firmly planted in his mind was the belief that at Rome everything could be bought. He now sent his son and two intimate friends as ambassadors to the Senate, and instructed them, as he had done those sent after the murder of Hiempsal, to attack every soul in Rome with bribes. On their drawing

Chap.
XXVIII. nigh to the city, the Senate was consulted by Bestia as to whether it was their pleasure that the ambassadors of Jugurtha should be received within the walls, and a decree was passed that, unless they had come to surrender his kingdom and person, they should leave Italy within the next ten days. The consul ordered notice to be given to the Numidians pursuant to the decree, and accordingly they departed home with their mission unfulfilled.

Meanwhile Calpurnius, now that his army was ready, chose for his staff party men of noble birth, whose authority he hoped would shield any misconduct of his own. Among them was the Scaurus, of whose disposition and character I have spoken. As for our consul, he had many good qualities, both of mind and body, but his avarice hampered the exercise of them all ; he had great power of endurance, a keen intellect and considerable forethought, was not ignorant of war, and never dismayed by danger or sudden attack. The legions were taken through Italy to Rhegium, thence to Sicily, and from Sicily to Africa. After organising his commissariat, Calpurnius at first vigorously attacked Numidia, capturing many prisoners and taking several Chap.
XXIX. towns by storm. When, however, Jugurtha began through ambassadors to tempt him with bribes, and to shew him the difficulty of the war he was conducting, his resolution, weakened by covetousness, readily succumbed. As colleague and assistant in all his proceedings he adopted Scaurus, who, though at first, when many of his party had already been perverted, he had strenuously resisted the king, was now by the magnitude of the bribe offered seduced from the path

of virtue and integrity into that of dishonour. Jugurtha began by purchasing no more than a delay in the
war, thinking that in the meanwhile his bribery or
influence might effect something at Rome. But the
news that Scaurus was taking part in the intrigue led
him to form the highest hopes of regaining peace, and
he determined to treat with the commissioners personally on all the conditions. Meanwhile, to inspire confidence, the consul sent his quaestor, Sextius, to Vaga,
a town of Jugurtha's, ostensibly to receive the corn
which Calpurnius had openly demanded of the ambassadors in return for the grant of a truce till the
surrender should be made. On this the king, in pursuance of his plan, came to the camp, and after saying
a few words in the presence of the council about the
ill-will excited by his deed, and his desire to be allowed
to submit, arranged all other points in a secret conference with Bestia and Scaurus. · On the following
day the opinion of the council was taken amid an
irregular discussion, and Jugurtha's submission was
received. In accordance with a command given in
the presence of the council, thirty elephants, a large
number of cattle and horses, together with a small
sum in silver, were delivered to the quaestor. Calpurnius then set out for Rome to hold the elections, and
peace was observed in Numidia and in our army.

When rumour spread the news of the events in
Africa, and of the way in which they had been brought
about, the conduct of the consul was discussed at every
place and in every assemblage in Rome. Among the
common people his unpopularity was great, while the
senators were anxious and undecided whether they

should sanction so serious a crime or annul the consul's ordinance. The chief obstacle to their following the true and upright course was the influence of Scaurus, the reputed adviser and accomplice of Bestia. But while the Senate was hesitating and raising delays, Gaius Memmius, of whose independent character and hatred of the power of the nobility I spoke above, roused the people to vengeance by his addresses, bade them not to betray the republic and their own freedom, exposed many instances of the pride and cruelty of the nobility, and in fine shewed great energy in exciting the populace by every possible means.

As the eloquence of Memmius was at that period renowned and influential in Rome, I have thought it well to set forth one of his numerous speeches, and I shall report by preference one which he delivered at a public meeting after the return of Bestia, somewhat as follows :—

"There is much, Romans, to dissuade me from espousing your cause, were it not that my patriotism is proof against every attack. There is the power of a cabal, your own submissiveness, the absence of justice, and, above all, the fact that political honesty involves more danger than recognition. I refrain, for very shame, from dilating on how for the last fifteen years you have been the sport of an arrogant faction ; how your champions have perished shamefully and unavenged ; how you have suffered cowardice and sloth to weaken your courage ; and even now do not rise against your enemies though they lie at your mercy ; even now tremble before men who ought to tremble before you. All this is as I have said, and yet my spirit forces me to oppose the tyranny of the cabal. I, at least, will make use of the freedom which was bequeathed to me by my father, whether in vain or to some purpose it lies with you to determine.

"I do not advise you to do as your ancestors often did, and take up arms against your wrongs. There is no need for violence, no need for secession; your enemies' own behaviour is certain to work their ruin. After the murder of Tiberius Gracchus, whom they accused of aiming at kingly power, they set their commissions to work against the party of the commons in Rome. Again, after the slaughter of Gaius Gracchus and Marcus Fulvius, many men of your station were put to death in prison, and in neither case was it the law but the victors' caprice that brought the massacre to an end. Let us grant, however, that to give the people back its own is equivalent to aiming at kingly power, and that deeds that cannot be avenged without bloodshed are constitutionally done. In former years you chafed in silence at the sight of the treasury being rifled, of kings and free people paying tribute to a clique of nobles, of the highest glory and the greatest riches being confined to them. Now, not satisfied with having committed these crimes with impunity, they have even presumed to betray to the enemy the laws, your dignity, things human and things divine, in fine, our all. And the men who have done these things feel neither shame nor repentance; they flaunt their splendour before your eyes, displaying their priesthoods and their consulships, and some their triumphs, as if they held them as honours to which they were entitled, not as spoils they had seized.

Slaves that are bought for money rebel at unjust commands of their masters: will you, Romans, who are born to rule, patiently submit to servitude?

"But what manner of men are these who have taken possession of the state? They are the mcst wicked of mortals, men of bloodstained hands and monstrous avarice, the most criminal and arrogant of their kind, men who would sell their word, their loyalty, their affections, and seek a profit alike from honour and from shame. Some of them find their safety in having murdered tribunes of the people, others in having held oppressive trials, many in the slaughter of your class. The worse their crimes the greater their safety; the fears that they should feel for their own guilt they have inspired in you in your cowardice. Common desires, common hatreds, and common fears, have united them together in an alliance which between good men would be friendship, but between bad is a cabal. Were but your anxiety for your freedom equal to their zeal for power, the state would assuredly not be the prey it now is, and your benefits would be enjoyed by your best men, not by your boldest criminals. To win their rights and establish their dignity your ancestors twice seceded in arms and seized Mount Aventine; will you not strive to the utmost of your power to maintain the liberty which you received from them? Will you not strive for it with a vigour made fiercer by the thought that it is more shameful to lose a possession once won than never to have gained it.

" ' But what do you propose ? ' some one will ask me; ' ought we to take vengeance on the men who have betrayed the state to its enemy ?' Not, CHAP. XXXI I answer, by force or by violence, which it is more disgraceful for you to use, than for them to· suffer, but by legal trial, and the witness of Jugurtha himself. For if he has really surrendered, he will undoubtedly pay obedience to your commands ; if he despises them, you will know how to judge of the peace and surrender which has secured to Jugurtha impunity for his crimes, immense sums to a few powerful men, and to the state nothing but loss and dishonour. Perhaps, however, you have not even yet had enough of their tyranny, and like the present times less than the days of old when kingdoms and provinces, law, justice, and judgment, peace and war, and all things both human and divine were held in the hands of a petty class, while you, you who are the Roman people, conquered by no enemy, the lords of every race, thought it enough if you kept your lives. For who among you dared to refuse the yoke of slavery ?

" But, despite my belief that for one who bears the name of man to sit quiet beneath a wrong is the deepest disgrace, I would yet be content that you should pardon these, the wickedest of their race, since they are your fellow-citizens, were it not that your compassion would turn to your own destruction. So great is these men's shamelessness that it will not be enough that you have forgiven their offences in the past, you must also, deprive them of the power of offending in the future ; if you do not, you will be kept in constant anxiety, for you will discover that you must either submit to slavery or keep your freedom by means of force. Of force, I say; for what hope is there of mutual trust or concord ?   They wish to rule, you to be free, they to inflict wrong, you to prevent it; while, finally, they treat your allies as enemies, and your enemies as allies.   With purposes so different, can there be either friendship or peace?

"I, therefore, warn and urge you not to allow so great a crime to go unpunished.   This is no case of fraud on the treasury, or of money extorted by force from your allies.   Heavy crimes as these are, custom by this time has taught us to count them mere nothings.   No; it is the powers of the Senate that have been sold to our bitterest enemy; your sovereign rights have been betrayed, at home and abroad; our country has been bought and sold.   If these things be not enquired into, if the guilty go unpunished, what is there left for us but to live in bondage to the men who have done them?   For what is kingship, but the power to work your will with impunity ?

"I do not, however, exhort you, Quirites, to be glad that fellow-citizens have done the wrong rather than the right.   I only exhort you, not to set about destroying the good by pardoning the bad.   In matters of state, I must add, it is much better to be forgetful of a service than of an injury.   Neglect only makes the good man slower to serve you, it makes the bad worse than he was before.   See to it that none do you wrong, and you will not often stand in need of others' help."

By frequent speeches to this and the like effect, Memmius persuaded the people to despatch Lucius Cassius, then praetor, to bring Jugurtha to Rome, pledging the public word for his safety, in order that by the king's testimony the misconduct of Scaurus and

the others who were arraigned for receiving bribes
might be more easily exposed.

While this was going on at Rome, the officers left by Bestia in command of the army in Numidia committed many scandalous crimes in imitation of their general. Some on receipt of bribes restored his elephants to Jugurtha, others sold him his deserters, others, again, plundered friendly lands: so violent was the avarice which had settled like a plague upon their minds.

Gaius Memmius carried his bill, and amid the dismay of the whole nobility, Cassius set out on his mission to Jugurtha. Finding the king full of fear, and prompted by his guilty conscience to despair, he persuaded him, since he had surrendered to the Roman people, not to prefer to learn their might rather than their clemency. For his safety, moreover, he privately pledged his own word, which, such at that time was Cassius' reputation, the king valued as highly as that of the people. Jugurtha therefore came to Rome with Cassius, in a guise so pitiful as to be the very opposite of royal state. He had himself no lack of courage, and was supported by all those whose influence or crimes had enabled him to accomplish all that I have above narrated. Nevertheless, he bought with a great bribe Gaius Baebius, a tribune of the commons, thinking that by his shamelessness he would be protected against both justice and violence. A public meeting was summoned, and the commons showed themselves very hostile to the king, some bidding him be put in chains, others that punishment should be inflicted on him as an enemy, according to ancient custom, unless he revealed who were his accomplices. Gaius Memmius, however, had more regard for their dignity than their wrath, quieted their commotion, softened their passions, and finally protested that, as far as he was concerned, the public word should not be broken. As soon as silence was gained he brought forward Jugurtha and addressed him, reminding him of his misdeeds in Rome and Numidia, and laying before him the crimes he had committed against his father and brothers. The Roman people, he continued, were not ignorant as to who were his helpers and agents in all this. They wished, however, to have it somewhat more clearly stated from his own mouth. Should he reveal the truth, there rested a great hope for him in the honour and merciful disposition of the Roman people. Should he withhold the information, he would not save his accomplices, but would ruin him-

self and his own hopes. Memmius finished his speech, and Jugurtha was ordered to make answer, when Gaius Baebius, the tribune of the commons whose corruption I have mentioned, ordered the king to be silent, and although the crowd which was present at the meeting in a frenzy of rage tried to terrify him by shouts, by gestures, by frequent assaults, and by every other ebullition which anger is wont to produce, his shamelessness, nevertheless, won the day. The people quitted the meeting where they had been thus mocked, and Jugurtha, Bestia, and the others whom the investigation was disquieting, felt their courage increase.

There was at this time in Rome a certain Numidian, by name Massiva, a son of Gulussa, and grandson of

Massinissa. In the struggle between the kings he had opposed Jugurtha, and, on the surrender of Cirta and murder of Adherbal, had fled from his country into exile. Spurius Albinus, consul with Quintus Minucius Rufus in the year after Bestia, now persuaded him, since he was of the stock of Massinissa, and Jugurtha for his crimes was loaded with odium and fear, to beg the kingdom of Numidia from the Senate. The consul was eager to conduct a war, and so preferred a general agitation to letting the matter lose its interest ; for the province of Numidia had fallen to himself, that of Macedonia to Minucius. On Massiva beginning to stir in the matter, Jugurtha, who found no sufficient defence in his friends, some of whom were embarrassed by their consciousness of guilt, others by their ill repute or their own fears, ordered Bomilcar, his most intimate and trusty attendant, to employ the bribery by which he had accomplished so much, in hiring assassins to attack Massiva, and to kill the Numidian, secretly if he could, or, failing this, by any means whatever. Bomilcar speedily carried out the king's commands, and, by means of men skilled in such business, gained information as to his victim's journeys and departures, and, in fine, as to all the places he was in the habit of frequenting, and the hours which he observed. He then directed the attack as the circumstances made advisable. One of the band who were hired to commit the murder rushed upon Massiva somewhat hastily, and though he cut him down, was himself seized. At the instance of many advisers, and especially of the Consul Albinus, this man turned informer, and Bomilcar was made to stand a trial,

CHAP.
XXXV. rather on considerations of equity than by the law of nations, since he was in attendance on one who had come to Rome under the public guarantee. Though detected in so great a crime, Jugurtha did not abandon the struggle against facts until he perceived that the odium of his deed was too great for either influence or money to overcome. On the first hearing of the case he had given fifty sureties from among his friends, but now, thinking more of his kingdom than his sureties, he privily despatched Bomilcar to Numidia, in the fear that, should he be punished, the rest of his accomplices might be seized with a dread of obeying him. A few days afterwards he himself set out on the same journey, as he was commanded by the Senate to leave Italy. When he had passed out of Rome, he is said, after often looking back on it in silence, at last to have cried: "A city for sale, soon to fall if once it find a buyer."

CHAP.
XXXVI. Meanwhile the war had been resumed, and Albinus hastened to convey to Africa provisions, and pay, and other requisites for his soldiers' use. He himself set out immediately, hoping either by arms, a capitulation, or some other means to finish the war before the date of the elections, which was now not far distant. Jugurtha, on the other hand, pursued a policy of delay, assigning now one cause and now another, promising to surrender and then pretending distrust, retreating before Albinus' advance, and a little while after, to keep his followers from despair, himself advancing. Thus, now by warlike, now by peaceful means, he secured delay, and baffled the consul. Some at the time thought that Albinus was privy to the king's design, and refused to believe that a war so vigorously begun was thus easily prolonged by sloth rather than treachery. Anyhow, time slipped away, and the date of the elections drew near at hand. Albinus, therefore, left his brother Aulus as pro-praetor in the camp, and departed for Rome.

CHAP. XXXVI.

Just at this time at Rome the state was being violently excited by dissensions among the tribunes, two of whom, Publius Lucullus, and Lucius Annius, were striving, despite the opposition of their colleagues, to extend their term of office. This disagreement prevented the elections being held throughout the year, and Aulus, who, as I said above, had been left as pro-praetor in the camp, was led by this delay to entertain a hope of either bringing the war to an end, or extorting money from the king by the terror of his army. Summoning the soldiers from their winter quarters for a campaign in the month of January, he arrived by means of forced marches in most inclement weather at the town of Suthul, where the king's treasures were deposited. The bitterness of the season, and the natural advantages of the place, made its storm or blockade impossible. Around its wall, which lay on the edge of a steep cliff, a swampy plain had been turned by the rain into a lake. Yet Aulus, either as a pretence by which to increase the king's alarm, or blinded by his eagerness to gain the town for the sake of the treasures, brought up mantlets, threw up a rampart, and hastily made other provisions such as might forward his undertaking. Aware of the folly and unskilfulness of the legate, Jugurtha craftily fostered his madness, sent a succession of beseech-

CHAP. XXXVII.

CHAP. XXXVIII.

 ing embassies, and, as if to avoid him, kept leading his army amid forests and bypaths. At last he enticed Aulus by the hope of a secret agreement, to leave Suthul and follow him in his pretended retreat into remote regions. ' [There his misconduct was to be more screened from observation.] Meanwhile he employed skilful agents to tamper with the praetor's army night and day, and bribed the centurions and squadron-leaders, some to desert, others at a given signal to abandon their post. When everything was arranged to his wish, in the dead of night he suddenly surrounded the camp of Aulus with a host of Numidians. The Roman soldiers were panic-stricken by the unwonted uproar; some seized their arms, others sought concealment, others again tried to encourage their frightened comrades ; everywhere there was confusion. The force of the enemy was large, the sky was darkened by night and clouds, their danger was critical, it was doubtful whether to flee or to remain was the safer course. Of those whom I stated to have been recently bribed, one cohort of Ligurians, with two squadrons of Thracians and a few private soldiers, deserted to the king, and the chief centurion of the third legion gave an entrance to the enemy over the rampart of which he had been entrusted with the defence ; by this road all the Numidians burst into the camp. Our men, in a disgraceful rout, many of them after throwing away their arms, gained a neighbouring hill. Night, and the plunder of the camp, withheld the enemy from making use of their victory. On the next day, Jugurtha, in a conference with Aulus, expressed himself to the effect that, although he held him and his army in the toils of famine and sword, he was yet mindful of human fortunes, and, if Aulus would enter into a treaty, would dismiss his whole force unharmed beneath the yoke ; with the further stipulation that he was to leave Numidia within ten days. The terms were grievous and shameful, nevertheless, with the fear of death before their eyes, peace was concluded according to the king's pleasure.

When information of this was received at Rome, fear and grief fell upon the state. Some sorrowed for the glory of their empire, others, in their ignorance of the affairs of war, feared for their freedom. Every one, and especially those who had often gained distinction in war, was bitter against Aulus for having, though possessed of arms, sought safety in dishonour rather than the sword. The consul Albinus, in his fear of odium and consequent danger from his brother's misconduct, consulted the Senate as to the peace. Meanwhile, he levied reinforcements for the army, summoned contingents from the allies and the Latin citizens, and in fact showed energy in every possible way. The Senate, as was their duty from the first, decreed that without the consent of itself and the people no agreement could have had the force of a treaty. The consul was prevented by the tribunes of the people from taking the forces which he had levied with him, but started himself in a few days to Africa, for his entire army in accordance with the agreement had evacuated Numidia and was now in winter quarters in the province. He arrived there, burning to pursue Jugurtha and so relieve his brother's unpopularity, but the sight of his soldiers, disorganised

CHAP.
XXXIX. not only by their route but by the disorder and luxury of a relaxed state of discipline, convinced him that with the means at his disposal nothing was to be done.

CHAP.
XL. Meanwhile at Rome Gaius Manilius Limetanus, a tribune of the commons, proposed to the people that an enquiry should be held as to all persons by whose advice Jugurtha had disregarded the decrees of the Senate, who had received bribes from him when on embassies or military commands, or who had restored to him his elephants and deserters, and also as to all who had made agreements with an enemy either for peace or war. Some in their consciousness of their guilt, others in their fear of danger from party hatred, finding themselves unable to openly resist the bill without arousing their favour for these and similar malpractices, prepared secretly to obstruct it by means of their friends, and particularly by the help of men from the Latin towns and the Italian allies. It is impossible, however, to relate with what determination and violence the commons supported the bill, and this, such was the passion that possessed the contending parties, rather from hatred of the nobility, against whom these penalties were aimed, than from any patriotic feeling. While all others were stricken with dismay Marcus Scaurus who, as I related above, had been Bestia's lieutenant, amid the triumph of the commons and the rout of his own party, in the confusion which still prevailed in the state, managed to have himself appointed one of the three judges created in accordance with the bill of Manilius. The enquiry, however, was conducted with harshness and violence according to the reports and caprices which prevailed among the commons, who at this crisis were possessed by the same insolence in their good fortune as had so often governed the nobility in theirs.

A few years before this, party divisions and cabals, with all the bad qualities they bring with them, had become common at Rome in a period of peace and of the abundance of such things as men esteem the first of blessings. Down to the destruction of Carthage, the people and Senate of Rome between them administered the state peacefully and soberly; there was no strife among the citizens for glory or supremacy, and fear of its enemies kept the state to the exercise of honourable qualities. When, however, men's minds were relieved of this fear, as a natural consequence, wantonness and arrogance, the favourite vices of prosperity, made their appearance. Thus the repose, for which amid their calamities they had longed, proved, when they had obtained it, more troublesome and bitter than calamity itself. The nobility now made dignity, the people freedom, the objects of party passion, and every one seized, plundered, and robbed, for his own hand. Thus everything was drawn to one or other side, and the state, which had stood between them, was torn asunder. Of the two parties the nobility were the stronger, owing to their power of common action; the force of the commons, weakened and scattered in a multitude of hands, was less effective. All action, both in war and in home affairs, was taken at the discretion of a clique. The same party controlled the treasury, the provinces, and civil offices and the awards of reputation and triumph. The people

CHAP.
XLI.

were ground down by military service and want; the spoils of war were seized by the generals and shared with a few accomplices, and meanwhile the parents and little children of the soldiers were thrust from their homesteads by their more powerful neighbours. Hand in hand with power, avarice, unlimited and unrestrained, spread abroad, and, while it caused general pollution and devastation, held nothing as estimable, nothing as sacred until it worked its own ruin. As soon as members of the nobility were found to prefer true glory to unjust dominion, the state was shaken and civil strife sprang into being like some convulsion

CHAP.
XLII.

of the earth. Tiberius and Gaius Gracchus—men whose ancestors had done much to advance the state in the Punic and other wars—first asserted the liberty of the commons and exposed the crimes of the clique. The nobility, in guilty terror, opposed their proceedings at one time by means of the allies and the Latin citizens, at another by the Roman knights who had been drawn from the side of the commons by the hope of an alliance with themselves. First they cut off Tiberius, and then, a few years afterwards, his brother Gaius, who was entering on the same course—the one a tribune, the other a commissioner for establishing colonies; and besides these they killed Marcus Fulvius Flaccus. The Gracchi, in their desire for victory, had certainly shown a too intemperate disposition. It is better, however, to be defeated by a good precedent than to crush a wrong by means of a bad one. As it was, the nobility used their victory to indulge their own passion, made away with many persons by sword or banishment, and for the future gained in the terror they inspired rather than in real power. Such conduct has often proved the ruin of great states. Each party is ready to use any means to defeat the other, and to punish the defeated too severely. But were I to set about treating of party passions and the condition of public morals in any detail, or in proportion to the importance of the question, my time would fail me sooner than my material. I therefore return to my task.

After the treaty of Aulus and the disgraceful flight of our army, the consuls Quintus Metellus and Marcus Silanus, in accordance with a resolution of the Senate, had settled on their respective provinces, and that of Numidia had fallen to Metellus, a man of energy, whose reputation, though he was an opponent of the popular party, was unshaken and unblemished. No sooner had he entered office than, while accounting everything else as duties to be shared with his colleague, he concentrated his attention on the war which he was about to conduct. Placing little confidence in the old army, he levied soldiers and summoned troops from all quarters; made ready armour, weapons, horses, and the other instruments of warfare, with an abundance of provisions, and everything in fact which in a war of variable character and of many requirements, is wont to be of service. The Senate by its influence, the allies, Latin citizens, and dependent kings, by freely sending contingents, and above all, the whole state by the earnestness of its zeal, used every exertion to complete these measures. When everything was prepared and arranged to his wish, the consul set out for Numidia amid the high hopes of the citizens,

CHAP.
XLIII.

which were roused not only by his talents but especially by the unswerving resolution with which he resisted the temptations of wealth, and by the fact that it was by the greed of our officers in Numidia that our strength had hitherto been crushed and that of our enemies augmented.

CHAP.
XLIV.

On the arrival of Metellus in Africa, he received from Spurius Albinus, the proconsul, an indolent and cowardly army, unable to bear either danger or toil, readier of tongue than of hand, the spoiler of its allies and the spoil of its enemies, without government and without discipline. Thus more anxiety fell to the new general from the bad character of his soldiers than reinforcement or hope from their numbers. The delay of the elections had shortened his time for a campaign, and he suspected that the minds of the citizens were strained with expectation of some decisive action. Nevertheless, he determined not to engage in active war before he had forced his men to endure toil by reviving the ancient discipline. Stunned by the defeat of his brother Aulus and his army, Albinus, after coming to the determination not to advance beyond the province, for the part of the usual campaigning time during which he was in command, kept his soldiers, as a rule, in fixed camps, except when the effluvium or a scarcity of food compelled him to change his position. These camps were not entrenched, nor were watches set according to military custom. The men left the standards at their own pleasure ; camp followers mingled with the soldiers and roamed about with them by day and night. In their excursions they wasted the land,

plundered the country houses, vied with each other in
carrying off cattle and slaves, and bartered them away
to traders for foreign wine and the like.   The corn with
which the state supplied them they sold, and bought
their bread from day to day.   In fine, there is no
shameful outcome of wantonness and sloth that words
can express or imagination figure that was not to be
found in that army, and more besides.   I find, however, that Metellus showed his greatness and wisdom
no less in this difficulty than in dealing with an
enemy; with such self-command did he keep the
mean between popularity-seeking and severity.   As
his first step, he abolished by edict all the appliances
of sloth, forbidding the sale in the camp of bread or
any other cooked food, the presence of camp-followers
in the track of the army, or the possession by a common soldier of any slave or beast of burden either in
camp or on the march.   On all other points he laid
down strict rules.   Moving along cross roads, he
shifted his camp from day to day, fortified it with
rampart and trench, as if in presence of the enemy,
set numerous watches, and went the rounds in person
with his officers.   On the march he was now in the
van, now in the rear, often, too, with the main body;
and saw that no one left the ranks, that the soldiers
marched in close order with the standards, and that
each man carried his own food and arms.   By this
course of restraining rather than punishing offences,
he soon gave stability to his army.

Meanwhile Jugurtha, on hearing the report of what
Metellus was doing, and being assured from Rome of
his integrity, despaired of his fortunes, and now at

last tried to make a real surrender. With this object he sent an entreating embassy to the consul to beg only life for himself and his children ; everything else they were to surrender to the Roman people.

Experience, however, had long ago convinced Metellus that the Numidians were a faithless and unstable race, ever eager for change. He therefore approached the ambassadors independently of each other, and tampered with them by degrees. Finding them favourable to his purpose, he persuaded them, by large promises, to surrender Jugurtha to him, if possible alive, but, failing that, dead. Publicly, he bade them take back an answer such as might satisfy the king. A few days later he invaded Numidia with an army prepared for fighting, and in hostile array. No signs of war were apparent ; the cottages were occupied, cattle and husbandmen in the fields. The king's officers advanced from their towns and dwellings to meet him, ready to provide corn, convey provisions, and in fact to do whatever they were ordered. None the less Metellus advanced guardedly as if in the presence of an enemy, sent his scouts far and wide in every direction, and believed these marks of submission to be a mere show, and that an opportunity was being sought for a sudden attack. He himself, with the light cohorts, and a chosen body of slingers and bowmen, was in the front. In the rear his lieutenant, Gaius Marius, was in command with the cavalry. The auxiliary cavalry Metellus had divided between the two flanks under the several tribunes of the legions and officers of the cohorts, in such a manner that skirmishers were mingled with it to repulse the cavalry of the enemy at whatever point it might attack. Such was the treachery of Jugurtha and such his acquaintance both with the country and with the art of war, that it was a question whether he were more dangerous absent or present, in peace or in war.

Not far from the road along which Metellus was marching was a Numidian town named Vaga, the most frequented market of the whole kingdom ; and here many Italians had been wont to settle and trade. On this town the consul imposed a garrison, partly for the sake of seeing whether the inhabitants would submit to it, partly on account of the advantage of the place. He further demanded that they should bring in corn and other stores useful for the war, thinking, as he had reason, that the number of traders would both aid the army with provisions, and would help to secure what he had already won.

While Metellus was busied with this, Jugurtha, with increasing earnestness, was sending submissive embassies, entreating for peace and offering to surrender everything except the lives of himself and his children. As he had done to their predecessors, the consul before dismissing the ambassadors suborned them to betray their master, neither refused nor promised the king the peace he asked, and amid these delays awaited the fulfilment of the ambassadors' promises. Jugurtha, when he came to compare the words of Metellus with his actions, perceived that he was being assailed with his own devices. As far as words went peace was offered him, as a matter of fact the war was being hotly pressed ; an important city had been won from him, the enemy had learnt the nature of the land, and the loyalty of his country-men had been tampered with. Forced by necessity, he determined on a struggle. A knowledge of the enemy's route led him to hope for victory from the favourable nature of the ground, and, raising as great forces of every kind as he could, by means of little known paths he got the start of the army of Metellus.

In the part of Numidia of which Adherbal had gained possession at the time of the partition there was a river named the Muthul, which took its rise from the south. Some twenty miles from this stream, and following the same direction, lay a barren and un-cultivated mountain ridge. Almost in its midst there rose a hill stretching to an immense distance, and clothed with wild olives, myrtles, and trees of such other kinds as grow in a dry and sandy soil. Between the hills and the Muthul was a plain, barren from want of water, except in the neighbourhood of the river, where it was planted with trees and thickly occupied by cattle and husbandmen.

 On this hill, which, as I said, lay at right angles to the road, Jugurtha took up his position in a very ex-tended line. Giving Bomilcar the command of the elephants and a part of his infantry, he instructed him what to do, while he himself remained at a point nearer the mountain with the whole body of cavalry and the pick of the infantry, and there posted his men. Then, visiting the several squadrons and companies, he urged and conjured them to be mindful of their ancient valour and of victory, and to shield himself and his kingdom against the greed of the Romans. The men, he said, against whom they had to fight were those whom they had formerly beaten and led beneath the yoke, and though they had changed their general they had not changed their spirit. Everything which the Numidians had a right to expect from their commander he had provided ; they would hold the higher ground, their knowledge would be matched with inexperience, they would not join in conflict as a weaker force against a stronger, or as raw recruits with men better versed in war. They must therefore, he said, hold themselves ready and on the alert to burst upon the Romans at the given signal. That day would either crown all their toil and victories, or be the beginning of the greatest miseries! Besides this, he addressed singly each man whom he had rewarded with money or distinction for some warlike exploit, reminding him of his favour, and pointing him out as an example to others. In fine, he suited his words to each man's character, and used the various incentives of promises, threats, entreaties. As he was thus engaged, Metellus was seen descending the mountain with his army, unaware of the enemy's presence. At first he was baffled by the strange appearance of the country, for the cavalry and the Numidians had taken up their position in the brushwood, and owing to the lowness of the trees were not altogether hidden, but yet were difficult to distinguish for what they were, as their own bodies and their military ensigns were masked, both designedly and by the nature of their position. He soon, however, discovered the ambush, and ordered a short halt. Changing his formation on the right flank, which was nearest the enemy, he drew up his line with a threefold reserve, distributed slingers and bowmen among the companies, placed all his cavalry on the wings, and, after a few words of suitable encouragement to his soldiers, led his force in its new formation, with the front ranks at right angles to the line of march, down to the level ground. He remarked that the Numidians remained quiet and did not descend the hill, and in that season, and in the scarcity of water, felt a fear lest his army should be exhausted by thirst. He therefore sent forward his lieutenant, Publius Rutilius, with some light cohorts and a part of the cavalry towards the river, to seize a position for a camp, expecting that the enemy would hinder his own advance by frequent charges and flank attacks, and, in their distrust of the sword, would try what the weariness and thirst of his soldiers would avail them. He himself then made a gradual advance, such as his means and situation allowed, in the same order in which he had descended the hill. Marius was behind in command of the troops facing the enemy, he himself with the cavalry of the left wing, which in the new order of marching was become the van.

As soon as Jugurtha marked that Metellus' rear had passed his own front ranks he occupied the hill, at the point where Metellus had descended, with a force of about two thousand foot, so as to prevent it serving as a refuge and subsequent stronghold to his adversaries in a retreat. He then suddenly gave the signal, and rushed upon the enemy. Some of the Numidians cut down our rear ranks, others assailed us on either flank, everywhere the enemy was upon us, and pressing us hard. The Roman ranks were thrown into disorder at every point, and even soldiers who had resisted the

enemy with unusual resolution found themselves thwar- CHAP.
ted by the baffling nature of the fight, and while they   L.
were being wounded from a distance, had no means of
striking a blow in return, or coming to close quarters.
As often as one of our squadrons began to pursue,
Jugurtha's horsemen, according to their instructions,
did not retreat in a body or to any one place, but
scattered themselves as widely as possible. They
were superior in numbers, and whenever they had
failed to deter the enemy from pursuit, surrounded
them on their rear and flanks when their order was
broken. When, again, the hill offered a readier retreat
than the plains, the Numidian horses, accustomed to
such riding, easily made their way amid the brushwood, while ours were held back by the rough and
unusual nature of the ground. The whole en-   CHAP.
gagement, in its changeful and indecisive aspect,   LI.
was such as to arouse both shame and pity. Separated from their comrades, some retreated, others
pursued ; heedless of standards and ranks, each
man made his stand where danger had overtaken him,
and there tried to avert it. Swords and javelins,
horses and men, foes and countrymen, were mingled
in confusion ; no plan was followed, or order obeyed ;
chance was supreme over all. The fourth part of
the day had passed in this way, and even yet the issue
was uncertain. At last, when all were faint with toil
and heat, Metellus marked that the onset of the
Numidians was less vigorous, and, gradually getting
his men together, re-formed their ranks, and posted
four cohorts of legionaries to resist the enemy's
infantry, of which a great part, out of sheer weariness,

CHAP.
LI. had seated themselves on the higher ground. At the same time he begged and exhorted his men not to show themselves wanting, nor to suffer the flying enemy to win the day, reminding them that they had no camp or fortifications of any kind to which to retreat, and that all their hopes lay in their arms. Meanwhile, Jugurtha, on his side, did not remain inactive. He visited and encouraged his men, renewed the battle, and, backed by his chosen followers, left no means of attack untried. He relieved his own troops and pressed on the enemy when they wavered, where he saw them making a firm stand he hampered them CHAP
LII. by distant assaults. Thus did the two generals, both of them men of high ability, vie with each other in their efforts. Personally they were a match, but the resources at their disposal were unequal. Metellus could count on the courage of his troops, but the ground was against him. Jugurtha, on the other hand, had everything in his favour save the quality of his men. At last the Romans understood that they had no place of escape, and that the enemy was avoiding a regular battle. When evening had already arrived, they carried out their orders and stormed the hill. The Numidians, on losing their position, fled in confusion. A few were killed, but the majority were protected by their own fleetness, and by their enemies' ignorance of the country.

Meanwhile, as soon as Rutilius had marched past him, Bomilcar, who, as related above, had been placed by Jugurtha in command of the elephants and a part of the infantry, slowly led his men down into the plain, and, while the Roman officer continued his hasty

advance towards the river to which he had been des- CHAP. LII.
patched, marshalled his army as noiselessly as the occasion demanded, and kept ceaseless watch on every
movement of the enemy. Learning that Rutilius had
already encamped and was quite off his guard, and at
the same time that the din of the battle in which
Jugurtha was engaged was increasing, he now feared
lest the lieutenant should discover what was happening, and assist his hard-pressed comrades. In his distrust of his men's courage he had drawn up his line in
close order, but he now extended it so as to block the
enemy's march, and in this order advanced against
the camp of Rutilius. The Romans, whose view was CHAP. LIII.
shut off by a plantation of trees, were suddenly aware
of a great cloud of dust. At first they thought it was
the dry soil being blown about by the wind; they
noticed, however, that its advance was steady and like
that of an army in battle order, and that it approached
ever nearer and nearer. At last, understanding what
was really happening, they hastily seized their arms,
and, in obedience to order, took up a position in front
of the camp. The distance between the two armies
diminished, and they charged each other with a loud
shout. The Numidians stood their ground only as
long as they thought to find help in their elephants;
as soon as they saw them entangled in the branches
of the trees and thus scattered and surrounded, they
took to flight, and most of them, with the loss of their
arms, escaped whole and sound under cover of the hill
and of the night, which was now falling. Of the elephants four were captured, the rest, to the number of
forty, were killed.

M

CHAP.
LIII. The Romans were tired with marching, camp-making, and fighting, and were flushed with their victory. The arrival, however, of Metellus was unexpectedly delayed, and they advanced to meet him ready for battle and on the alert; for the stratagems of the Numidians forbade any relaxation of vigilance. The night was dark, and the two armies, when now not far apart, each inspired the other with terror and confusion by its noise as if of an enemy's approach. In this state of ignorance a pitiable disaster was on the point of happening, when the horsemen who were despatched from both armies discovered the truth. As it was, fear was suddenly exchanged for joy. The soldiers hailed each other in triumph, and heard and related their several exploits; each man was loud in praising his prowess to the skies. Thus is it in the affairs of men ; in victory even the cowards may boast, while calamity casts a slur even on the brave.

CHAP.
LIV. Remaining four days in the same encampment, Metellus made the recovery of the wounded his care, rewarded those who had done good service in the battles according to military custom, and praised and thanked the whole body of his troops in a public speech. He exhorted them to maintain a like spirit in the face of the easy tasks which still remained, and assured them that they had already fought enough for victory, and that the rest of their toils would be for booty. In the meantime, however, he sent deserters and other suitable agents to discover where Jugurtha might be living, and how he was employed ; whether he was at the head of a few followers or of an army, and how he bore himself under a defeat. The king, I should men-

tion, had withdrawn to a woody country of natural
strength, and was there collecting an army, greater in
numbers, but without vigour or strength, and composed of men more skilled in the art of the husband-
man or shepherd than in that of war. The cause of
this was, that with the exception of the royal cavalry,
no Numidian attends the king after a rout; they dis-
perse to whatever quarter they severally feel inclined,
and this is not esteemed a military offence, but is the
custom of the country.

Metellus saw that Jugurtha's spirit was still high,
and that a war was being renewed the conduct of
which must depend on his adversary's pleasure; between himself and his enemies the contest was
unequal, for their defeats were less costly than his own
victories. He determined, therefore, to carry on the
war not by battles nor in battle array, but in another
fashion altogether. Accordingly he marched into the
richest parts of Numidia, wasted the country, captured
and burnt many strongholds and towns which had
either been hastily fortified or left without a garrison,
slew all the adult males, and ordered everything else
to be the soldiers' booty. Amid the terror thus inspired, many persons were surrendered to the Romans
as hostages, corn and other useful provisions were
supplied in abundance, and a garrison was stationed
wherever there seemed occasion. This policy had a
much greater effect in frightening the king than any
battle lost by his soldiers. He whose whole hope lay
in flight found himself obliged to pursue, and though
he had been unable to protect his country when his
own, he had now to wage war in it when the enemy

was its master.   He embraced the course which seemed best with the means at his disposal, and ordered the greater part of his army to conceal itself in a fixed position, while he himself with some picked cavalry pursued Metellus.   By a series of night marches along unfrequented roads he escaped notice and suddenly attacked a straggling body of Romans.   Most of them were cut down in their defenceless condition, many were captured, and not one of the whole number made his escape unhurt.   Before relief could arrive from the camp, the Numidians, according to their orders, withdrew to the neighbouring hills.

Meanwhile at Rome great rejoicing arose on the intelligence of the doings of Metellus, of his adherence to ancient custom in his government of himself and his army, of the victory which, though in an unfavourable position, his valour had won him, of his mastery of the enemy's country, and of how he had reduced Jugurtha, whose glory had been raised so high by the carelessness of Aulus Albinius, to place his hope of safety in a retreat to the deserts.   The Senate, therefore, decreed thanksgivings to the immortal gods for the campaign so happily conducted, and the citizens, who had been alarmed and anxious as to the issue of the war, regained their cheerfulness.   Of Metellus men spoke in the most distinguished terms.

The general now redoubled his efforts for victory and used every means of despatch ; he was cautious, however, nowhere to expose himself to the enemy, and remembered that envy follows close upon reputation.   The more his fame increased the greater was his anxiety, and, after Jugurtha's treacherous attacks,

he no longer scattered his army on plundering expeditions. When corn or fodder were needed certain
cohorts of infantry, together with the whole of the
cavalry, acted as a guard. Part of the army he
led in person, the rest were under Marius, but it
was rather by fire than by rapine that he wasted
the country. The two generals pitched their camps
at no great distance from each other; where
strength was required they united their forces, on
other occasions they kept apart, so as to spread
flight and terror the wider. At this period Jugurtha
was following them along the hills, seeking a suitable
line and position for a fight. Ascertaining what was
to be the route of the enemy, he would destroy the
fodder as well as the springs, of which there was a
scarcity. Showing himself at one time to Metellus,
at another to Marius, he would attack their rear-ranks
and immediately retreat to the hills, to recommence
his threatening demonstrations first in one quarter,
then in another. He neither gave battle nor allowed
the enemy rest, and contented himself with hampering
them in their projects.

The Roman general saw that he was being exhausted by this strategy, and that no offer of battle
was made by the enemy. He determined, therefore,
to besiege a large town named Zama, the key of that
part of the kingdom in which it was situated, thinking
that, as the occasion demanded, Jugurtha would come
to the relief of his subjects in their strait, and that
there would be a battle before the place. The king,
however, was acquainted of this plan by deserters, and
by forced marches outstripped Metellus, exhorted the

inhabitants to defend their walls, reinforced them with a contingent of deserters (the troops who, since they could not play him false, were the most trustworthy of the royal forces), and promised in addition, that in due course he would himself come to their help with his army.

After making these arrangements Jugurtha retired to the most secret recesses he could find. A little while afterwards he learnt that Marius, with a few cohorts, had left the line of march on a mission to Sicca, there to collect corn. This town had been the first to secede from the king after his defeat. He now marched thither by night with his chosen body of horse, and attacked the Romans in the gateway as they were in the act of departure. At the same time he loudly called on the men of Sicca to surround the cohorts in the rear; fortune, he shouted, was giving them the chance of a noble achievement, if they accomplished it, henceforth he should live in fearless enjoyment of his kingdom and they of their freedom. Marius hastened to advance and get clear of the town; had he not done so the whole or a great part of the people of Sicca would assuredly have played him false. With such fickleness do the Numidians behave. As it was, Jugurtha kept his soldiers for a short while in their ranks. As soon as the enemy began to press them harder, they scattered in flight after losing a few of their number.

Marius next arrived before Zama. This town, situated on a plain, was strong rather by art than by nature, was abundantly provided with every requisite, and well supplied both with arms and men. After making such preparations as his circumstances and the nature of the ground allowed, Metellus surrounded the whole extent of the walls with his troops, and assigned to each of his officers his post of command. At a given signal a shout rose simultaneously from every quarter, but without terrifying the Numidians, who stood their ground without confusion, hostile and on the alert. The battle then began. The Romans fought each according to his temper. Some discharged bullets and stones from a distance, others advanced close to the wall and tried now to undermine it, and now to storm it with ladders, showing great anxiety to bring the fight to close quarters. On the other side, the townsmen rolled down stones on their nearest assailants, and flung pointed stakes and javelins, and torchwood dipped in burning pitch and sulphur. Even those who had remained at a distance found but slight protection in their timidity, for many of them were wounded by javelins hurled either from engines or by the hand, and thus brave and cowardly shared the same peril, though with very different renown.

CHAP.
LVII.

While this conflict was raging around Zama, Jugurtha suddenly attacked the enemy's camp with a large force, and burst upon the gate at a time when the garrison had grown careless, and were expecting anything rather than a battle. Astounded by the sudden alarm, our men consulted their safety in such ways as their several characters inclined them; some fled, others seized their arms, while many were by this time wounded or killed. Out of all that host, however, not more than forty took thought for the honour

CHAP.
LVIII.

CHAP.
LVIII.

of Rome. These formed themselves into a body, and seizing a position a little higher than the rest, defied all efforts to dislodge them, hurling back the darts discharged at them from a distance, and, as a few men amid a host, more rarely missing their aim. Whenever the Numidians attacked them at close quarters they displayed prodigies of valour, and slaughtered, scattered, and routed them with the greatest vigour. Meanwhile, Metellus, as he was pressing on the siege with much energy, heard the noise of an attack in his rear. Turning his horse, he observed that the flight was towards himself, which showed the fugitives to be his own soldiers. In all haste he despatched the whole of his cavalry to the camp, followed immediately afterwards by the cohorts of the allies under Gaius Marius, whom, with tears in his eyes, he besought, in the name of their friendship and of the state, not to allow reproach to cleave to their victorious army, nor to permit the enemy to escape unpunished. Marius quickly carried out his orders. Jugurtha found himself entangled in the entrenchments of the camp, and seeing some of his men hurled headlong over the ramparts, and others, in their hurry, blocking each other's way amid the narrow paths, withdrew, with a heavy loss, to his strongholds. Metellus, whose own operations had been unsuccessful, on the arrival of night returned with his army to the camp.

CHAP.
LIX.

The next day, before marching out to the attack, he ordered the whole of the cavalry to patrol before the camp, on the side by which the king had made his approach, and assigned the charge of the different gates and the neighbouring points to the different

tribunes. He then marched up to the town and at- CHAP. LIX.
tacked the wall as on the former day. While he was
so engaged, Jugurtha suddenly dashed upon our men
from an ambush. Those who had been posted nearest
to his point of attack were for the moment frightened
and thrown into confusion ; the rest, however, quickly
came to their aid. The Numidians could now have
no longer stood their ground had not their infantry
mingled with the horsemen made great havoc in the
encounter. In reliance on these, instead of following
the usual cavalry tactics of alternate pursuit and retreat, they charged horse against horse, and entangled
and confused our ranks, and thus, by the help of their
light infantry, almost defeated their enemy. Mean- CHAP. LX.
time the conflict was raging around Zama. The
struggle was fiercest at the several points where a
lieutenant or tribune was in command, and no one
trusted to his neighbour's valour instead of his own.
The townspeople showed no less vigour. At every
point there was assault and preparations to meet it.
On each side men were more eager to wound their
opponents than to defend themselves. Shouts of encouragement, joy, and pain arose to heaven amid the
din of arms, while darts were flying from side to side.
When the enemy for a while slackened in their attack,
the defenders of the wall watched with eagerness the
distant cavalry engagement. As Jugurtha's fortunes
rose and fell you might mark them now rejoicing
and now in fear. As if they could be heard or seen
by their comrades, some shouted warnings, others encouragement, while they beckoned and gesticulated,
and swayed their bodies, as if to avoid or hurl the

darts. Marius, who was in command at this point, marked their behaviour, and feigning despair, purposely slackened the attack, and suffered the Numidians to gaze without disturbance at the king's encounter. As soon as they were strongly engrossed in anxiety for their comrades, he suddenly assaulted the wall with the utmost violence, and his soldiers had already climbed their ladders and almost seized the battlements, when the townspeople rallied and met them with a shower of stones, fire, and other missiles. Our men at first stood their ground; then, as one ladder after another was broken, and those who had stood on them dashed to the ground, the remnant, some whole and sound, but many sorely wounded, made their retreat as best they could. At last night broke off the engagement.

Metellus saw that his attempt was vain. The town was not captured, Jugurtha never gave battle except in surprises or on ground of his own choosing, and the summer was already past. He now retreated from Zama, and, after placing garrisons in such of the towns which had seceded to him as were sufficiently protected by their position or fortifications, led the rest of his army to its station in that part of the province which borders on Numidia. He did not, however, follow the custom of other commanders and surrender that season to repose and luxury, but, since the war was little advanced by force of arms, aimed a secret attack against the king by means of his friends, and prepared to use their treachery instead of arms. The man who, as Jugurtha's greatest friend, had the greatest power of deceiving him, was Bomilcar, the same who had been with him at Rome, and, after giving sureties in the matter of Massiva's death, had fled to escape trial. To this man Metellus now applied with many promises, and induced him as a first step, to visit him secretly for the sake of a conference, and then pledged his word that on his surrendering Jugurtha dead or alive, the Senate would grant him a full pardon and possession of all his goods. These offers easily won over the Numidian, who, besides his natural inclination to treachery, was alarmed lest in the event of peace being concluded with Rome, his own surrender for punishment might be one of the terms of the treaty. On the first favourable occasion, Bomilcar approached Jugurtha at a moment when he was troubled and lamenting his fortunes, and advised and conjured him with tears at last to take thought for himself and his children and the Numidian people who had deserved so well of him. He reminded him that they had been beaten in every battle, their country wasted, many of his subjects made prisoners or killed, and the resources of his kingdom utterly impaired; the courage of his soldiers and the favour of fortune had already been tried sufficiently often; he implored him to be on his guard lest, while he was hesitating, the Numidians should take counsel for themselves. By these and other like arguments, Bomilcar incited the king to surrender, and ambassadors were despatched to the general to announce that Jugurtha was ready to comply with his orders, and offered to surrender himself and his kingdom to his protection without any stipulation. Metellus hastily ordered all persons of senatorial rank to be summoned from their winter

CHAP.
LXI.

CHAP.
LXII.

CHAP.
LXII.

quarters, and held an assembly of these and such other persons as he himself thought fit. According, therefore, to ancient custom, by the decree of his council he sent through the ambassadors his commands to Jugurtha to deliver up two hundred thousand pounds of silver, all his elephants, and a large number of horses and suits of armour. These commands were complied with without delay, and he now ordered that all his deserters should be brought to him in chains. The greater number were delivered to him in obedience to these orders; a few, as soon as the surrender began, had escaped to Mauritania, to king Bocchus. After being thus plundered of arms, men, and money, Jugurtha was summoned in person to Tisidium, there to await further orders. On this he began once more to waver in his resolution, and, in consciousness of his guilt, to fear the punishment he deserved. After wasting many days in hesitation, during which at one moment in disgust at his ill-fortune he thought anything preferable to war, at another he considered how great would be the fall from king to slave, he at last resumed the war, after vainly sacrificing many of his chief means of defence. At Rome the Senate, when consulted as to the disposition of the provinces, had decreed Numidia to Metellus.

CHAP.
LXIII.

About the same time it happened that, as Gaius Marius was invoking the gods in sacrifice, the diviner informed him that there were portents of great and wonderful events, and that he should therefore carry out in reliance on the gods whatever projects he had in his mind; let him try fortune as often as he would, the issue would always be favourable. Even before this, Marius had been tormented with a great desire for the consulship, for attaining which he was, indeed, well endowed with every qualification except that of ancient family. He was energetic, upright, of wide experience in warfare, and immense courage in battle. In domestic life he was frugal, unconquered by lust and riches, and only covetous of glory.

The birthplace of Marius was Arpinum, and there he spent his boyhood. As soon as he was of an age for military service, he practised himself not in Greek oratory or in elegant accomplishments, but in campaigning; and thus amid honourable pursuits his character quickly developed, unimpaired. On his seeking election as a military tribune few people even knew him by sight, but the fame of his exploits procured his return by every tribe. Beginning with this, he won successive magistracies, and always so conducted himself in office as to be esteemed worthy of a more important post than the one he held. Such was the quality he had shown hitherto (for afterwards his thirst for popularity worked his ruin), and yet he did not dare to stand for the consulship. Even as late as this the commons had entrance to other magistracies, but the consulship was preserved by the nobility as the hereditary possession of their order. No self-made man was so distinguished or had performed such noble deeds as to be held worthy of that office, or other than unclean.

When Marius saw that the words of the diviner pointed in the same direction as his own desires were spurring him, he asked leave of absence from Metellus,

CHAP. LXIII.

CHAP. LXIV.

in order to stand as a candidate. Metellus was eminently endowed with courage, renown, and much else that good men might desire ; he had, however, that evil so common with men of rank, a scornful and haughty temper. At first, astonished by so unusual an occurrence, he expressed his surprise at Marius' project, and advised him, with an appearance of friendship, not to enter upon so improper a course, nor to cherish thoughts above his fortunes ; it was not everything, he said, that all men were free to desire ; Marius ought to be content with his position, and, in fine, should be careful not to demand from the Roman people a favour which they would rightly deny him. Finding that these and other arguments did not change Marius' resolution, Metellus answered him with a promise to do what he asked, as soon as the public business would allow. When, however, the request was subsequently repeated with some frequency, he is said to have remarked that Marius should be in no hurry to depart, as it would be time enough for him to stand for the consulship in the same year as his own son, a youth of about twenty, who was serving at the time in the war and sharing his father's tent. This remark, as was afterwards seen, strongly excited Marius to efforts to gain the office to which he aspired, and to enmity towards Metellus. He set to work under the influence of ambition and anger, those worst of counsellors, and refrained from no act or speech that might gain him popularity. He treated the soldiers whom he commanded in the winter quarters with more indulgence than before ; and, at the same time, spread slanderous and boastful insinuations about the war among the

traders, of whom there were many at Attica. Were but
the half of the army, he said, entrusted to him, in
a few days he would have Jugurtha in chains: the
general was purposely procrastinating war in the
excessive delight which a frivolous man of regal
haughtiness took in authority. These insinuations
seemed to the traders all the better grounded, inasmuch as the length of the war had impaired their
fortunes, and to the eager mind no haste is sufficient. There was, moreover, in our army a Numidian
named Gauda, a son of Mastanabal and grandson of
Massinissa, whom Micipsa, when spent with disease,
and with his mental powers thus somewhat impaired,
had appointed in his will as his second heir. Gauda
had requested Metellus to assign him, as a prince, a
seat next his own, and, again, on a subsequent occasion, to grant him a squadron of Roman cavalry as a
bodyguard. Both of these requests Metellus refused—
the seat of honour, because, by custom it belonged only
to those whom the Roman people recognised as kings;
the guard, inasmuch as it would be an insult to Roman
cavalry to consign them as attendants to a Numidian.
Marius made advances to Gauda in his trouble, and
encouraged him to try, with his help, to avenge himself
on the general for these insults. Inflating with fair
speeches a mind which diseases had enfeebled, he
represented to Gauda that he was a king, an important
person, and the grandson of Massinissa; should Jugurtha be captured or slain, he would have immediate
possession of the kingdom of Numidia, and this
might quickly be brought to pass, if he himself were
despatched as consul to direct the war. In this way,

CHAP.
LXV.

not only Gauda but the Roman knights, the soldiers, and traders, were incited, some by Marius personally, many by the hope of peace, to speak bitterly of Metellus' conduct of the war in their letters to their connections at Rome, and to ask for Marius as general. It thus came to pass that many persons sought to gain the consulship for him with the most honourable recommendations, while, just at this period, the commons, after routing the nobility by the Mamilian law, were supporting men of no birth as candidates; thus everything combined to favour Marius.

CHAP.
LXVI.

In the meantime Jugurtha, after breaking off his surrender and renewing the war, was zealously making all possible preparations, showing great activity, and collecting an army. He tried by threats and by holding out rewards to gain over the cities which had deserted him, fortified his own positions, replaced by manufacture or purchase the armour, weapons, and other material which he had sacrificed in the hope of peace; attracted bodies of Roman slaves, and with his money tampered even with the Roman garrisons. In a word, he left nothing untried, no stone unturned, but adopted every possible expedient. When Jugurtha had first opened negotiations for peace, Metellus had imposed a garrison on the town of Vaga. At the importunate entreaty of the king, to whom, at heart, the inhabitants had never been disloyal, the chief citizens now formed a conspiracy. As for the common people, they, as usual, especially with Numidians, were of an inconstant temper, rebellious, and full of discord, eager for change, the enemies of peace and quietness. Arranging their plans among themselves, they agreed to carry them out on the third day, which was one observed as a festival throughout all Africa, and promised rather sport and wantonness than alarm. When the time arrived the centurions, military tribunes, and the governor of the town, Titus Turpilius Silanus, himself, were invited by different citizens to their homes, and all, with the exception of Turpilius, massacred in the course of the banquet. The conspirators then attacked the soldiers who were wandering about unarmed as was natural on such a day, and in the absence of their officers. The common people followed their example, some instructed by the nobles, others urged only by their zeal for such work; these were ignorant of what had been done and the purpose of it, but found in the mere rioting and revolution enough to content them. The Roman soldiers, baffled by so unexpected an alarm, and not knowing what best to do, fell into confusion. A force of the enemy barred their path to the citadel, where their standards and shields were deposited ; the gates, previously closed, prevented their flight, and the women and children standing on the edge of the roofs zealously hurled at them stones and such other missiles as were at hand. Against so baffling a danger no precautions could be taken, and the bravest soldiers could make no resistance to these weakest of opponents. Good and bad, stout and cowardly were alike massacred unavenged. Amid these outrages, when the cruelty of the Numidians was at its height and every gate shut, the governor, Turpilius, was the single Italian who escaped unharmed. Whether this was the result of his host's compassion, of a bargain, or of chance, I cannot assure

N

CHAP.
LXVI.

CHAP.
LXVII.

CHAP.
LXVII. myself. Inasmuch, however, as in such a calamity he preferred a shameful life to unspotted honour, he seems to have been a worthless and execrable character.

CHAP.
LXVIII. Metellus, on receiving news of the event at Vaga, for a short while retired in sorrow from the public gaze. As soon as anger began to mingle with his grief, he hastened with the utmost zeal to avenge the wrong. Exactly at sunset he led out the legions with which he was in winter quarters, and as many Numidian horsemen as he could muster, lightly equipped. About the third hour of the next day he arrived at a plain surrounded on all sides by somewhat higher ground. His soldiers, tired with their long march, were inclined to be mutinous, when Metellus laid the matter before them, told them that Vaga was not more than a mile distant, and that they ought cheerfully to submit to the rest of their toil so long as they could avenge their fellow citizens, those bravest and most unfortunate of men. In addition, he generously promised them the booty. After thus raising their spirits, he ordered the cavalry to go in front in skirmishing order, and the infantry to follow with their ranks as close as possible, and their ensigns concealed. The

CHAP.
LXIX. people of Vaga, on perceiving that an army was marching in their direction, at first conjectured rightly that it was Metellus, and closed their gates. When, however, they noticed that their lands were not being wasted, and that the van was composed of Numidian cavalry, they changed their minds, and, thinking it was Jugurtha who was coming, went forth to meet him with great rejoicing. Suddenly, part of the

cavalry and infantry at a given signal cut to pieces
the crowd which had poured out of the town, while
others hurried to the gates, and others seized the
towers ; rage and the hope of plunder overcame
their weariness. The men of Vaga rejoiced in their
treachery for only two days ; the whole of that great
and wealthy city was now given over to vengeance
and plunder. Turpilius, the governor of the town, who,
as explained above, was the only man who escaped
the massacre, was ordered by Metellus to stand his
trial. He excused his conduct but lamely, was condemned and, as a Latin citizen, punished by scourging
and decapitation.

About the same time Bomilcar, at whose instigation
Jugurtha had begun the surrender which he afterwards
abandoned through fear, having incurred the king's
suspicion, and being suspected by him in turn, was now
desirous of a change of affairs. After wearying his
mind day and night in seeking some plot to work
Jugurtha's destruction, he at last, in the course of his
innumerable efforts, took to himself as an accomplice
a noble named Nabdalsa, (a man of great wealth,
and beloved and esteemed by his countrymen,) who
generally held an independent command, and carried
out all tasks which Jugurtha, either from weariness or
from attention to weightier matters, had left unfulfilled.
In this way he had acquired both renown and wealth.
By agreement between the two conspirators, a day was
fixed for their treachery; everything else they thought
best to arrange at the moment, as occasion might demand. Nabdalsa set out for his army, which, according to his orders, he was keeping between the outer

CHAP.
LXX.
stations of the Romans, to prevent the enemy from ravaging the country with impunity. Confounded by the greatness of the crime, he did not appear at the time agreed on, and his cowardice prevented the execution of the plot. Bomilcar was eager to carry out his designs, but at the same time was disconcerted by the timidity of his accomplice. Fearful lest, now that Nabdalsa had abandoned his original plan, he might form some new one, he despatched a letter to him by trusty messengers. In this letter, after reproaching him for his lack of resolution and energy, and calling to witness the gods by whom he had sworn, he warned him not to turn the bribes of Metellus to his destruction, and showed that Jugurtha's ruin was near at hand, and that the only question was whether he should perish by their courage or by that of Metellus: Nabdalsa should consider, therefore, whether

CHAP.
LXXI.
he preferred rewards or a miserable death. When this letter was delivered, Nabdalsa happened to be fatigued, and was resting on a couch. After acquainting himself with the message of Bomilcar, at first anxiety, and then, as often happens, sleep took possession of his troubled spirit. In his service was a certain Numidian who took charge of his affairs, much trusted and esteemed by him, and the sharer in all but this latest of his designs. Hearing that a letter had been brought, and custom making him think that his own help and ability would be needed, this man now entered the tent, took the letter while his master slept, as it lay carelessly on a cushion above his head, read it through, and, learning the treachery intended, hastened to the king. Shortly afterwards Nabdalsa

awoke, and, on failing to find the letter, understood exactly what had happened. At first he tried to overtake his betrayer, then, finding the attempt fruitless, he approached Jugurtha with the object of appeasing him, declared that the treachery of his retainer had anticipated the step which he had himself determined to take, and tearfully besought him by their friendship, and by the proofs which he had hitherto given of his loyalty, not to suspect him of such an enormity. Dissembling his real feelings, the king returned him a mild answer. After putting to death Bomilcar, and many others whom he discovered to have shared in his treachery, he seems to have stifled his anger for fear lest the matter might give rise to a rebellion. From that time no day or night brought peace to Jugurtha; he never trusted place, man, or season, feared his countrymen no less than the enemy, pried into every corner, and was terrified at every sound. At night he rested sometimes at one place, sometimes at another, often where it little fitted his royal dignity, and now and again, on waking from sleep, would seize his arms and raise an outcry; so tormented was he by a terror which verged on madness.

On hearing from deserters of the fate of Bomilcar, and the betrayal of the plot, Metellus once more made every preparation, and hastened to renew the war. Marius was wearying him as to his departure, and was, at the same time, hateful and hostile to him personally; thinking him, therefore, an unsatisfactory lieutenant, he dismissed him home.

At Rome, the commons, on learning the purport of the letters which had been despatched on the subject

CHAP.
LXXIII.

of Metellus and Marius, had very readily believed the characters respectively assigned them. The noble birth which had hitherto been an honour to the general now made him unpopular, while humble descent brought his rival into favour. In each case men's judgment was guided rather by party spirit than by the good or bad qualities of these two officers. Turbulent magistrates, moreover, excited the crowd, impeached Metellus at every public meeting, and exaggerated the merit of Marius. At last the commons were so aroused that all the artisans and country people, whose fortunes and credit lay only in their hands, abandoned their work to attend on Marius, and thus postponed their own necessities to his dignity. The nobility were defeated, and the consulship after many years was entrusted to a man of no birth. Later on, the tribune of the commons, Titus Manlius Mancinus, demanded of the people whom they wished to conduct the war with Jugurtha, and in a full assembly the people ordered that Marius should have the command. I should mention that, a little before this, the Senate had decreed that Gaul should be his province ; but this measure was useless.

CHAP.
LXXIV.

At the same time, Jugurtha, who had lost his friends, many of whom he had himself put to death, while of the rest, some in their terror had escaped to the Romans, others to king Bocchus, now found that it was impossible to carry on the war without lieutenants. Amid such treachery, however, on the part of his old officers he thought it dangerous to try the loyalty of new ones, and was changeable and uncertain in his plans. Discontented with every man, measure, and counsel, he changed his route and his officers from day to day; marched now against the enemy, and now into desert places, often rested his hopes in flight, and then, a moment afterwards, in arms. He doubted whether he could trust the courage or the loyalty of his countrymen the less, and thus, to whatever quarter he turned, found everything opposed to him. While he was in this state of inactivity, Metellus suddenly appeared at the head of an army, and Jugurtha equipped and marshalled the Numidians as well as time would allow; and the battle then began. In the quarter where the king was taking part in the fight the conflict lasted some time; the rest of his troops were all driven back and routed at the first charge. The Romans captured a considerable quantity of standards and arms, but only a few prisoners, for in all their battles the Numidians, as a rule, are protected rather by their feet than their swords.

By this defeat, Jugurtha was led to still deeper distrust of his fortunes. Taking with him the deserters and a part of his cavalry, he made his way to the wastes, and thence to Thala, a large and wealthy town where he had great treasures, and where his sons were passing their boyhood amid much splendour. When Metellus discovered this movement, although he knew that between Thala and the nearest river there lay fifty miles of parched and barren desert, yet in the hope that by gaining possession of the town he might put an end to the war, he applied himself to surmount every difficulty, and conquer even nature herself. He ordered all the beasts of burden to be relieved of their packs, with the exception of provisions for ten days,

CHAP.
LXXV. and that only skins and other vessels suitable for holding water should be carried. He collected also from the fields as many trained oxen as he could, and on these placed vessels of every description, but mostly wooden, which he had got together from the huts of the Numidians. He then ordered the men of the neighbourhood (who, after the king's defeat, had made submission to Metellus) to bring, each of them, as much water as he could, and announced the day and place for them to appear. He himself loaded his beasts from the river, which, as I mentioned above, was the nearest water to the town; and, thus equipped, set out for Thala. On arriving at the place where he had enjoined the Numidians to meet him, the camp was hardly pitched and fortified when suddenly so much rain is said to have fallen from the heavens that this alone provided the army with water enough and to spare. Their supplies, too, surpassed their expectation, for the Numidians, like most newly-submitted peoples, had exceeded the services required of them. The soldiers, however, from a religious feeling, preferred to use the rain water, and its fall added greatly to their courage by making them think themselves under the protection of the immortal gods. On the next day, to the surprise of Jugurtha, they made their way to Thala. The inhabitants, who had deemed themselves protected by the difficulties of the country, were astounded by so great and unusual a feat. They prepared, however, for the conflict with undaunted

CHAP.
LXXVI. energy, and our men did the same. The king now believed that nothing was impossible to Metellus, whose energy he had seen overcome all things—arms and weapons, situations, and seasons, and even nature CHAP. LXXVI. herself, who ruled all other men. He, therefore, made his escape from the town by night, taking with him his children, and a great part of his money. Henceforth, he never abode in any place for longer than a single day or night, pretending that he was hurried away by business, but really from fear of treachery. This he thought he might avoid by the quickness of his movements, as such designs require leisure and a favourable occasion for their achievement. To return to Metellus; on seeing that the townspeople were ready for battle, and, at the same time, that the town was protected both by its works and its situation, he surrounded the walls with a rampart and ditch. He then pushed forward mantlets at the most suitable points that offered, threw up a mound, and by erecting towers on it protected his work and his helpers. To meet these measures the townspeople were active in their preparations; nothing, in fine, on either side was left undone. At last the Romans, wearied by much previous toil, and by the battles they had fought, on the fortieth day after their arrival gained possession of the town, and that alone; all the booty had been destroyed by the deserters. These, on seeing that rams were battering the wall, and that their fortunes were ruined, brought the gold, silver, and whatever else was of highest value, to the royal palace. There they ladened themselves with wine and the banquet, and then destroyed the booty, the house, and their own lives, by fire ; they thus voluntarily paid the very penalty which they had feared to receive from their enemies in case of defeat.

CHAP.
LXXVII. Simultaneously with the capture of Thala, deputies had come to Metellus from the town of Leptis, beseeching him to send thither a garrison and governor. According to their account, a certain Hamilcar, a man of good birth and intriguing disposition, was eager for a change in affairs, and the commands of the magistrates and the authority of the law were powerless against him ; should Metellus delay, their safety, allies of Rome as they were, would be in the greatest danger. The people of Leptis, I should mention, long before this, at the very beginning of the [Jugurthine] war, had sent to the consul Bestia, and subsequently to Rome itself, to request friendship and alliance. On obtaining their prayer, they remained ever honest and loyal, and had strenuously carried out all the commands of Bestia, Albinus, and Metellus. The general, therefore, readily granted their petition, and sent to their town four cohorts of Ligurians, and Gaius Annius as governor.

CHAP.
LXXVIII. Leptis was founded by Sidonians who, as I learn, were exiled on account of internal dissensions, and came to these parts by sea. It is situated between the two Syrtes, whose name was given them from their nature. These are two bays which lie almost on the verge of Africa, of unequal size but like character. Near land they are very deep; elsewhere, as it chances, in some places deep, in others, when a storm is blowing, full of shoals. When the sea gets high and struggles with the wind, the waves draw down mud, sand, and huge stones ; and thus the appearance of these parts changes with every change of the wind. It is this power of suction from which they are called

Syrtes. Intermarriage with the Numidians changed nothing more than the language of the people of Leptis; the greater part of their laws and civilization is Sidonian, and this they have the more easily retained owing to their distance from the king's government, for between them and the more populous part of Numidia lay many miles of desert.

As the affairs of the people of Leptis have taken me into these regions, it seems not unbecoming to record a splendid and memorable deed of two Carthaginians, of which the mention of the country has reminded me. In the period when the Carthaginians were rulers over the greater part of Africa, Cyrene also was a great and wealthy city. The intervening country was sandy and monotonous, without river or mountain to mark the boundary of their dominions. This fact kept them in a desperate and prolonged war; armies and fleets had often been defeated and routed on either side, and each had considerably impaired the other's strength. At last, in the fear lest some third power should presently attack both victors and vanquished in their exhausted condition, they agreed in a time of truce that on an appointed day deputies should set out from either city, and the place where they met be held the common boundary of the two peoples. Two brothers, called the Philaeni, were sent from Carthage, and these made good speed in their journey. The progress of the Cyrenians was slower, whether through laziness or accident I have not clearly ascertained; for in these parts, storms are as wont to delay the traveller as on the sea. Gathering as it sweeps across the flat and lifeless country, the wind tosses up the sand from the soil, and this is then blown along with tremendous force, and fills the face and eyes, and hinders progress by shutting off all view. The Cyrenians saw that they were somewhat behindhand, and, in their fear of being punished on their return for their failure, accused the Carthaginians of having left home before their time, tried to upset the whole proceedings, and, in fact, shewed a determination to do anything rather than come off the worst. The Carthaginians then asked them to propose any other terms so long as they were fair, and on this the Greeks gave them their choice of either being themselves buried alive at the point where they demanded that their country's boundary should be set, or allowing them to advance as far as they like on the same condition. The Philaeni approved of the terms, and sacrificed their own persons and lives to the public good. Accordingly they were buried alive. The Carthaginians dedicated altars to the brothers on the spot, and other honours were ordained to them in the city. I now return to my subject.

 After the loss of Thala, Jugurtha thought he had no sufficient safeguard against Metellus. He set out, therefore, with a few companions, and made his way through vast deserts to the Gaetulians, a wild and uncivilized tribe, at that time ignorant of the name of Rome. Of this people he collected a host, and in a short time accustomed them to keep the ranks, follow the standards, obey commands, and behave in other respects like regular soldiers. Besides this, by means of great gifts and greater promises, he prevailed on those immediately about King Bocchus to be zealous in his

service, and, with these to aid him, approached the
king and induced him to take up arms against the
Romans. This task was the more easily and readily
accomplished, inasmuch as Bocchus, at the outset of
this war, had sent an embassy to Rome to ask for a
treaty of friendship. The conclusion of such a treaty,
which would have been most advantageous for the war
then newly begun, was prevented by the blind avarice
of a clique accustomed to sell every service, whether
honourable or the reverse. Bocchus, moreover, had
previously married a daughter of Jugurtha, though
this tie is held of slight importance among Numidians
and Mauritanians, inasmuch as every one has as many
wives as he can afford, some ten, some more, and the
kings a proportionately greater number. The mind is
thus distracted by numbers; no wife holds the place
of a partner, but all are held equally cheap. The two
kings now assembled their armies at a place they had
agreed on. Pledges were there given and received,
and Jugurtha roused the spirit of Bocchus by an
harangue. The Romans, he said, were unjust, of
fathomless greed, and the common enemy of all
peoples; they had the same reason for a war with
Bocchus as with himself and other races—their lust,
namely, for empire, which made them see an enemy
in every kingdom; it was now himself who was the
Roman's foe, a little before it had been the Carthaginians, then King Perses, and thereafter it would
always be the richest victim they could find. After
these and similar speeches, they determined on a
march against the town of Cirta, as the place where
Metellus had deposited his spoil, captives, and heavy

CHAP.
LXXXI. baggage. Jugurtha thought that they would either be rewarded by the capture of the town, or that, should the Romans advance to its relief, a battle would be fought. In his crafty policy, the only thing for which he was eager was to lessen Bocchus' chance of peace, lest, if there should be any procrastination, he might prefer some other course to war.

CHAP.
LXXXII. On learning of the alliance between the kings, the general no longer offered battle rashly, or, as after his many defeats of Jugurtha, he had been wont to do, in every position. He awaited the two kings in a fortified camp not far from Cirta, thinking it would be better to fight at his convenience after learning the quality of the Mauritanians, since they had joined in the war as a new enemy.

Meanwhile he was informed by despatches from Rome that his province had been assigned to Marius, the news of whose election to the consulship he had received previously. These events affected him more than was either right or honourable; he could neither restrain his tears nor govern his tongue. Though distinguished in other accomplishments, he bore vexation in too womanish a manner. Some construed his behaviour as a mark of pride; others as the outcome of a noble spirit inflamed by insult; many, again, as caused by the feeling that the victory he had practically won was being wrested from his hands. For myself, I am assured that it was rather the honour conferred upon Marius than his own wrongs which tormented him, and that he would have borne the blow more equably if the province of which he was deprived had been assigned to any other than Marius.

Burdened by this grief, and thinking it foolish to charge himself with another man's work to his own peril, Metellus sent ambassadors to Bocchus to desire him not to become an enemy to the Roman people without a cause. They were to urge that the king had at this time an opportunity of cementing a friendship and alliance; that this was far preferable to war, and that, despite his confidence in his resources, it was unwise to exchange the certain for the doubtful; every war was easy to enter on, most difficult to abandon; to begin and to end it were not in the power of the same person; even a coward might do the first, the time for the second was fixed by the victor's will; Bocchus, therefore, should take thought for himself and his kingdom, and should be careful not to involve his own prosperity in the ruined fortunes of Jugurtha. To this message the king returned a conciliatory answer, to the effect that he was desirous of peace, but pitied the misfortunes of Jugurtha. If the same opportunity were given to the latter, a treaty was assured. The general sent fresh messengers in reply to the proposals of Bocchus, who accepted some of his terms, and declined others. In this manner the time passed in the frequent interchange of messages, and the war, as Metellus wished, was prolonged without activity on either side.

As I narrated above, Marius, to the great delight of the commons, had been elected consul. Previously hostile to the nobility, after his appointment by the people to the province of Numidia, he attacked them with even greater vigour and spirit, railing, now at individuals, and now at the whole body, boasting that he had won the consulship as his spoil after their defeat, and in other ways exalting himself and annoying them. Meanwhile, he attached most importance to the necessary provision for the war, demanded that the strength of his legions should be raised, and summoned reinforcements from the tributary peoples and kings, and from the allies. He invited, moreover, all the bravest men from Latium, with most of whom he had been acquainted in the field, while a few he knew by report. His solicitations also constrained veterans who had served their time to set out under his command. The Senate, though hostile to him, did not dare to deny him on any point. The reinforcements it had voted with actual pleasure, under the idea that military service was distasteful to the commons, and that Marius would lose either the requisites of war or the favour of the crowd. This hope, however, was vain, so great a desire for accompanying Marius had seized men's minds. Everyone thought that he would be enriched with booty and return home victorious, and pondered over other like ideas in his mind. They had been, moreover, not a little excited by a speech of Marius; who, after all his demands had been voted, and his desire was now to enlist soldiers, summoned a meeting of the people, in order to encourage them and at the same time to indulge in his usual invective against the nobility. His speech was as follows :—

"I am aware, Romans, that the qualities which most men show in their behaviour after election are very different from those with which they sought your suffrages; and that the energetic, humble, and un-

ambitious character of their previous life is then
changed for sloth and insolence. My views, however,
are very different from theirs ; for in proportion as the
state as a whole exceeds the consulship or praetorship
in importance, by so much ought our diligence in its
government to exceed that with which we seek these
offices. I am not insensible to the greatness of the
burden which, by your distinguished favour, I have to
bear. To prepare for war without straining the treasury, to press into service men whom one is unwilling
to offend, to superintend every detail at home and
abroad, and to do all this amid the jealousy of hostile
intriguers, is harder, Romans, than can be conceived.
Again, if others commit an error, their ancient family,
the brave deeds of their ancestors, the wealth of their
kinsmen and connections, and troops of clients are all
at hand to defend them. I have to place my whole
hopes in my own person : I must needs protect them
by my merit and integrity, for I have no other help in
which I can trust. I understand, too, Romans, that
the eyes of all men are upon me, and that, while,
inasmuch as my services advance the state, fair and
honest men are in my favour, the nobility are seeking
some point of attack. I must, therefore, strive with
the greater energy both that you may not be deceived
in me, and that your enemies may be disappointed.
My life, from boyhood to the present day, has been
such as to make me familiar with every toil and
danger ; nor, Romans, do I intend, now that I have
received my reward, to abandon the course of conduct
which, previously to your kindness, I voluntarily
pursued. Men who, in their desire for popularity,

O

have assumed the mask of virtue, find it hard to restrain themselves when in power; I, who have passed my whole life in the most honourable pursuits, now find that uprightness has passed from habit into nature.

"You have commanded me to conduct the war with Jugurtha, and at this the nobility have taken deep offence. Consider, I pray you, whether it would be a change for the better were you to despatch either on this or on any like commission, some member of that ring of nobles, some scion of an ancient house who could boast of the effigies of his many ancestors, but of never a campaign; and allow him on an affair of this importance, to hurry and bustle about in his utter ignorance and take some man of the people to instruct him in his duty. For, I assure you, it is nothing uncommon for the man to whom you have given command to look to some other for his orders. I myself, Romans, have known cases of consuls who, after their election, have begun to read the old chronicles and the Greek manuals of warfare; men, these, who begin at the wrong end, for though the conduct of wars follows the appointment to them in order of time, in the order of nature and experience it precedes it. With these proud ones, Romans, compare me, the self-made man. The things of which they are wont to hear or read, I have either seen or have myself performed; and the knowledge which they get from books, I have acquired by active service. I leave it to you to consider whether deeds or maxims are the more important. They despise my lack of family; I their cowardice. In my teeth men cast my fortune ; in theirs, their infamous deeds. For my own part I think that all men have one common nature, and that it is the bravest who are the noblest. If to the fathers of Albinus or Bestia the question could now be put whether they would prefer me or them as their descendants, what other answer think you they would return than that they wished to have the best for their children? Again, if these men are right in despising me, let them do the same to their ancestors, whose nobility, like my own, sprang from their merit. They are jealous of the dignity conferred on me ; why are they not jealous of my energy, my integrity, yes, and of my dangers, since it is by these that I have gained it? Rotten with pride, they pass their days, as if they despised the 'dignities you can confer ; yet they demand them with the air of men who have lived an honourable life. Surely they are deceived who thus hope to unite the two things of all others the most opposed—the pleasure, namely, of sloth and the rewards of merit. Again, in their speeches before yourselves or the Senate, the greater part of their harangue is a eulogy of their ancestors ; for they think by dwelling on their brave deeds to increase their own reputation. Yet the very reverse often is the result, for the nobler the life of their ancestors, the more shameful is their own sloth. Indeed, the glory of forefathers is really to their descendants as a burning light, which allows neither their good deeds nor their bad to remain unnoticed. I confess, Romans, I have nothing of this kind, but I have something which is far nobler, the power, namely, to tell of doings of my own. See, then, the unfairness of these men. The privileges which they claim for themselves in right of another's merit, they do not allow me in right of my own, and this because I have no effigies of ancestors to show, and because the nobility I have is a thing of to-day. Yet surely to have won nobility is better than to have received and shamed it.

"I am aware that my enemies, should they wish to answer, will be at no loss for an eloquent and studied reply. Now, however, that I am so favoured by you, they attack me on every occasion ; and I have, therefore, chosen not to remain silent, lest my self-restraint should be mistaken for a consciousness of guilt. For myself, indeed—I say it from my heart—no speech can hurt me ; truth can speak no otherwise than favourably ; falsehood is foiled by the evidence of my life and character. They impugn, however, your policy in assigning me so high an office and so weighty a task ; and, so, I ask you again and again to consider whether you ought really to repent it. To inspire your trust I have no statues, triumphs, or consulships, of my ancestors, to which to point ; but, if need be, I can show spears, a standard, medals, and other prizes soldiers earn, and scars dealt full upon my breast. These are my statues, these my title to nobility, and one which was not left me as a bequest, as in the case of my enemies, but which I won for myself by my many toils and dangers. My words have no studied grace ; of that I think little ; merit needs no help to display it, though my enemies must use their tricks of rhetoric to conceal their base deeds behind a mass of words. Again, I have learnt no Greek ; I was not anxious to gain a knowledge which had done nothing to help its teachers in the pursuit of virtue. In the knowledge, however, which is far the most important for the state, I am a master. To strike the foe, to keep good watch, to fear nothing save disgrace, to bear heat and cold with equal patience, to make my bed on the ground, to undergo toil and hunger together, all this I know, and with this teaching I shall exhort my soldiers. Nor will I treat them with stringency, myself with indulgence, nor claim the glory and leave them the toil. To refrain from such conduct is to rule with efficiency and moderation. To live in luxury yourself while you coerce your army by punishments is to act the tyrant, not the general. By such conduct as I have praised your ancestors won renown for themselves and the state. In reliance on their glory a nobility, their very opposite in character, now scorns us who emulate these men of old, and claims of you every post of honour, not for any service rendered, but simply as its due. Truly these arrogant nobles make a deep mistake. Their ancestors left them everything that could be left—wealth, pedigree, and their own glorious memory. Their merit they did not, and could not bequeath them ; that alone is neither given nor received. They call me mean and unpolished, because I am no adept at tricking out a feast, keep no actor, no cook more highly paid than my bailiff. Romans, I am proud to confess such conduct. The lesson I learnt from my father and other pious men was that graces befitted a woman, toil a man, and that the good should be always richer in glory than in wealth ; arms, not ornaments, are the true honours. Let the nobles, then, continue to follow the course they delight in and prize ;

let them live and drink; in the scenes of rivalry where they spent their youth there let them pass their old age, the slaves of their belly and their lust; and the sweat and dust, and the like, let them leave to us who find more joy in them than in the feast. But this they will not do. When they have disgraced themselves with every crime, these vilest of men come to seize the prizes of the good. In defiance of all justice, those outrageous vices, luxury and sloth, are no obstacle to the men who practise them, while they are the destruction of the guiltless state.

"I have answered my enemies with a brevity which suits my own character better than such a theme as their misconduct; I will now say a few words on public affairs. In the first place, Romans, be of good heart as regards Numidia. Hitherto Jugurtha has been protected by the avarice, unskilfulness, and arrogance of your generals, and all these you have now removed. In the second place, you have an army there, acquainted with the country, but, I profess, more vigorous than fortunate; for a great part of it has been wasted away by the corruption or rashness of your commanders. I ask such of you, therefore, as are of military age to join your efforts with mine, and protect the state. Let no one take alarm from the misfortunes of others, or from the arrogance of generals. I shall be with you in person on the march, and in the field, at once to consult your interests and to share your dangers; I shall treat you in all respects the same as myself; and with the help of the gods, victory, booty, renown, are all ready to our hand. Even were they doubtful or distant, it would yet be the duty of every honest man to support the state. Cowardice never yet gained a man immortality, nor has any parent yet asked for his children that they might exist for ever; they ask that they may live out their life in uprightness and honour. Romans, I would say more, could words inspire the timid with courage ; for the brave man I think I have said fully enough."

After a speech of this kind, Marius, when he saw the enthusiasm of the commons aroused, hastily loaded ships with provision, pay, arms, and other requisites, and ordered his lieutenant, Aulus Manlius, to set out in charge of them. Meanwhile he himself levied soldiers, not, according to ancient custom, from the classes, but simply as they volunteered, and, for the most part, men of no fortune. Some asserted that this course was taken owing to the scarcity of respectable recruits, others traced it to the consul's desire for popularity, inasmuch as it was by men of this description that his renown and dignity had been given him, while the seeker for power ever finds his readiest instrument in the needy wretch, who, in his destitution, has no home to hold dear, and thinks everything honourable that brings him gain.

Marius, therefore, set out for Africa with a force slightly in excess of that decreed him, and after a few days landed at Utica. The army was delivered to him by Publius Rutilius, the lieutenant of Metellus; for the general himself had avoided the sight of Marius, lest he should see the things of which his resolution had been unable to support the mere hearing.

With his legions and auxiliary cohorts at their full

CHAP.
LXXXV.

CHAP.
LXXXVI.

CHAP.
LXXXVII.

CHAP.
LXXXVII. strength, the consul marched upon a fertile district, well stocked with booty. He gave the whole of the plunder there taken to his soldiers, and then attacked some fortresses and towns which were neither well situated, nor manned for defence; he also fought many petty engagements at various points. Meanwhile his raw soldiers joined in battle without alarm, and saw that the runaways were either captured or killed, that the bravest man was the safest, and that the power of protecting his freedom, country, parents, and every other blessing, and of winning glory and wealth, all lay in a man's arms. In this way, recruits and veterans were soon welded together, and all became equally courageous.

On learning of the arrival of Marius, the kings separated, and made their way to inaccessible districts. Jugurtha had determined on this course in the hope that it might be possible to attack the enemy in detail, and that the Romans, like most other soldiers, when relieved of alarm, would grow careless and disorderly.

CHAP.
LXXXVIII. Meanwhile, Metellus had started for Rome, and was there, contrary to his expectation, received with the utmost rejoicing. Now that his unpopularity had faded away, he was equally beloved by the commons and the Senate.

Marius now gave his mind with energy and foresight to the position alike of his own and the enemy's army, ascertained their respective advantages and drawbacks, set spies to watch the movements of the kings, forestalled their plans and treacheries, and left nothing unlooked to on his own side, or unmenaced on theirs. He had thus often attacked and routed on their march both the Gaetulians and Jugurtha, as they tried to plunder our allies ; and, not far from Cirta, had stripped the king himself of his arms. Finding, however, that these exploits served rather to gain glory than to finish the war, he determined to invest, one after another, the cities which from their garrison or situation were most adapted for helping the enemy and injuring himself; Jugurtha would thus be deprived of his strongholds should he not interfere, or, if he did, would have to fight a battle. As for Bocchus, that king had sent numerous embassies to him, expressing his desire for the friendship of the Roman people, and assuring him that he need fear no attack from his quarter. Whether in this he was feigning in order to make an assault the more dangerous because unexpected, or whether it was an outcome of the fickle character which made him love to be now at peace, and now at war, has not been ascertained. The consul carried out his plan, and by marching on the fortified towns and strongholds wrested them from the enemy, in some cases by force, in others by threats or promise of reward. At first he confined himself to insignificant ventures, thinking that Jugurtha would give battle in defence of his subjects. When he learned that the king was far away and engaged on other business, it seemed time to attempt greater and more difficult undertakings.

In the midst of vast deserts there lay a strong and important town, named Capsa, founded, so tradition said, by the Libyan Hercules. Jugurtha had exempted its citizens from tribute ; his yoke was light, and they were, therefore, the most loyal of his

CHAP. LXXXIX.

subjects. Against their enemies they were protected by walls, arms, and men, and, above all, by their inaccessible position. With the exception of the immediate neighbourhood, the whole country was desolate, untilled, without streams, and made unsafe by serpents, which, like all savage creatures, become more dangerous by lack of food, while their nature, of itself a deadly one, is more quickened by thirst than by anything else. A great desire of mastering this place had seized Marius. It would be useful for the war, and at the same time the exploit appeared difficult, and Metellus, with great glory to himself, had taken the town of Thala, whose position and fortifications were very like those of Capsa, except that at Thala there were some springs not far from the walls, while the people of Capsa had only a single fount of running water, and that within the town ; the rest of their supply came from rain. This inconvenience, both at Capsa and in all parts of Africa where men lived amid deserts far from the sea, was the more easily borne owing to the Numidian habit of feeding chiefly on milk and game, while they avoid salt and other stimulants of the palate. Food is to them the antidote of hunger and thirst, not an object

CHAP. XC.

of passionate extravagance. To resume, the consul made every enquiry, and then, I suppose, placed his trust in heaven, for no forethought could enable him to make sufficient provision against such obstacles. Besides those I have mentioned, he was assailed by a scarcity of corn ; for the Numidians apply themselves more to raising fodder for their cattle than crops, and by command of the king had conveyed every blade to

their strongholds ; it was now, also, the height of summer, and the country at this season was parched and
barren. In spite of these difficulties, Marius made
such arrangements as his means allowed with great
forethought ; he assigned to the auxiliary cavalry the
task of conveying all the cattle that had been captured on the previous days, ordered his lieutenant,
Aulus Manlius, with some light cohorts, to proceed to
the town of Laris, where he had stored pay and provisions, and announced that in a few days he would
come to the same place in person in the course of his
pillaging. With his real object thus concealed, he
advanced towards the river Tanais. On his march he
had each day equally portioned out the flocks among
his army by centuries and squadrons, and saw that
leather bottles were made out of the hides. In this
way he lessened the effects of the scarcity of corn, and
at the same time, in perfect secrecy, made preparations, soon to be of use, while finally, by the sixth day,
when they reached the river, a great quantity of skins
had been got ready. Marius now pitched his camp with
only a slight fortification, and ordered the soldiers to
take their food and be prepared to march exactly at
sunset ; all their baggage was to be thrown away, and
they were to load themselves and their beasts with
nothing but water. When it seemed time, he marched
out of the camp, advanced throughout the night, and
then came to a halt. He followed the same plan the
next night, and on the third arrived, long before dawn,
at some downs, distant not more than two miles from
Capsa ; there he concealed himself and all his forces
as closely as he could. Day dawned, and the Numid-

CHAP.
XC.

CHAP.
XCI.

CHAP.
XCI.

ians, who dreaded no attack, issued in numbers from the town, when suddenly Marius ordered all his cavalry and the swiftest of his foot soldiers to advance at full speed upon Capsa, and seize the gates. He himself hurried eagerly after them, and forbade the soldiers to go after booty. The towns-people became aware of his attack and the peril of their position; their great alarm, the suddenness of the calamity, and the fact that a part of their citizens were outside the walls and in the enemy's power, all compelled them to surrender. The town was, nevertheless, burnt, the adult Numidians slaughtered, all the others sold, and the spoil divided among the soldiers. This outrage on the laws of war was not caused by any avarice or wickedness on the part of the consul; it was due to the fact that the place, while useful to Jugurtha, was difficult for us to reach, and its inhabitants a fickle and treacherous race, restrained neither by kindness nor fear.

CHAP.
XCII.

Even before this Marius had been regarded as a great and illustrious general; now that he had accomplished such an exploit without loss to his soldiers, his fame rose still higher. Every error in his judgment was interpreted as a merit; the soldiers, who were mildly governed and at the same time enriched, praised him to the skies; the Numidians feared him as something more than man ; and, in fine, all, allies and enemies alike, believed that he was either inspired or that, by the will of heaven, all things were foretold him.

After the success of this undertaking, the consul marched upon other towns, captured by storm a few where the Numidians resisted, but found a greater

number abandoned owing to the terror inspired by
the fate of Capsa; these he destroyed with fire, and
filled the whole land with sorrow and bloodshed.
After gaining possession of many places, and mostly
without loss to his army, he applied himself to another
exploit, not, indeed, so perilous as that of Capsa, but
no less difficult to achieve.

Not far from the river Muluccha, which separated
the kingdom of Jugurtha and Bocchus, there rose amid
the surrounding plain a rocky mountain, broad enough
at the summit for a fort of moderate size, and reaching to an immense height. A single narrow approach
was left; all the rest was as precipitous naturally as
if labour and design had been employed to form it.
The fact that the king's treasures were stored in this
place now led Marius to concentrate all his energies
on its capture. Chance, however, was more instru-
mental than skill in bringing about a happy result.
The fort was well supplied with men and arms, and
had an abundance of provisions and a spring of water;
the ground, too, was unsuited for the employment of
ramparts, turrets, and other means of attack; and the
path used by the garrison was extremely narrow, with
a sheer descent on either side. Penthouses were
brought up at great risk, but with no result; as
soon as they had made a slight advance, they were
destroyed by fire or showers of stones. The ruggedness of the ground prevented the soldiers from
making a stand in front of their works, and they
could not even labour amid the penthouses without
danger. The bravest men were wounded or killed,
and their loss increased the terror of the rest. After

many days had been spent in fruitless toil, Marius anxiously debated whether he should abandon the attempt, since all his efforts were in vain, or wait for the fortune whose favours he had often experienced. He had pondered his situation for many restless days and nights, when a certain Ligurian, a private in one of the auxiliary cohorts, happening to leave the camp to fetch water, at a point not far from the side of the fort, opposite to that on which the combatants were engaged, noticed some snails crawling amid the rocks, and, as he went after first one, then another, and then a larger number, in his eager gathering gradually climbed nearly to the summit. He at last remarked the loneliness of his situation, and man's inborn love of the difficult made him change his purpose. It happened that, just where he was, a huge holm oak had sprung up amid the rocks, growing for a little way horizontally and then taking a turn, and springing aloft in the natural direction of all plants. Clinging sometimes to the branches of this tree, at others to the jutting rocks, the Ligurian made his way to the level summit of the mountain, for the attention of all the Numidians was occupied with the combatants. After satisfying himself on all points which he thought might presently be of use, he now returned by the same way; not, however, carelessly, as he had ascended, but testing and examining every inch. He then hastily sought an interview with Marius, informed him of his adventure, and advised him to assail the fort on the side by which he had made the ascent, offering himself to act as guide on the perilous journey. Marius sent some of those about him with the Ligurian to test

his assurances, and these, according to their several
characters, variously reported the undertaking as
difficult or easy. The spirit, however, of the consul
was somewhat raised. From the trumpeters and
hornblowers at his disposal he chose five of the
swiftest, and sent with them . . . four centurions
as a guard. He ordered the whole force to obey the
Ligurian, and fixed the following day for the attempt.
When he saw that the appointed time had arrived,
and all the arrangements were complete, Marius advanced against the place. Meanwhile the scaling
party, instructed by their leader, had changed their
armour and accoutrements, and had bared their heads
and feet, so as more easily to see and keep their footing amid the rocks. On their backs they carried their
swords and shields, but these last were of Numidian
make and formed of leather, both as being lighter and
making less noise when struck. The Ligurian led the
way and fastened nooses round the rocks and the pro-
jecting roots of ancient trees, so as by these supports
to assist the soldiers in their ascent. Some were
frightened by the strange nature of the track, and
these, from time to time, he helped along with his
hands. Whenever the ascent was somewhat steeper,
he sent them on in front, one by one, without their
arms, and then followed with these himself. Where
the footing seemed doubtful, he was the first to test it,
and by repeatedly climbing up and down in the same
way, and then suddenly standing aside, inspired the
rest with boldness. After a long and exhausting
climb they at length arrived at the fort, and found it
undefended on this side; its garrison, as on other days,

CHAP.
XCIV. had all gone to face the enemy. On hearing from messengers of the success of the Ligurian, Marius, although he had kept the Numidians fully engaged in battle the whole of the day, now redoubled his exhortations to his soldiers, and himself issuing beyond the penthouses, made his men advance under cover of their locked shields, and at the same time terrified the enemy from a distance by means of his catapults, bowmen, and slingers. The Numidians on previous occasions had often overthrown or burnt the Roman penthouses, and were no longer in the habit of sheltering themselves behind their ramparts. Alike by day and night they moved to and fro before their wall, insulted the Romans, scoffed at Marius as a madman, threatened our soldiers with being made slaves to Jugurtha, and displayed all the insolence of success. Meanwhile, when all, both Romans and Numidians, were occupied in the battle, and our men were fighting vigorously for fame and dominion, the others for their own safety, the trumpets suddenly sounded in the rear. The women and boys, who had issued forth to see the fight, were the first to fly, and they were followed by those of the defenders nearest the wall, and finally by the whole body of armed and unarmed men. On this the Romans redoubled their efforts, scattered the enemy, whom for the most part they were content only to wound, made their way over the bodies of the slain, strove, in their eagerness for glory, each to be the first to reach the wall, and in not a single instance allowed plunder to delay them. Marius' rashness was redeemed by his fortune, and his fault redounded to his fame.

While this affair was in progress, the quaestor, Lucius Sulla, entered the camp with a large force of cavalry, which he had been left behind at Rome to levy from Latium and the allies. Our subject thus brings this remarkable man to our notice, and it, therefore, seems fitting briefly to describe his character and accomplishments, as we shall have no other opportunity of speaking on Sulla, and Lucius Sisenna, who has composed the best and most painstaking treatise of any writer on this subject, seems to me hardly to have spoken his mind with freedom.

Sulla, then, was nobly born, of a patrician house, and a family which the indolence of his ancestors had reduced to obscurity. He was as well versed in the literatures of Greece and Rome as the most learned, a man of great aspiration, eager for pleasure, yet more eager for fame, luxurious in his leisure, yet never suffering pleasure to withdraw him from his duties, except that he might have better consulted his honour in his married life. He was eloquent, shrewd, and an obliging friend, with a quite incredible skill in feigning and concealment, and of great generosity in many matters, and especially with regard to money. Before his triumph in the civil war, though the most fortunate of men, his luck never surpassed his energy, and many doubted whether he could more rightly be called the fortunate or the brave. As to his subsequent conduct I do not know whether its narration would be a more shameful or a more disgusting task.

When, as narrated above, he arrived with the cavalry in Marius' camp in Africa, Sulla was quite ignorant and unpractised in war. In a short time, however, he

CHAP.
XCV.

CHAP.
XCVI.

P

CHAP.
XCVI.

became the most skilful soldier in the army. He addressed the men with kindness, granted many favours, both by request, and of his own accord, and was unwilling to receive those offered by others, though he returned these more readily than he did his loans; for his own part he never sought repayment, but rather was anxious to increase the number of his debtors. He would talk, both gravely and gaily, with the humblest, frequently visited the men at their work, on the march, and on guard, and all the time refrained from the vice of the meanly ambitious, and never injured the character of the consul or any man of honour; he contented himself with allowing none to excel him in counsel or action, and with himself outstripping most competitors. By these services and accomplishments he quickly endeared himself to Marius and the soldiers.

CHAP. XCVII. Jugurtha had lost the town of Capsa and many other fortified important places, and with them great treasures; he now sent messengers to Bocchus, bidding him lead his forces into Numidia with all speed, as the time for battle had arrived. Learning that the king was hesitating and pondering in doubt on the respective advantages of peace and war, he again, as he had done before, bribed those about him, while to the Mauritanian himself he promised a third part of Numidia, to be surrendered on the expulsion of the Romans from Africa or the conclusion of a peace which should leave his dominions intact. Bocchus was enticed by the bribe, and joined Jugurtha with a great host.

The two kings united their armies and attacked

Marius, who was already setting out for his winter
quarter, when hardly a tenth part of the day was left,
thinking that the night, which was already falling,
would protect them if worsted, while, if victorious,
their knowledge of the country would prevent its
hampering them; the Romans, on the other hand,
they thought, would in either event find their difficulties increased in the darkness. The consul had
no sooner been warned from many quarters of the
approach of the enemy than the enemy himself was
upon him, and, before the army could be marshalled
or collect its baggage; indeed, before it could receive
any signal or command, the Mauritanian and Gaetulian cavalry in no line or order of battle, but in
troops, just as chance had thrown them together,
charged down upon our men. These were confused
with the suddenness of the alarm, but nevertheless
each remembered his courage, and either seized on
his armour or sheltered from the enemy others so
engaged. Some mounted their horses and advanced
against the enemy, and the fight assumed the character rather of a contest with brigands than a battle. Foot and horse were mingled together without
standards or ranks, slaughtering others and being
themselves cut down. Many who were fighting
desperately against the foe in front found themselves
beset in the rear. Neither valour nor armour gave
any real security, our men were outnumbered by their
enemy and surrounded on every side. At last the
Romans [whose knowledge, as a body, of war, was increased by the present mixture of] veterans and recruits,
formed in rings, as chance, or the nature of the ground

threw them together, and being in this way sheltered and in good order on every side, beat off the enemy's attack. Though beset by such a calamity, Marius was neither downcast nor inclined to despond. At the head of his own troop, which he had formed of brave soldiers rather than personal friends, he ranged over the field; at one moment helped some hard-pressed Romans; at the next charged into the thickest of the foe. His thought for his soldiers he showed by his valour, for in the general confusion he could give them no commands. The day was now spent, and the barbarians relaxed no effort, but rather pressed on more vigorously, believing, as the kings had told them, that night was in their favour. At this point Marius took the best course the situation allowed, and, in order to provide his men with a refuge, seized on two neighbouring hills, the one of which, though too small for a camp, possessed a bountiful spring of water, while the other was suited to his purpose, being for the most part lofty and steep, and thus requiring little entrenching. Ordering Sulla to bivouac near the spring with his cavalry, he himself gradually concentrated his scattered troops, whose confusion was fully equalled by that of the enemy, and led the whole force at a rapid pace to the hill. The difficult nature of the ground compelled the kings to desist from the battle; they did not, however, permit their men to retire to any distance, but encamped in loose order with their hosts surrounding the two hills. The barbarians then lit numerous fires, and throughout the greater part of the night rejoiced, according to their custom, with vaunts and shouts; even their leaders grew insolent, and behaved themselves as conquerors, merely because they had not fled. The Romans, who were themselves in darkness and on higher ground, could easily watch their behaviour, and were greatly cheered by it. Marius, most of all, was encouraged by the inexperience the enemy betrayed, and ordered perfect silence to be kept, forbidding even the ordinary calls to be sounded at the different watches. As daylight approached and the enemy, already wearied out, had been now for some little while overpowered by sleep, [he suddenly ordered] the watches and, with them, the trumpeters of the cohorts, squadrons, and legions, all simultaneously [to] sound an alarm, and the soldiers [to] raise a shout and sally forth from the gates. The Mauritanians and Gaetulians, suddenly roused by an unfamiliar and terrifying din, could neither flee nor seize their arms, nor, in fact, take any action or measures for defence, to such an extent had the din and outcry, the absence of help, and the onset of our men, the confusion and panic, caused them all to be seized as with a kind of madness. To conclude, the whole army fled in utter rout ; many arms and ensigns of war were captured, and more of the enemy were killed in this battle than in all those that preceded it. Sleep and an unwonted panic hampered their flight.

Marius now resumed his march to his quarters for the winter, which he had determined to pass in the seaports, for the sake of provisions. His victory made him neither remiss nor arrogant, and, as if in the presence of the enemy, he marched with his army in a hollow square; Sulla, with the cavalry, was on the

CHAP.
C.

extreme right ; on the left was Aulus Manlius, with the slingers and bowmen, in charge also of the Ligurian cohorts ; tribunes, with companies of light troops, were posted in the van and rear ; while deserters, the men least valued and best acquainted with the country, spied out the enemy's line of march. At the same time the consul looked to every point himself, as if none other had charge of it ; visited all the men, and distributed praise and blame as they were severally deserved. He compelled the soldiers to be armed and on the alert like himself, fortified the camp with the same care he displayed on the march, drafted cohorts from the different legions to keep guard at the gates, and cavalry from the auxiliary forces to patrol before the camp, and posted other troops on the rampart ; the watches he went the round of in person, not so much from any mistrust as to the fulfilment of his orders, as from the desire to increase the willingness of his soldiers by showing them that their general shared equally in their toil. In fact, both at this and other periods [of the Jugurthine war], Marius maintained discipline rather by appealing to his men's sense of honour than by punishments. This conduct many traced to his desire for popularity, while some thought that he had been from boyhood so inured to hardship and other miseries, as they are mostly accounted, that he now regarded them as pleasures. Be this as it may, the public interests were as well and honourably served as under the most tyrannical of commanders.

CHAP.
CI.

At last, on the fourth day, not far from Cirta, the scouts from all quarters presented themselves in haste, a certain sign that the enemy was at hand. Pouring in, as they did, from every side, and all with the same intelligence, they rendered it impossible for the consul to decide how to draw up his army for the battle ; he therefore made no change in his formation, but stood his ground prepared for all emergencies. He thus baulked Jugurtha, who had divided his forces into four, under the idea that one or other of them must in any case take the enemy in the rear. Meanwhile Sulla, who was the first to be attacked, cheered on his men, and at the head of a troop formed in the closest order, charged the enemy in person, while the rest of his soldiers kept their position, sheltering themselves from the javelins darted from a distance, and cutting down any of the enemy who attacked them at closer quarters. While the cavalry were thus engaged, Bocchus, with the infantry whom his son Volux had brought up, and who, owing to a delay in the march, had been absent from the former battle, charged his Roman rear. Marius at this moment was occupied in the front, as there Jugurtha was attacking with the strongest division. The Numidian now learnt that Bocchus had arrived, and, with a few attendants, wheeled round, unnoticed, to the infantry. There he shouted in Latin, a tongue which he had learned to speak at Numantia, that our soldiers were fighting in vain, as a moment before he had slain Marius with his own hand, at the same time displaying a dripping sword, which in the course of battle he had stained gallantly enough with the blood of our infantry. On hearing his words, our men were panic-stricken, though rather by the hideousness of such a calamity than

CHAP CI.

from belief in the news. The barbarians at once plucked up their courage, and pressed the frightened Romans more fiercely. They had nearly reduced them to flight, when Sulla returned from crushing the enemy against whom he had ridden, and charged the Mauritanians on their flank. Bocchus rode off immediately, but Jugurtha, in his eagerness to uphold his men and to cling to the victory he had so nearly won, was hemmed in by the cavalry, and when all, both to his right and left, had been cut down, eluded the enemy's javelins and broke alone through their midst. Meanwhile Marius, after routing the cavalry, hastened to the assistance of his comrades, of whose straits he had just been informed. This completed the rout of the enemy. A dreadful scene then ensued in the open plains; there was flight and pursuit, slaughter and capture, horses and riders dashed to earth, and many a wounded man, with no strength to fly or patience to lie still, struggling to rise and forthwith fainting back; as far as the eye could reach, the whole country was strewn with weapons, armour, and corpses, and between them appeared the blood-stained earth.

CHAP. CII.

Henceforth indisputably victorious, the consul now made his way to Cirta, whither from the outset he had directed his march. To this place, five days after the second defeat of the barbarians, came ambassadors from Bocchus entreating Marius in the king's name to send him two trusty envoys, as he wished to confer with them both on his own position and on the interests of the Roman people. Marius immediately ordered Lucius Sulla and Aulus Manlius to proceed to the king, and they, although they had come by request, nevertheless determined to address the king in order to alter his disposition if hostile, or if they found him desirous of peace, to further kindle his eagerness. Accordingly, Sulla, to whose eloquence, not to his years, Manlius gave way, spoke briefly to the following effect :—

"We greatly rejoice, King Bocchus, that heaven has warned a man of your parts at last to prefer peace to war, and, by avoiding the pollution of your own nobility by association with the utter vileness of Jugurtha, to release us from the cruel necessity of bringing your mistake and his wickedness to a common punishment. From the very beginning of their empire the Roman people has thought it better to seek friends than slaves, and has deemed it safer to rule by goodwill rather than compulsion. To yourself, nothing can be more convenient than our friendship ; in the first place, our distance from you will make collisions almost impossible, while our goodwill will be as effectual as were we your neighbours ; in the second, we have subjects in abundance, of friends neither we nor any that ever lived have had enough. Would that you had seen the wisdom of this course from the beginning ! Had you done so, you would by this time assuredly have received more favours from the Roman people than, as it is, you have suffered ills. Fortune, however, is ruler over all, and she, it séems, has seen fit that you should experience both our power and our goodwill. Now, therefore, that you have her permission, hasten and advance on the road you have entered. You have in your power

Chap. CII. many means of outweighing your errors by your services. Let this thought sink into your breast, that the Roman people was never outdone in a contest of kindness; its power in real war you have learnt for yourself."

To this speech Bocchus made a peaceful and courteous reply, and at the same time touched briefly on his offence. He had taken up arms, he said, in no hostile spirit, but for the defence of his kingdom; a part of Numidia, whence, as he contended, he had forcibly expelled Jugurtha, had, according to the laws of war, become his own, and it was impossible for him to allow Marius to lay it waste. He alluded also to the refusal of alliance when he had previously sent an embassy to Rome, but expressed a wish to bury the past, and, for the present, if he had Marius' permission, to send an embassy to the Senate. Leave was granted; but Jugurtha had learnt of the embassy of Sulla and Manlius, and, fearing the very projects which were actually on foot, had bribed the friends of Bocchus, and these now led the barbarian to alter his resolve.

Chap. CIII. Meanwhile Marius, after settling his army in huts for the winter, marched with the light cohorts and a part of the cavalry to the desert country to besiege one of the royal forts, in which Jugurtha had placed the whole of his deserters as a garrison.

Bocchus now once more, either from considering what had been the issue to him of the two battles, or by the advice of other friends whom Jugurtha had left unbribed, chose from among his intimates five of proved loyalty and great ability, and bade these proceed as ambassadors to Marius, and subsequently, if advisable, to Rome ; giving them full power of treating and of concluding the war in any way they could. The ambassadors set 'out betimes for the Roman winter quarters, but on their way were beset and plundered by Gaetulian brigands, and escaped trembling and in sorry plight to Sulla, whom the consul, on setting out for his expedition, had left in command as pro-praetor. Sulla received them not as their condition warranted, as impostors and enemies, but with an elaborate and unstinted courtesy, which made the barbarians believe that the reputation of the Romans for avarice was undeserved, and that Sulla, since he showed them such generosity, was their friend. Even as late as this many still understood nothing about bribery, and thought that no one was generous except out of a corresponding goodwill, and regarded all gifts as tokens of kindness. The ambassadors explained to the quaestor the instructions they had received from Bocchus, and at the same time begged of him his patronage and advice, magnified the king's resources, loyalty, and greatness, and touched on other points which they thought likely to be of use or to conciliate. Sulla promised them everything, and, instructed by him how to address both Marius and the Senate, they remained where they were for about forty days.

CHAP.
CIII.

On returning to Cirta, unsuccessful from his enterprise, Marius was informed of the arrival of the ambassadors, and ordered them to accompany Sulla to Utica. He also summoned Lucius Belienus, a praetor, and all persons in the country of senatorial rank, and in the presence of these received the

CHAP.
CIV.

CHAP.
CIV.

message of Bocchus. The consul granted the ambassadors leave to proceed to Rome; meanwhile, they asked for a truce. This Sulla and the majority of the council were in favour of granting; a few voted for a more arrogant course, ignorant, we may presume, of human fortunes, which in their unstable and fluctuating nature are ever shifting to opposite poles. After obtaining all their requests, three of the Mauritanians set out for Rome with Gnaeus Octavius Ruso, who, as quaestor, had brought pay-money to Africa; the other two returned to the king. From these Bocchus heard with pleasure all their news, and especially of the kindness and zeal of Sulla in his service. At Rome, his ambassadors, after owning that the king had erred and been led away by the wickedness of Jugurtha, entreated for an alliance of friendship, and received as answer that " The Senate and people of Rome are wont to remember services both good and ill. To Bocchus, inasmuch as he repents, they accord pardon for his fault; an alliance of friendship will be granted when he has deserved it."

CHAP.
CV.

Immediately on learning this answer, Bocchus besought Marius by letter to send Sulla to him, that under his guidance measures might be taken to settle the points at issue. Sulla was now despatched with an escort of cavalry [foot soldiers], and Balearic slingers, and with these there went a force of bowmen and a cohort of Paeliginians who, for the sake of expedition, wore the armour of skirmishers, by which they were as well protected as by any other kind against the [light] weapons of their enemies. When they had now been five days on the march, Volux, the son of

Bocchus suddenly appeared on the open plain with not more than a thousand horsemen; but these by their confused and disorderly advance seemed both to Sulla and every one else more numerous than they really were, and inspired a fear of hostilities. Each man, therefore, held himself in readiness, tested his armour, and prepared his weapons for use; some little fear was felt, but hope prevailed, as was natural with conquerors when confronted with an enemy they had often defeated. Meanwhile the horsemen who had been sent to the front to reconnoitre, reported, and truly, that the encounter was a peaceful one. Volux approached, and, addressing the quaestor, informed him that he had been sent by his father Bocchus at once to meet and escort him. During this and the following day the two forces mingled fearlessly together, but later on, when the camp had been pitched, and it was now evening, the Mauritanian suddenly hastened to Sulla with an agitated and frightened countenance, and, announcing that he was informed by the scouts that Jugurtha was not far distant, prayed and entreated him to escape secretly with himself under cover of night. Sulla haughtily replied that he had no fear of the oft-defeated Numidian, and had full confidence in his men's courage; even, he added, were certain destruction imminent, he would rather stand his ground than betray his soldiers and disgrace himself by flight in order to prolong the uncertainty of a life which soon, perchance, disease might terminate. Advised, however, by Volux to set out by night, he approved the plan, and immediately ordered that when the soldiers should have finished their suppers in camp, a number of fires be lighted, and the departure effected in silence in the course of the first watch. Exactly at sunrise, when all were tired with their night march and Sulla was measuring out a camp, the Mauritanian cavalry reported that Jugurtha was encamped in advance of them at a distance of about two miles. The news became known, and now indeed our men were seized with terror, believing themselves betrayed by Volux and beset by an ambush, nor were there wanting some who demanded that he should be summarily punished and that so great a crime on his part should not be left unavenged.

Sulla, however, although he took the same view of the case, defended the Mauritanian from harm. He exhorted his soldiers to keep a brave heart, and told them that a few men of energy had often fought with success against a host, that the less they spared themselves in the battle the safer they would be, and that no soldier who had armed his hand ought to seek for safety from his unarmed feet, while, in the height of his terror, he exposed the blind and undefended side of his body to the foe. He then, after loudly invoking heaven to witness the crime and treachery of Bocchus, ordered Volux, since he was found plotting against them, to leave the camp. Volux besought him with tears not to hold such a belief; no deceit, he assured him, had been used; the catastrophe had been brought about by the cunning of Jugurtha, whose spies had apparently acquainted him with their route. The king, however, he continued, had no large force at his disposal, he was dependent for all his hopes and resources on his father Bocchus, and, he believed, would not venture on any open attack in the presence of the latter's own son; the best course, it seemed to him, that they could take was to march openly through the midst of Jugurtha's camp; and he would either send his Mauritanians on in front or leave them where they were, and himself accompany Sulla without any escort. Under such circumstances his proposal was approved, and a start was at once made; their approach was unexpected, Jugurtha waited and hesitated, and, meanwhile, they passed him in safety. A few days afterwards they reached their journey's end.

On their arrival they found in frequent and familiar intercourse with Bocchus a certain Numidian, named Aspar, whom Jugurtha, on hearing of the summons to Sulla, had despatched as an ambassador and secret spy upon the designs of Bocchus. They found also a certain Dabar, a son of Massugrada, and of the family of Massinissa, but of low birth on his mother's side [she having been his father's concubine], whose many good qualities had made him beloved and esteemed by the Mauritanian. Bocchus had proved this Dabar's loyalty to the Romans on many occasions, and therefore chose him to convey a message to Sulla announcing that he was ready to do whatever the Roman people wished. He further asked the general himself to fix a day, place, and hour, for a conference, and assured him that he had violated no single detail of their agreement, and that he need have no fear of Jugurtha's ambassador, who had been received solely to enable them to conduct their business with greater freedom, for this was the only way by which they could guard against the king's subtle attacks. I gather, however, that Bocchus was actuated rather by considerations of " Punic honour " than by these which he professed, and was at the same time amusing both the Romans and the Numidians with the hopes of peace ; he deliberated often and deeply whether he should deliver Jugurtha to the Romans or Sulla to him, and while his inclina-

tion was hostile, his fears pleaded our cause. Sulla replied to his message that he would speak briefly with him in the presence of Aspar, and hold the rest of their discussions in private or with as few witnesses as possible ; at the same time he instructed him what answer to return. The meeting took place in the way he wished, and Sulla announced that he had come on a mission from the consul to ask whether Bocchus intended to maintain peace or war. On this the king, according to his instructions, bade him return after ten days ; he had even yet not come to any resolution, but would give him an answer on the day named. They then separated and returned each to his own camp. When the night was far advanced Sulla was secretly summoned by Bocchus. Only trusty interpreters were admitted by either party, and, besides these, Dabar, a man of high character and liked by both parties, as a go-between. The king immediately began the following speech :—

" I never thought that it could happen that I, the greatest king in this land, and of all princes of whom I know, should owe gratitude to any private person. Indeed, Sulla, I profess that before I knew you, though I helped many at their prayer and others of my own accord, I myself needed the assistance of none. At the breach of such a custom others are wont to grieve,

to me it is a pleasure; I am content that it may be
my lot to have needed for a moment this friendship of
yours, than which my heart holds nothing dearer. And
this profession it is open to you to test: take and use
my arms, men, money, whatever in fact you will, and
never, while you live, think that my debt of gratitude
to you is discharged. It will ever remain with me
undiminished, and, in a word, you shall never to my
knowledge wish for anything in vain. To my thinking,
it is less dishonourable for a king to be surpassed in
arms than in generosity. As for your commonwealth,
as guardian of whose interests you have been sent
hither, listen to the few words I have to say: I neither
made war upon the Roman people, nor did I ever wish
it to be made; I only used arms to protect my territory against an armed invader. This question, however, since you wish it, I pass over; as for your war
with Jugurtha, carry it on as long as you please. I
for my part will not cross the river Muluccha, the
ancient boundary of my kingdom and that of Micipsa,
nor will I allow Jugurtha to come on this side of it.
Furthermore, if you make any request which you can
worthily prefer and I accord, you shall not leave my
presence unsatisfied."

To this speech Sulla replied briefly and moderately
as touching himself, but spoke at length on the subject
of the peace, and their common interests. As the
upshot he made it clear to the king that the Senate and
people of Rome, inasmuch as they had proved their
superiority in arms, would not regard his promises as
any favour; that he must do something which they
might see had been to their advantage rather than his

own, and that this was perfectly easy for him since he had Jugurtha in his power : let him deliver Jugurtha to the Romans and their debt would be great; their friendship and alliance, and the part of Numidia which he was at present trying to obtain, would all come to him as a matter of course. The king at first gave a firm denial, alleging that the bonds of kinship and marriage, besides a solemn treaty, prevented his compliance ; he had fears too, he said, lest if he should act treacherously, he might alienate the affection of his people, who loved Jugurtha and hated the Romans. At last, after many importunities he gave way, and promised to do everything as Sulla desired. They made such arrangements as seemed expedient for counterfeiting the peace for which the Numidian, in his weariness of war, was most desirous, and then after concerting their plot, departed their several ways.

On the next day Bocchus summoned Aspar, Jugurtha's ambassador, and informed him that through Dabar he had learnt from Sulla that the war could be brought to an end on certain conditions, and that he therefore wished him to ascertain the views of his king. Aspar was overjoyed and set out for the camp of Jugurtha. When he had been duly instructed on all points by that king, after eight days he returned in haste to Bocchus, and informed him that Jugurtha was anxious to comply with every demand, but had little faith in Marius as he had often made previously fruitless treaties of peace with Roman generals : if Bocchus wished to act in the interests of both and gain a secure peace, he should contrive a meeting of all the parties as if for a conference on the question of peace, and should then betray Sulla to himself: when he had a man of such importance as a prisoner, a treaty would soon be concluded at the bidding of [the Senate or] people [of Rome]; a man of noble birth would not be left in the hands of enemies, into whose power he had fallen, by no cowardice of his own, but in the service of the state.

CHAP.
CXII.

The Mauritanian long deliberated on this proposal, and at length promised to carry it out. Whether in this case his hesitation was real or assumed my information does not say. The caprices of kings are as unstable as they are strong, and often clash with each other. Later on, the time and place for the assembly of the conference on the subject of peace were settled, and Bocchus addressed himself now to Sulla, now to the envoy of Jugurtha, treated each with courtesy, and made them both the same promise. They, on their side, were equally delighted and full of hope. On the night which preceded the day appointed for the conference, the Mauritanian is said to have first summoned his friends, and then, suddenly changing his mind, to have bidden them withdraw, and to have long debated the problem with himself, while his countenance and glance changed with each turn of his thought, and, despite his silence, laid bare the secrets of his breast. At last he ordered Sulla to be summoned, and planned the treachery against the Numidian, according to his wish. At last day came, and it was announced to him that Jugurtha was not far off. Accompanied by a few friends, and by our quaestor, as if to pay the king the compliment of

CHAP.
CXIII.

 meeting him on his way, he advanced to a hillock within easy view of the men in ambush. The Numidian, with most of his intimates, approached the same place, according to the agreement, unarmed. The signal was immediately given, and he was attacked by the ambush upon every side. His companions were all cut down ; Jugurtha himself was delivered in bonds to Sulla, and by him conducted to Marius.

 During this same period the Roman generals Quintus Caepio and Gaius Manlius were defeated in a battle against the Gauls, and all Italy trembled in the panic thus occasioned. From that day down to our own times the Romans have believed that, while their courage can surmount all else with ease, with the Gauls their contest is for preservation, not for fame. In the present crisis, when it was announced that the war in Numidia was ended, and that Jugurtha was being brought in chains to Rome, Marius was elected consul in his absence, and Gaul decreed to him as his province. On the first of January the general who had won such renown, and was now consul for the second time, celebrated his triumph. At that crisis the hopes and the resources of the state were alike centred in him.

NOTES TO THE JUGURTHINE WAR.

CHAP.
IV.

These I would ask to remember the character of the men who were unsuccessful as candidates at the times when I obtained my several offices, and the classes who subsequently gained admittance to the Senate. . . . (Qui si reputaverint, et quibus ego temporibus magistratus adeptus sum, quales viri idem assequi nequiverint, et postea quae genera hominum in senatum pervenerint. . . .)

Marcus Cato was an unsuccessful candidate for the praetorship shortly before Sallust's election as tribune, and it is to this, possibly, among other cases of which we do not know, that the historian is supposed to refer. As the sentence stands its language is singularly infelicitous, for to have succeeded where a Cato failed should have been a cause rather for shame than for rejoicing ; and yet it is of such a success that Sallust seems to boast. It is possible, however, that he really meant to point out that Cato's rejection convinced him that he himself could not hope for a continued success, and thus afforded a reason for abandoning politics ; if so, he expresses himself very obscurely.

The allusion to the "*genera hominum*" who subsequently gained admittance to the Senate is usually referred to the policy of Caesar ; some, however, think

CHAP.
IV.

that it was the measures of the triumvirs which Sallust had in mind; others, again, take *postea* to mean "lastly," and think that he refers to some particular instance at an earlier date.

CHAP.
V.

Massinissa . . . after the conquest of the Carthaginians and the capture of Sufax . . . was rewarded by the Roman people with a gift of all the cities and lands which they had conquered. (Victis Carthaginiensibus et capto Suface . . . populus Romanus quascunque urbis et agros manu ceperat, regi dono dedit.)

Massinissa (born B.C. 238) was a son of Gala, king of the Massylians. In the second Punic war he fought on the side of Carthage against Sufax, king of the Massaesylians or Western Numidians, and afterwards in Spain against the Romans themselves, until their decisive victory at Silpia in B.C. 206. During the next two years he was engaged in a fruitless contest for the possession of his father's kingdom with Sufax, now the ally of Carthage. In this war he suffered three crushing defeats, and when Scipio landed in Africa in B.C. 204, could only join him as the landless chief of a few freebooters. His genius, however, for African warfare enabled him to do the Romans good service, and he took a prominent part in the surprise of Sufax's camp by which that king was captured, and his army of fifty thousand foot and ten thousand cavalry, completely destroyed. On the conclusion of the war, Massinissa, besides being confirmed in his possession of his father's kingdom, was rewarded by Scipio with a grant of the greater part of the territory of Sufax. In the treaty, moreover, which was concluded with Carthage, it was stipulated that he should retain all the possessions which he or his predecessor had held within the boundaries of Carthage, and also that Carthage should not make war upon any ally of Rome. Of the means of annoyance thus placed in his hand Massinissa availed himself to the full, and during his long reign of more than fifty years made perpetual encroachments on the Carthaginian territory, especially in the fertile district of Emporia. Confirmed by the Romans in possession of this district in B.C 161, he proceeded to attack that of the Bagradas, and in B.C. 152 Carthage prepared for armed resistance. The Numidian appealed to Rome for protection, and after the Carthaginians had been defeated by him, the Senate declared war on them for disobeying their commands. At this conjuncture Massinissa's long life of ninety years (B.C. 238-148) came to a close, and Scipio divided his kingdom among his three sons, Micipsa, Gulussa, and Mastanabal, giving to the first the residency and state chest, to the second the command in war, and to the third the administration of justice. On the destruction of Carthage, the dominions which that city had held in its latest days, the lands along the coast opposite to Sicily, from the rich Tusca as far as Thenae, were formed into a Roman province, but the Numidian princes were formally confirmed in their possessions on the Bagradas and in Emporia, and their kingdom stretched from the rich Muluccha as far as the great Syrtis, touching Mauritania on the one side, and Cyrene and Egypt on the other. Gulussa and Mastanabal both died during their brother's life ;

and though the first in Massiva, and the second in Gauda, left behind him a legitimate son, Micipsa became sole king. He himself was of a quiet and peaceable disposition, and we hear of no remarkable occurrence during his reign.

Micipsa, on sending to Spain a contingent of Numidian foot and horse to the help of the Roman people in the Numantine war, placed Jugurtha in command of this force. (Bello Numantino Micipsa, cum populo Romano equitum atque peditum auxilia mitteret (Jugurtha) praefecit Numidis quos in Hispaniam mittebat.)

The siege of Numantia formed one of the principal incidents of a twenty years' war in Spain (B.C. 154-133) which afforded even more striking proof of the treachery and incapacity of the Roman generals than that with Jugurtha. Fulvius Nobilior was defeated under its walls in B.C. 153, and a similar ill success in B.C. 141 induced Quintus Pompeius to offer terms to the inhabitants. Pompeius subsequently, with the sanction of the Senate, repudiated the treaty, and the war went on until B.C. 137, when the consul G. Hostilius Mancinus was forced to surrender, and agree to terms of peace dictated by the Numantines. This treaty also was repudiated and the war again resumed. In 134 B.C. Scipio Æmilianus, the first general of the day, received the command, and in the following year reduced the town, not by assault, but by an elaborate blockade. The inhabitants were then sold into slavery, the city levelled with the ground, and its territory divided among the neighbours. Such was the fate awarded by the Romans to an enemy who throughout the struggle had displayed a courage and honour far superior to their own.

It was only within the last three years that Jugurtha [by his adoption] had been admitted to authority. (Nam ipsum illum tribus proxumis annis [adoptatione] in regnum pervenisse.)

Numantia fell in B.C. 133, and Sallust, two chapters back, has asserted that on Jugurtha's return Micipsa "adopted him immediately." The king's death, though Sallust speaks of it as occurring "a few years afterwards," did not take place till B.C. 118, that is at least fourteen years after what we should have imagined from the historian's language was the date of Jugurtha's adoption. We have here, therefore, another instance of our author's gross carelessness in matters of chronology. Dietsch, to save Sallust's credit, brackets "*adoptatione*" as a stupid gloss. If it be omitted, "*in regnum pervenisse*" must be referred to the position assigned to Jugurtha by Micipsa's will, or by some other measure of which we do not know; but the historian has sinned too deeply in other places for his credit to be allowed to outweigh that of the manuscript.

My family formed its friendship with the Roman people in the Carthaginian war, when we could hope to find in you no more than a loyal though luckless ally. (Familia nostra cum populo Romano bello Carthaginiensi amicitiam instituit, quo tempore magis fides ejus quam fortuna petenda erat.)

The assertion which Sallust here puts into the mouth

of Adherbal is in outrageous opposition to facts. Massinissa fought on the side of the Carthaginians till their decisive defeat at Silpia in Spain, B.C. 206. He then formed a secret alliance with Scipio, but did not finally break with the Carthaginians until the Romans landed in Africa, B.C. 204. In the intervening two years he himself had been three times defeated by Sufax, while the long campaign in Italy had terminated with the expulsion of the Carthaginians. Massinissa's personal ability made him a valuable ally to the Romans, but he joined them as the chief of a mere band of marauders at a time when fortune was entirely on their side.

Of these the most conspicuous was Marcus Æmilius Scaurus, a man of high birth, an energetic partisan, greedy for power, office, and wealth, and an adept in concealing his personal vices. (Sed ex omnibus maxume M. Æmilius Scaurus, homo nobilis, impiger, factiosus, avidus potentiae honoris divitiarum, ceterum vitia sua callide occultans.)

From the way in which Sallust speaks of him it is evident that Scaurus had by this time already attained a considerable position at Rome ; we do not, however, possess much information as to how he gained it. He was born in B.C. 163 of a patrician family, but of one so poor that it could not have been by his profusion that he gained popularity. In his youth he served in Spain, probably in the siege of Numantia, and we hear of him in Sardinia in B.C. 126. In B.C. 115 he obtained the consulship, and distinguished himself by passing two laws, one to restrain the growing luxury, the other

to check the power of the freedmen.   In the following
year he gained some victories over the Inalpini, a
mountain tribe, and for these paltry successes was
allowed the honour of a triumph.   In B.C. 109 he was
censor, along with M. Livius Drusus, and made an
unsuccessful attempt to retain his office after his colleague's death.   He was a second time consul in
B.C. 107, and in B.C. 100 took an active part in opposing Saturninus.   Ten years later we hear of him
triumphantly resisting the attacks of his enemies, and
his death, which seems to have taken place a little
before B.C. 88, brought to a close a career of uniform
success.   The character which Sallust here assigns to
Scaurus is possibly slightly coloured by the historian's
democratic partialities, but Mommsen is probably right
in surmising that neither in morality nor genius did
he rise above " respectability."   He was, however, one
of Cicero's heroes, and his success, despite his aristocratic policy, in obtaining popularity ought to count
in his favour.

*At the head of this commission was Lucius Opimius,
a man of distinction, and at that time of great influence
in the Senate owing to the stern use which he had made
as consul of the victory of the nobility at the time when
Gaius Gracchus and Marcus Fulvius Flaccus were murdered.   (Cujus legationis princeps fuit L. Opimius, homo
clarus et tum in senatu potens, quia consul, C. Graccho et
M. Fulvio Flacco interfectis, acerrume victoriam nobilitatis in plebem exercuerat.)*

Lucius Opimius, as praetor in B.C. 125, had received
the surrender of Fregellae from the traitor Numitorius.

CHAP.
XVI.

In B.C. 122, the efforts of Gaius Gracchus procured his defeat when a candidate for the consulship, but in the following year he was duly elected and entrusted by the Senate with extraordinary powers against the democrats. These he so used as to make an appeal to arms inevitable, and, after the murder of Gracchus and Marcus Flaccus, put himself at the head of a commission by whom over three thousand of the popular party are said to have been strangled in prison. On laying down office he was accused of treason to the state, but the aristocrats had no difficulty in procuring his acquittal. It is satisfactory to know that Opimius was one of those condemned under the bill of Limetanus, in B.C 109, and that he died in exile at Dyrrachium. Cicero, of course, praises him as a champion of order.

CHAP
XVIII.

As it was interpreted to me from the Punic books said to have belonged to King Hiempsal. (Uti ex libris Punicis, qui regis Hiempsalis dicebantur, interpretatum nobis est.)

The Hiempsal here mentioned is the father of Juba, Caesar's opponent. The account which the books "said to have belonged" to him give of the history of Africa is of course quite valueless. Other and more trustworthy authorities which Sallust may have consulted in compiling his narrative are the history of Sisenna mentioned in chapter 95, the autobiography and Roman history of P. Rutilius Rufus, who served in the war as Metellus' legate, and the memoirs of Sulla and Marcus Aemilius Scaurus. Besides these he might have referred to the annal writers, such as G. Licinius Macer, and to the reports sent to the Senate by the various generals, which may still have been extant.

That Sallust did avail himself of some, if not all of
these materials, there is abundant evidence in his work
to prove ; he was too young, however, to be able to
supplement them from the conversation of men who
had fought in the campaigns, and seems to have made
little use of the opportunities for research afforded by
his stay in Africa.

Near the town of Cirta, not far from the sea. (Haud
longe a mari prope Cirtam oppidum.)

Cirta, the modern Constantina, lies in the upper
part of the river Ampsager, by which one side of the
town is protected from attack. Mr Long (History, i.
392-395), quotes a long description of its situation from
an Arab geographer of the sixth century, and con-
cludes from his account that Sallust " evidently knew
nothing of the position of the town, and his description
of the siege of Cirta is a fiction." The sentence
quoted as a heading to this note is itself a proof of our
author's carelessness or ignorance, as Cirta instead of
being near the sea is at least forty miles inland. Sallust,
indeed, seems to be singularly unhappy in the part of
his work relating to this town, as in chapter 81 he
speaks of it as in possession of Metellus, without giving
us any information as to how it passed out of Jugurtha's hands. It is about the siege of Cirta, moreover, that the chief chronological difficulties in his
narration present themselves. We know that Micipsa
died in B.C. 118, and that Bestia, the first general who
acted against Jugurtha, was one of the consuls for B.C.
112. In the interval of six years between these two
dates, we have to place the murder of Hiempsal,

Adherbal's visit to Rome, the commission for dividing Numidia between Adherbal and Jugurtha, Jugurtha's predatory raids on his cousin's kingdom, and the five months' siege of Cirta. Kritz makes all these events to have happened in a single year, B.C. 116, but this may fairly be described as a physical impossibility, and even if his theory were put in a more reasonable form it would leave an interval of over three years between the massacre of the Italians and the Roman measures of vengeance. That such an interval was allowed to elapse is not only intrinsically improbable, but in direct contradiction to the statement of Sallust that Jugurtha's partisans failed in their efforts to gain time. There are, moreover, two positive reasons for assigning the siege of Cirta to a later date than B.C. 116. In the first place, M. Aemilius Scaurus is spoken of as of consular rank at the time of his mission during the siege, and his consulship did not take place till B.C. 115. It is true that "*consularis*" seems sometimes to be loosely used to include a "consul-designatus," which Scaurus would have been in B.C. 116, and that in so careless a writer as Sallust too much stress must not be laid on a chance expression; the epitomizer, however, of Livy mentions the fall of Cirta after the defeat of Cn. Papirius Carbo in B.C. 113, and this evidence turns the scale decidedly in favour of the date B.C. 112. The murder of Hiempsal, and flight of his brother to Rome, probably took place in B.C. 107, and the arrival of Opimius' commission in the following year. There is nothing strange in supposing that the efforts of Jugurtha to provoke Adherbal into a war, were continued for three years before they met with success.

Gaius Memmius, a tribune elect, an active man, and an enemy to the power of the nobility. (G. Memmius, tribunus plebis designatus, vir acer et infestus potentiae nobilitatis.)

This Gaius Memmius subsequently deserted the democratic party, and was killed in B.C. 100 by the mob of Saturninus. He and his brother Lucius were two of the most celebrated orators of the time, though Cicero speaks disparagingly of such specimens of their eloquence as were extant in his time. The word (*perscribere*) which Sallust uses in chapter 30, ought to denote that the speech which follows is written out as Memmius actually delivered it; it is unlikely, however, that Sallust resisted the temptation of trying to improve another man's oratory.

In accordance with the Sempronian law Numidia and Italy were assigned to the consuls of the next year as their provinces. (Lege Sempronia provinciae futuris consulibus Numidia atque Italia decretae.)

In the law here referred to Gaius Gracchus endeavoured to loosen the hold which the Senate possessed over the consuls by virtue of its power of fixing their respective spheres of duty. He did not altogether deprive the Senate of this power, but prevented its being used for purposes of reward or retaliation by ordaining that the consuls should have their provinces fixed for them before they entered upon office, and thus be rendered independent of the favour of the Senate.

CHAP.
XXIX.

The consul sent his quaestor Sextius to Vaga, a town of Jugurtha's. (Mittitur a consule Sextius quaestor in oppidum Jugurthae Vagam.)

Vaga or Vacca is one of the few places mentioned by Sallust of which we are able to fix the site. It lay a long day's journey to the south-west of Utica, on the borders of what are now Tunis and Algiers. In chap. 47 Sallust mentions that it was the resort of many Italian traders, and it was probably, therefore, commercial reasons which impelled the Romans to restore it after its destruction by Metellus. (Chap. 68.) By Justinian it was surrounded with a wall and renamed Theodosia in honour of his wife. Its modern name is Baja.

CHAP.
XXIX.

After saying a few words in the presence of the council. (Pauca praesenti consilio locutus.)

The functions and constitution of a provincial governor's council are among the points illustrated by Sallust's history of this war. From chapters 62 and 104 we learn that all persons in the province of senatorial rank would be expected to attend, together with the general's staff, and any other persons whose advice he chose to ask. Measures adopted after a discussion would apparently be announced in the name of the council, and not of the individual commander, and for the latter to conclude any negotiation on his personal responsibility would be a breach of ancient custom. The expression "*per saturam sententiis exquisitis*" is variously taken to refer to a vote passed by acclamation or to a desultory discussion.

Calpurnius then set out for Rome to hold the elections. (*Calpurnius Romam ad magistratus rogandos proficiscitur.*)

CHAP. XXIX.

Calpurnius' colleague in the consulship, Publius Scipio Nasica, had died during his year of office, hence Calpurnius' presence in Rome was actually necessary. He was subsequently one of those condemned under the bill of Mamilius Limetanus, but is mentioned as living in Rome in B.C. 90. He was compelled, however, to retire into exile in the course of that year, in order to avoid condemnation under the Varian law against intrigues with the Italians.

I refrain for very shame from dilating on how for the last fifteen years you have been the sport of an arrogant faction. (*Nam illa quidem piget dicere, his annis quindecem quam ludibrio fueritis superbiae paucorum.*)

CHAP. XXXI.

This speech of Memmius was delivered in B.C. 111, and it is difficult to see why he speaks of the democracy as having been oppressed for fifteen years rather than ten or twenty. Ten years would have recalled his hearers' minds to the time of Gaius Gracchus; twenty, to that of his brother Tiberius; fifteen can have reminded them of no measure of greater importance than the exclusion of the Italians from Rome by the bill of Junius Pennus (B.C. 126), which, although a blow to the democrats, certainly did not constitute an epoch in their struggle with the aristocracy. Mr. Long, in his paraphrase of this speech (*History*, i. 403), actually gives the number as twenty, but Dietsch mentions no alternative reading.

R

CHAP.
XXXI. *They set their commissions to work against the party of the commons in Rome.* (*In plebem Romanum quaestiones habitae sunt.*)

P. Popillius Laenas and P. Rutilius, the consuls for 132, with C. Laelius and P. Scipio Nasica, the Pontifex Maximus, were at the head of this commission. Its members did not set to work with anything like the ferocity which distinguished Lucius Opimius in trying the partisans of Gaius Gracchus eleven years later; and indeed it is chiefly memorable for the intrepid behaviour of Blossius, Tiberius' teacher and friend, when summoned before it.

CHAP.
XXXIII *Jugurtha therefore came to Rome with Cassius, in a guise so pitiful as to be the very opposite of royal state.* (*Igitur Jugurtha contra decus regium cultu quam maxume miserabili cum Cassio Romam venit.*)

The assumption of the outward signs of mourning by persons who wished to excite compassion was common both in Greece and Rome; it was this practice which Jugurtha now followed, apparently in a somewhat extravagant manner. When Adherbal addressed the Senate, and spoke of himself as "deformatus aerumnis," he was probably attired in a similar fashion.

CHAP.
XXXVI. *Anyhow time slipped away, and the date of the elections drew nigh at hand. Albinus, therefore, departed for Rome.* (*Sed postquam dilapso tempore comitiorum dies adventabat, Albinus Romam decessit.*)

The return of Albinus to Rome was rendered necessary by the absence of his colleague, M. Minucius Rufus, in his province of Macedonia.

Just at this time at Rome the state was being violently excited by dissensions among the tribunes. (Ea tempestate Romae seditionibus tribuniciis atrociter respublica agitabatur.)

It is not likely that " continuare magistratum " refers to any attempt on the part of the tribunes to hold office for, say, fifteen months instead of the legal twelve. Just as in the "Catiline" Sallust uses the phrase " continuare domos " of joining two houses under one roof, so here he means that some of the tribunes were seeking re-election, and endeavouring to add a second term of office to that which was about to expire. Gaius Gracchus, in accordance with a bill which he himself brought forward, had held the tribunate for two successive years, B.C. 123, 122, and was only defeated in his third candidature by the knavery of the magistrate presiding at the election. He had, in fact, in some measure anticipated the policy of the empire, and was endeavouring to make the tribunate the basis of a personal rule. The eligibility of tribunes for re-election was a standing menace to the Senate, and we are therefore not surprised to find from this passage of Sallust that after the death of Gracchus it had been annulled.

He arrived by means of forced marches in most inclement weather at the town of Suthul. (Magnisque itineribus, hieme aspera, pervenit ad oppidum Suthul.)

Sallust's authorities apparently did not like dwelling on such a disaster to the Roman arms as the surrender of Aulus, and it is evident that Sallust is chiefly indebted to his imagination for the account which he

CHAP.
XXXVII.

gives. It is absurd to suppose that in such a place and season Aulus set about besieging a town in the regular Roman fashion, and equally absurd to suppose that guilty negotiations could be carried on more secretly in any one place in a desert than any other. The situation of Suthul is not known to us; the actual surrender, according to Orosius, took place at Calama, the modern Guelma, about forty miles from the sea. The strength of the Roman army which thus disgracefully capitulated Orosius estimates at 40,000 men.

CHAP.
XXXIX.

The Senate decreed that, without the consent of itself and the people, no agreement could have had the force of a treaty. (Senatus decernit suo atque populi injussu nullum potuisse foedus fieri.)

The conscience of the Senate in the matter of the disavowal of treaties grew more and more pliable with the course of time. When they repudiated that concluded with the Samnites after the disaster of the Caudine Forks, all the officers of the army were surrendered to their vengeance. Again, some eight-and-twenty years before the present occasion Mancinus was similarly given up to the Numantines, though his officers were held guiltless. Now the treaty was simply disowned as soon as the Romans had obtained full benefit from it, and no further steps were taken in the matter, the war apparently being renewed without any formal notice to Jugurtha. It is possible, as Mr. Long suggests, that the Senate may have justified its conduct by some legal or religious quibble, but it is noticeable that if perfidy was Jugurtha's natural weapon, throughout the war the Romans invariably excelled him in its use.

Meanwhile at Rome, Gaius Mamilius Limetanus, a CHAP. XL.
tribune of the commons, proposed to the people that an
enquiry should be held. (*Interim Romae G. Mamilius*
Limetanus tribunus plebei rogationem ad populum pro-
mulgat uti quaereretur.)

From Cicero we learn that the jury in the trials
held under this act of Limetanus was composed of
"equites," or capitalists, men who would be interested
in bringing the war to an end, from their connection
with the tax farmers and traders in Africa, whose
lives and fortunes were both endangered by its continuance, while many of their friends may have been
among the victims of the massacre at Cirta. Among
those whom the commission condemned Cicero mentions L. Calpurnius Bestia, G. Cato, G. Sulpicius Galba,
Sp. Albinus, and Lucius Opimius. What the punishment assigned to them was we have no means of
learning.

The nobility in guilty terror opposed their proceedings CHAP. XLII.
at one time by means of the allies and Latin citizens, at
another by the Roman knights, who had been drawn
from the side of the commons by the hope of an alliance
with themselves. (*Nobilitas noxia atque eo perculsa*
modo per socios ac nomen Latinum, interdum per equites
Romanos quos spes societatis a plebe dimoverat Grac-
chorum actionibus obviam ierat.)

The democratic leaders had had the unwisdom to
depart from the policy of Gaius Gracchus, who tried
to enlist the Italians on his side by offers of the full
Roman franchise. As, moreover, most of the privately

CHAP.
XLII.

owned land available for distribution had already been disposed of, the Latin and Italian communities feared, not without reason, that the democrats might proceed to confiscate the domains of which they held possession as corporate bodies, and as a means of protection against such measures were ready to ally themselves with the Senate. As they had no power of voting they could only have made themselves useful as mobs in the streets of the capital, and it is strange that the democrats did not now employ against the Senate the law of Junius Pennus, which had originally been passed as a party measure against themselves. As to the conduct of the knights, that class was always a shifting force in Roman politics, throwing its weight now on this side and now on that, according as it was exasperated at the moment by the exclusiveness of the nobility or the anarchist tendencies of the democrats. The Senate, however, always retained a hold over it owing to the services which the provincial governors would render to the tax-farmers and traders with whom they came in contact, though at present this advantage was counterbalanced by the equestrian control of the law courts.

CHAP.
XLIII.

Numidia had fallen to Metellus, a man of energy, whose reputation, although he was an opponent of the popular party, was unshaken and unblemished. (Metello Numidia evenerat, acri viro et quamquam advorso populi partium, fama tamen aequabili et inviolata.)

It is of this Metellus that the story is told that, when maliciously accused of malversation, on his producing his account books the jury refused to look at

them, holding his bare word sufficient to rebut the
charge. Three years after his return from Africa he
was allowed the honours of a triumph and the title
" Numidius " for his services in the war. In B.C. 102
he was one of the censors, and endeavoured to expel
Glaucia and Saturninus from the Senate. Two years
later, by an unprincipled manoeuvre on the part of
Marius, he was himself expelled from the Senate for
refusing to swear obedience to an agrarian law, and
retired into exile at Rhodes. He was recalled to
Rome the following year, but we hear nothing more
of him. A fragment of one of his speeches is preserved
by Gellius.

*The Senate by its influence, the allies and Latin
citizens and dependent kings by freely sending contingents. (Senatus auctoritate, socii nomenque Latinum
et reges ultro auxilia mittendo.)*

Another way of punctuating this passage is to place
the comma after " *Latinum*," instead of " *auctoritate*,"
when the translation becomes, " Contingents were sent
by the allies and Latin citizens in compliance with a
decree of the Senate, and by the dependent kings of
their own accord." This rendering is adopted by
Dietsch in his earlier edition, and it seems to fit in
better with what we know of the method of procedure
in such cases, than does the translation given in the
text.

*He therefore sent forward his lieutenant, Publius
Rutilius. (P. Rutilium legatum praemisit.)*

Publius Rutilius Rufus had been a military tribune

CHAP. L.

under Scipio during the siege of Numantia, was prac-
tor in B.C. 111, and consul six years later.   In B.C. 95
he accompanied the pro-consul, Q. Mucius Scaevola, to
his province of Asia, there to act as his legatus.   On
his return he was tried on a charge of extortion, and,
though his innocence was clearly established, a jury of
"*equites*," i.e. tax-farmers and capitalists, condemned
him in order to annoy the Senate.   Rutilius retired to
Smyrna, to live among the people whom he had been
accused of oppressing, and refused subsequently to
return to Rome when recalled.   Several of his speeches
were published, and he also wrote his autobiography,
and a history of Rome in Greek ; with these Sallust
was evidently acquainted, and it is to Rutilius that we
owe the unusual excellence of his description of this
battle.

CHAP LVI.

*He learnt that Marius had left the line of march on
a mission to Sicca.   (Cognoscit Marium ex itinere
Siccam missum.)*

Sicca is the modern El Kef, and lies on the river
Bagradas, not far from the boundary of the Roman
province.   It was built upon a hill, and was subsequently occupied as a Roman colony.   Besides Sicca
it had the name Veneria from a temple of Astarte
whom the Romans identified with their goddess
Venus.

CHAP LXII

*Jugurtha was summoned in person to Tisidium, there
to await further orders.   (Cum ipse ad imperandum
Tisidium vocaretur.)*

The locality of Tisidium is unknown.   It has been

proposed to substitute the reading "Thysdrum," but for this there is no authority, and Mr. Long, who has gone very fully into the geography of these campaigns, declares that there could be no reason for Metellus being there, and that the subsequent narrative of Sallust proves that Tisidium is not Thysdrus.

As Gaius Marius was invoking the gods in sacrifice *the diviner informed him that there were portents of great and wonderful events.* (*G. Mario per hostias deis supplicanti, magna atque mirabilia portendi haruspex dixerat.*)

Gaius Marius was born in the year B.C. 157 at Cereatae, near Arpinium. Like most of his contemporaries he first saw service during the siege of Numantia. In B.C. 119 he was one of the tribunes of the commons, and distinguished himself during his term of office by his freedom from party spirit, opposing the Senate when they attempted to interfere with the freedom of election, and the democrats in an endeavour to extend the corn laws. His career hitherto had by no means been one of triumphant success, as he had been twice defeated on the same day when a candidate for both aedileships, and in B.C. 115 had barely secured the praetorship. As Sallust remarks, it was probably chiefly the popular indignation against the nobility which now enabled him to obtain the consulship. He was the first "novus homo" who had held that office since B.C. 143, and after his death it was not again gained by any member of the class until Cicero's election for B.C. 63.

CHAP
LXV.

Whom Micipsa had appointed in his will his second heir. (Quem Micipsa testamento secundum heredem scripserat.)

According to Sallust, Micipsa had followed in his will the custom of Roman testators who named sometimes as many as two or three sets of heirs who were successively to be offered the inheritance should the original legatees be unable or decline to accept it. In most cases, of course, such mention would be purely complimentary. Thus Augustus appointed the chief men of the state as his heirs in ultimate default, according to Tacitus, out of simple vanity. In the present case the bequest took unexpected effect.

CHAP.
LXIX.

Turpilius was condemned and, as a Latin citizen, punished by scourging and decapitation. (Turpilius condemnatus verberatusque capite poenas solvit; nam is civis ex Latio erat.)

The Porcian law secured the backs of Roman citizens from the scourge, but the Latins had no other protection than could be found in a law of Drusius which ordained that they could only be scourged by the command of their own officers. As Turpilius was himself an officer, and probably the highest of the non-Romans, it seems that even this was disregarded. According to Plutarch, Turpilius was a personal friend of Metellus, and his condemnation was brought about by Marius out of hatred for the general. Turpilius Plutarch represents as really innocent.

I should mention that a little before this the Senate had decreed that . Gaul should be his province; but this measure was useless. (Sed paullo . . . . decreverat; ea res frustra fuit.)

The translation in the text is from Mommsen's conjecture, "Ei uti Gallia provincia esset paullo ante Senatus decreverat," which is preferable to filling in the hiatus with "ante Senatus Metello bellum." The sense in any case is evident, but it is more likely that the Senate would have tried to gain their ends by an indirect than by a direct method of opposing the evident wish of the people, and the need had already risen for a strong hand in Gaul.

Taking with him the deserters and a part of his cavalry he made his way to the wastes and thence to Thala. (Cum perfugis et parte equitatus in solitudinei, dein Thalam pervenit.)

In the midst of vast deserts there lay a strong and important town named Capsa. (Erat inter ingentis solitudines oppidum magnum atque valens, nomine Capsa.)

Thala and Capsa are two places in the south of the modern regency of Tunis. Capsa has been clearly shown to be the same as the modern Kafsa or Gafsa; the site of Thala, on the other hand, is still uncertain, as it has been variously identified with the modern Thelepte, and with two villages which still bear the name of Thala in its original form. Sallust's account of the two expeditions is very unsatisfactory, as he gives them as isolated incidents, without any information

CHAPS.
LXXV,
LXXXIX. as to the movements which followed or preceded them. The object of the Roman commanders was evidently to deprive Jugurtha of all his strongholds in the eastern part of his dominions; Mommsen, however, draws a distinction between the two undertakings, and says that "the expedition of Marius to Capsa was an adventure as aimless as that of Metellus to Thala had been judicious;" grounding this distinction on the hope which Metellus entertained of capturing Jugurtha's person.

CHAP.
LXXVIII. *It is this power of suction from which they are called Syrtes. (Syrtes ab tractu nominatae.)*

The name Syrtes is derived from the Greek σύρειν, to sweep or draw.

CHAP.
LXXXVI. *Meanwhile he himself levied soldiers, not, according to ancient custom, from the classes, but simply as they volunteered, and, for the most part, men of no fortune. (Ipse interea milites scribere, non more majorum neque ex classibus, sed uti cujusque lubido erat, capite censos plerosque.)*

Capite Censi were originally the sixth class of citizens at Rome, whose property, consisting of less than 11,000 asses (£43), did not bind them to enter the army. This minimum census long before the Jugurthine war was lowered from eleven to four thousand asses (£17), and in times of emergency freeborn citizens possessed of property rated at from 375 to 1500 asses (£1 10s.—£6) were also called upon to serve. In recruiting his army from volunteers without paying any attention to a property-qualification, Marius was only carrying to its logical conclusion a tendency which had long existed; none the less, this and his other measures of military reform completely revolutionized the Roman army.

From the trumpeters and hornblowers at his disposal, he chose five of the swiftest, and sent them . . . four centurions as a guard. (*Itaque ex copia tubicinum et cornicinum numero quinque quam velocissumos delegit, et cum eis praesidio qui forent . . . quatuor centuriones.*)

There is here evidently something wrong with the text, as four centurions by themselves would have been an absurdly insufficient guard, while the description of the ascent and in fact the whole nature of the attempt forbids us to suppose that they were at the head of their companies, for the force would then have been too numerous for such a surprise. Dietsch in his earlier edition supplied the words "et paucos milites," but, though this makes excellent sense, we have no reason for supposing that these were the particular words which Sallust used.

Lucius Sisenna, who has composed the best and most painstaking treatise of any writer on the subject. (*L. Sisenna, optume et diligentissume omnium, qui eas res dixere persecutus.*)

Lucius Cornelius Sisenna was a praetor in B.C. 78 and one of Pompey's lieutenants in B.C. 67. His history of Rome seems to have begun with the Marsic war, and was probably written in twenty-four books. Cicero mentions as its most striking peculiarity the strange words that are to be found in it.

CHAP.
LXXXVI.

CHAP.
XCIII.

CHAP.
XCV.

CHAP.
XCV.

Sulla, then, was nobly born, of a patrician house, and a family which the indolence of his ancestors had reduced to obscurity. (Igitur Sulla gentis patriciae nobilis fuit, familia jam prope extincta majorum ignavia.)

Sulla was born in B.C. 138, and, as Sallust says, had as yet done nothing to distinguish himself. He could not, however, have been so utterly unacquainted with military matters as the historian represents, as previous service in the cavalry was a necessary qualification for the quaestorship. The sketch which Sallust here gives of his character is, as having been given by a democrat, remarkable for its fairness, and it is very honourable to our author that he was fully alive to the good qualities of Sulla and to the bad ones of Marius. The allusion contained in the phrase "except that he might have behaved more honourably in the matter of his wife," cannot be satisfactorily explained. Sulla was married no less than six times, and Sallust may refer either to the generally scandalous character of his behaviour, or to some particular incident with which we are unacquainted.

CHAP.
XCVII.

At last the Romans [whose knowledge, as a body, of war, was increased by the present mixture of] veterans and recruits. . . . Denique Romani veteres novique [et ob ea scientes belli]. . . .

In his former edition Dietsch bracketed "novique" in this "et ob ea scientes belli." The latter may have been inserted as a gloss, the former have crept in as a part of a very common phrase. One of the two must certainly be omitted; as the sentence stands, it may suggest a meaning, but possesses none.

He need have no fear of Jugurtha's ambassador who   CHAP.
had been received solely to enable them to conduct their   CVIII.
business with greater freedom. (Neu Jugurthae legatum
pertimesceret. . . . quo res communis licentius gereretur.)

It has been proposed to omit any hiatus here, and
refer "quo" to Bocchus' request that Sulla should be
free from fear ; but this would make the reference in
the following clause extremely obscure. It seems,
better, therefore, to suppose that two or three words
with the meaning given in the text here dropped out.

During the same period the Roman generals Quintus   CHAP.
Caepio and Gnacus Manlius were defeated in a battle   CXIV.
against the Gauls. (Per idem tempus advorsum Gallos
ab ducibus nostris Q. Caepione et Gn. Manlio male
pugnatum erat.)

The defeat here referred to is that of the battle of
Arausio, fought October 6th, B.C. 105, in which the allies
of Quintus Caepio, and Gnaeus Manlius Maximus were
annihilated in succession by the Cimbrians, and 80,000
Roman soldiers lost their lives. As in the case of the
Numidian war, the military disaster was followed by
a storm of persecutions, which resulted in the condemnation not only of Caepio, whose folly had occasioned
the defeat, and who was also suspected of embezzle-
ment, but of Manlius and many other men of note.

When it was announced that the war in Numidia   CHAP.
was ended, and that Jugurtha was being brought in   CXIV.
chains to Rome. (Sed postquam bellum in Numidia
confectum, et Jugurtham Roman vinctum adduci nun-
tiatum est.)

Sallust had apparently become tired of his task

before he brought it to a close, as he has not taken the trouble to inform his readers of the subsequent fate either of Jugurtha or of his kingdom. From other sources we learn that a few days after Marius' triumph the prince was thrown into the Tullianum, and there either strangled or left to perish of cold or hunger. His kingdom passed into the hand of his half-brother Gauda, diminished on its western side by the country between Caesarea and the river Muluccha, which was granted to Bocchus in return for his treachery. Jugurtha may be said to have richly deserved the fate he met, but not at the hands of the Romans, who repudiated two treaties which their generals had concluded with him, tried to procure his assassination by his own servants, and only finally became possessed of his person by means of treachery. Marius celebrated his triumph on January 1st, B.C. 104. Like Metellus, he had assumed the command in Africa at the end of the year, and his two campaigns must therefore be placed not in B.C. 107, 106, but in B.C. 106, 105, and those of Metellus in B.C. 108, 107. The surrender of Jugurtha took place at the close of the summer of B.C. 105, and the news of his election to the consulship would naturally bring Marius to Rome without delay.

Printed at the University Press by
ROBERT MACLEHOSE, 153 WEST NILE STREET, GLASGOW.